WANTED: VAMPIRE'S ASSISTANT

MOONHAVEN COVE
BOOK ONE

DUSTY ROSE

ALSO BY DUSTY ROSE

A Waltz Through Time

Pixie Problems

CHAPTER 1
MIA

I was working the late evening shift at Happy's Diner. The owner, Happy, liked to stay open later than other diners to catch the people getting out of the bars and nightclubs down the street. Personally, I thought it was an idiotic idea. People getting out of bars and nightclubs were not generally good customers, and dealing with drunks was never my favorite idea, either.

As a matter of fact, I had an aversion to random people pinching my butt or coming in so tipsy that they crashed into their table, knocking the plates and glasses to the floor in a crescendo of broken china. And it *really* irritated me when Happy glared at me as if all of it were my fault.

I grumbled under my breath as I picked up the broken china and swept the area. You would think working mostly at diners for the last eleven years of my life would give me more than enough experience to be above the grunt work of certain diner jobs—to be a manager or owner—but nope. And it wasn't because I was a terrible worker. I was a dang good worker. It was for the simple reason that people and I did not mix well.

Being around people left me all jumbled and chaotic inside. There was this huge mix of feelings that swirled around and around inside me whenever I was around them. Like someone had taken a fireman's hose, opened it full throttle, and shoved it down my throat. It was not pleasant.

I'd really tried. I'd tried as a child, and then as an early teen to make friends. But I could tell when people were lying to me, and I could tell when people were saying something not because they felt it, but because they thought it would make me think better of them. I could tell when people were being insincere. And, the sad truth was, there was a lot of lying and insincerity out there in the world. So much of it, in fact, that I'd stopped trying.

It was a rare find to find a decent, truthful person who didn't live or die by others' opinions of them. People gravitated to people who made them feel better about themselves. And, sadly, that wasn't me for most people. Hence the no friends, and the cleaning broken china, and the leering man with crazy eyebrows and bloodshot eyes who tried to pinch my butt again.

I stood up and glared at him, my chest heaving. His cronies around the table were snickering into their food, watching the scene play out; none of them speaking up for me, none of them seeing anything wrong with putting your hands on someone else's butt when it was clearly not wanted. The man winked at me, and I saw red. I gently set the tub of broken china down on the table, fisted my hand, and punched him as hard as I could in the nose.

The man squawked, covered his nose, and said in a high-pitched, grating voice, "I didn't mean anything by it, idiot woman! Stop being so sensitive!" His cronies were cracking up now, guffawing into their waters, and I could tell the butt-pincher was getting embarrassed. I knew this would go one of two ways: One, he would drop it and slink away. Two, he would create a scene with my manager.

He went with option two.

"You're fired," Happy sneered. "Get your things and get out." The other servers and cooks avoided my eyes, and not one of them stood up for me. It hurt a bit. I knew I wasn't really friends with any of them, but we were at least friendly with each other most of the time. I tried to help my coworkers as much as possible, taking shifts when they were sick or had to take care of a sick child, and staying late so they could get home to families and kids.

But none of them stood up to Happy. I understood, or at least I tried to comfort myself that I understood. They didn't want to lose their jobs, either. And the economy was terrible. I sighed, glaring at Happy. His name was a huge misnomer. He should have been named Growly the Ghastly. It certainly would have fit better than Happy.

I gathered my things, glared at the table of guys in the corner who'd gone quiet, nodded at my coworkers, and left the diner.

The sky was thick with dark clouds, and it was starting to drizzle. I pulled the collar of my coat up and wrapped my scarf around my neck, tucking the ends inside my coat to keep myself as warm as possible.

The streets were deserted at this time of night. Occasionally a car passed, but I didn't look up and take note. I kept my nose down and my eyes on the sidewalk and walked as fast as I could toward my apartment building.

It wasn't the smartest idea to walk home at this time of

night. I knew that. But I had zero extra money for a cab, and I didn't own a car. Heck, I would just be grateful if I could scrounge up enough money for my rent. Right now, all of my money was going toward the business classes I was taking online. I juggled bills to pay the tuition each month, taking extra shifts at work whenever I could swing it.

Until last week, I'd been working two jobs: Happy's and The Juice Box, a juicing bar down the street that was always crazy busy. But I'd had to let that job go so I could focus on my upcoming finals. I was nearing the end; so close to my certification that I could almost taste it.

It had taken me two years of double shifts, night shifts, two jobs, extra jobs, and eighteen-hour days to get me to this point. The finals were on my laptop at home, waiting for me to send them in. I just had to proof them one last time and then I was done. I would never have to work a diner job for the rest of my life. I could polish up my resume, add in my education and certification, and get a better-paying job that would help me get out of the slums and into decent housing. Maybe afford a car, and an occasional meal out.

A car with very faded headlights passed close by me, spewing muddy water on my lower half. I growled and wanted to shake my fist at the driver, but I didn't bother. They probably couldn't see any better than I could in this wet weather.

A woman with a very bundled-up baby was up ahead on the sidewalk. He was in what looked like a snow suit, including a hoodie, and the woman had on two coats and what appeared to be three differently colored scarves, with boots up to her knees. I wanted to laugh. It wasn't *that* cold, but as she drew near, I felt a strange surge of peace. She smiled at me, despite the drizzle, and I felt warmth blossom inside of me.

I smiled back at her, despite the crappy day I was having. She was one of those rare types of people that made you smile simply because you couldn't help yourself. We nodded as we passed each other and went our separate ways. I didn't really find it odd that she was out in the drizzle at night with her baby. Or that she wasn't taking a cab, because there was what looked like a harried dad following her. He looked asleep on his feet; his tie was askew, his dress pants were wrinkled, and he quickly tried to catch up with her with a huge umbrella so she and baby didn't get wet.

I smiled and shook my head. Little family out for a walk? Maybe they were trying to calm junior so he could fall asleep? I didn't know. But it was interesting, and the woman seemed like a good person. The dad just seemed tired, and maybe a little frustrated that his wife was outstripping his pace. I looked at the apartment building they'd walked out of. It was brightly lit, and had a doorman just behind the glass doors, staying out of the rain. This was a better and safer part of the city. I purposely went out of my way to walk through the more affluent areas of town on my way home. I had no desire to be a statistic.

When I could no longer walk home via the affluent areas of town, I quickly marched down the streets closer to home. A homeless man was on the corner, babbling to himself, and empathy hit me hard. I'd been homeless once. I'd eaten out of dumpsters and begged for scraps and essentials from others.

I had five bucks in my pocket. It wasn't a lot, maybe enough to get a small meal, but it was all I had. I handed it to him as I passed, and he smiled a vacant, gap-toothed smile at me. As I turned the corner, I heard him singing.

I passed the alley right between my apartment building and another, and felt a chill skitter down my spine. I pivoted and saw a man leaning against the building, smoking a cigarette under an overhang that kept him dry. For no discernible reason, as the man's eyes met mine my insides turned to ice and I felt intense fear. He made no threatening move toward me—in fact, he didn't move at all—but I felt like my life was in jeopardy. I turned away from him quickly, and because I'd felt such things before and trusted my instincts, I bolted for my building, running flat out.

I opened the outer building's door with my key and slammed it shut behind me, breathing hard and looking out at the man who'd followed me so quietly I hadn't heard him. We stared at each other through the small patch of dirty glass, me with my heart beating like a runaway train, and him looking like he was contemplating nothing more dire than dinner. I palmed my phone, preparing to call nine-one-one, when he smirked and left.

I almost collapsed to the dirty floor in relief.

I had no idea how I knew he was bad news; I just did. I always did. A person could look like the most affluent businessman, but if they were a danger to me, I always knew. As a matter of fact, I'd had that happen in the past.

One of my night classes had been on a local campus, and it was a packed classroom. Most of the students had seemed and felt friendly to me, but one man hadn't. And the craziest part was that he'd been among the friendliest of the class. He'd laughed and joked with others, gone out to coffee with the group, and just generally seemed to get along with everyone. His eyes had looked bright and cheerful. His dress was always business casual, and I'd seen him drive home more than once in a nice late-model car. But every time I was around him, my heart had pounded, my chest had tightened, cold would pulse through my body, and I would shake. Which made it dang hard to take notes and pay attention to my instructor.

I sat on the opposite end of the class from him, and avoided him at all costs. Others eventually noticed my behavior and asked me about it, but I kept my mouth shut, refusing to explain why I avoided him like the plague. I still had nightmares about the look in his eyes when he realized I could see right through him. It had only been then that I could see the eyes of a killer. Later that year, the news outlets had screamed about his arrest. Eventually, he'd been convicted of fifteen counts of murder and sentenced to a life in prison without possibility of parole.

That incident proved to me in a very visceral way that you couldn't judge someone based upon looks and what they projected to the world. I'd felt icy fear around white-collar businesspeople, and I'd felt peaceful and happy around what most considered the dregs of society. It didn't matter your skin color, the money in your bank account, where you lived, or what you did for a living. There were good and bad people in all walks of life, and in every imaginable circumstance. Most people seemed to fall between the two extremes.

I stiffened my shaky knees and walked up three flights of stairs to my apartment. I let myself in and flicked the light switch closest to the door, fear still surging through me, making me compulsively check every nook and cranny of my tiny apartment for some crazy person intent on murdering me in my sleep.

I wanted to collapse on my dilapidated sofa, but I quickly showered the diner smell off me put on some fuzzy pajamas, and made some ramen before I sat down. I huddled under a blanket and slurped my noodles, watching a Disney movie on TV. Something light and happy that would help the feelings of the day to drain from me. I drank icy water from a water bottle and slumped into the cushions.

I couldn't ever remember feeling this defeated. I was a good worker, but I seemed to be cursed when it came to jobs. From my first job when I'd been a homeless sixteen-year-old, to this latest disaster at Happy's, I'd had twenty-three jobs. Some I'd left on my own because I'd been really uncomfortable with an employee or boss, but most I'd lost because of circumstances similar to tonight.

It was like I was a magnet for disaster. No matter where I went or what I did, I couldn't get ahead. Something would happen, and life would shove me down the stairs again, kicking me as I fell.

I didn't believe in the supernatural, but I didn't disbelieve either. And some of those lost jobs...they'd seemed unnatural. Occasionally people that I came across that felt different to me. And the strange thing was, they seemed to notice me as well. To be honest, it freaked me out that they seemed to see me clearly, when to me they were more murky. I couldn't make heads or tails of it. I relied on my sense of people. It had saved my life on more than one occasion. It bugged me that there were people out there that I couldn't get a good sense of. They were complete mysteries.

I fell asleep with this on my mind and woke to pounding on my door. The pounding had a certain sound of doom to it. I knew who was at the door, and I knew what he wanted.

My super, Lando, wanted the rent money. The problem was that I didn't have it. I wasn't usually late on rent, but I'd had a last payment for my tuition, and I couldn't graduate without being fully paid up.

Perhaps if I ignored him long enough, he wouldn't pitch me out into the streets.

Making a faint noise of disgust at my thoughts, I rose from the couch, drew in a big breath for courage, and flung open the door.

Lando had an unamused expression on his pinched, scowling face. His beady eyes looked carrion bird-ish, making me hold in an inappropriate snort at my doomsday thoughts.

"Rent money."

"I'm sorry, Lando, but I don't have all of it right now. I'll have it to you by the end of the week."

Somehow. I might have to find some under-the-table work for a few days to scrounge together the remaining two-hundred dollars. I dug into my purse for my wallet and handed him what I had. "This is all I have so far. I *promise* I'll get the rest to you this week." I wanted to plead with him to be patient, but knew better, even before he opened his mouth.

He squinted and pursed his lips. "I've already listened to five sob stories this morning; yours will not make a difference. If I don't have the rest by Friday, I'll deadbolt your apartment and lock you out."

Never mind that it was illegal to do that, and I should have had thirty days. It didn't matter. Housing in Manhattan was terrible in the slum areas. And it was rarely overseen by the city.

I was so screwed.

I nodded and shut the door in his face. It was only mildly satisfying, which was a sad commentary on my life at the moment.

I snatched another bottle of water from the fridge and stood in front of the mirror in my hallway.

I sighed and pushed my wavy dark hair away from my face. It was long and thick and so hot in the summer that it was not uncommon for it to be slapped up in a messy bun all the time. I had pale skin that veered into the porcelain range, and what some had dubbed "creepy bronze eyes".

Literally. They were bronze. That metallic looking brownish-goldenish-reddish color.

I actually liked them, but most people avoided my eyes like I was Medusa and would turn them to stone with one look.

Sometimes I wished I had that superpower.

I would totally use it judiciously.

Maybe.

Possibly.

Okay, probably not.

I sighed and plopped down onto my couch again to read the comics. Just because. I even had it in me to smile a little at *Dennis the Menace*.

Such a cool kid.

A handful, yes. But awesome.

For the thousandth time, I wished I had a brother. Even if he drove me insane with his shenanigans, I just knew that I would treasure him.

I wanted a home and a sense of belonging. I wanted warmth and light and love. I wanted family and friends. I wanted an amazing boyfriend. But the thought of the chaos that swirled inside of me whenever I was around people made me cringe and made me gun-shy. I'd tried and failed so many times that I'd given up. At least for now. Loneliness was eating at me again, and I knew I'd probably try again soon. There were times I thought I'd accept a feral cat if it meant having someone to talk to.

I didn't remember my birth parents; they'd died when I was very young, and I spent the early part of my life in foster or group homes. At fourteen, I'd been adopted by a kind family, but when I was sixteen they'd died in a helicopter accident. I had been stuck at home with the flu and unable to travel with them. Which, in retrospect, had saved my life. Who knew the flu could be lifesaving?

The days following were not so great and still felt like a fevered dream for me. My nanny was fired, the will and important papers were seized, the house was claimed, and my sick self was ejected from the house in short order.

Some still-living nephew had been the heir of their entire estate. It hadn't mattered at all to him that I was a minor. He'd just kicked me out of the house with no warning. Whenever I thought of him, my teeth ground together. Who did that to a sixteen-year-old girl? What a scuzz.

I still wasn't sure why my adopted parents had left me out of the will, but I hadn't quibbled or fought back against Glade. After living with a great family the prior two years, I hadn't wanted to go back into the system. Technically, my cousin should have gotten custody of me, but he'd felt like a rampaging bull in the short time I'd been around him and I'd had no desire to put myself into his care. Instead, I got a job at a diner in town that paid in cash, lied about my age to everyone I met, and lived on my own. It took months to scrounge together enough money for a down payment on an apartment. That was eleven years ago.

For a while after he inherited the estate, Glade had people following me.

At first, I thought I was losing my mind. I would get the distinct and creepy feeling of someone's eyes lasering into my shoulders or the back of my head. I'd turn and there would be no one there. Other times, I would see a familiar face hanging around outside the diner. Someone I'd seen on the streets in passing, but they would never come in, and they never bothered me.

To say that it had irritated me would be a vast understatement.

He'd kicked me out, dumped me in the rain while I was delirious with fever, and to top all of that off, he'd had people tailing me for months.

I didn't know what to make of it.

What was he worried about? That I'd set the house on fire? That I'd make a stink in the media about him stealing my home? I was sixteen. Far too young to take him on in court and win. Besides, I'd wanted to avoid him and avoid drawing attention to myself at all costs. I wasn't about to take on a dangerous man all over money and a big house.

It just wasn't me.

I huffed under my breath as I flipped the page and looked through the *Help Wanted* ads. I'd been looking at possible secretarial jobs for the last several months, just seeing what was out there and what they were paying, but I'd been waiting until I had my degree in hand before applying to anything. It was nice to see what the potentials were. But this ad was starting to tick me off. It had been running for a month now, and was still there in big, black and bold-as-you-please font, taking up nearly a quarter page of the paper. And it was completely and utterly ridiculous.

Wanted: Vampire's Assistant

Duties will include, but will not be limited to: shopping, banking, accounting, making travel arrangements, supplying a daily itinerary, correspondence and communications with all Excelsior acquisitions and its management teams, etc.

The best applicant for the job will be:

Loyal.
Quiet.
Fearless.
Possess the ability to keep the CEO's affairs private.
In good health.
Flexible.
Dependable.
Somewhat sturdy.

Applicant should also be intelligent and not prone to temper tantrums, moodiness or fits of terror.

Compensation commensurate with applicant's percentage of match affinity with the job and the qualifications.

If hired, living accommodations will be provided by Excelsior Inc.

All inquiries please apply at:
Draven Leto Industries
P.O. Box 727
Moonhaven Cove, Oregon
97579
or
Attn: Draven Leto
@
DravenLetoIndustries@excelsior.com

I HUFFED AGAIN. My current straits were dire. I needed money quickly, and after the week I'd had, it irritated me that this man kept putting out this ad that was so ridiculous it was an utter waste of space. And it was a huge ad! That space could have and should have been used by genuine people looking for employees for their business. I didn't know how it worked in newspapers, but what if real businesses were getting turned away for next week's paper because this yahoo kept running an ad that was clearly meant as a joke for some unsuspecting fool?

I frowned at the ad again, reading through it a second time, then fired up my laptop, and started an email. I was going to tell this Draven Leto person that his joke of an ad wasn't funny, and to please retract it. Placing a prank ad might be funny on any other day. A month ago, I might have laughed with the rest of Manhattan. I might have snickered into my favorite peppermint tea and rolled my eyes.

But today I was inches from getting kicked out of my apartment. I'd had to punch someone last night, who, yet again, didn't seem to appreciate the word "no", and I'd narrowly avoided what might have been a serial killer walking home. My hair was a tangle of wild in an I-will-tame-you-if-it's-the-last-thing-I-do bun, I was stressed out and so tired—even after sleeping all night—that I could barely see straight. My eighteen-hour days had more than caught up to me.

Attn: <u>DravenLetoIndustries@excelsior.com</u>

Subject: Your ad

Mr. Leto,

I realize your ad is probably one big joke for you. Its place-ment nationwide, and possibly worldwide, means that you at least have the means to back up your pranks, but I need to inform you that your prank ad reduces viable space where other companies, and those looking to hire, might find applicants.

Applicants such as myself.

Since we do not live in a fictional world, and since there are no such beings as vampires, I have to assume that this ad's audience was a person in your circle that you needed to get back at or have a little fun with.

Normally, that would be funny. Hilarious, even, as it shows a lightheartedness that I would usually appreciate. But, between the lecherous men at my previous place of employ-ment, my rent being past due, and there being zero food in my cupboards, I can tell you that your ad, on this side of the paper, was not at all funny.

In fact, I found it to be in poor taste.

Please, in the future, refrain from taking up valuable ad space with your pranks.

There are people out there that really need a job and roof over their head that legitimate ads provide the chance of. Thank you for your time.

P.S.

I hope your friend at least found it funny.

Sincerely, Mia Durran

I HIT send and scrounged up some more ramen. It was cheap and filling, and my cupboards usually overflowed with the stuff.

I needed a job, and fast.

I spent the day polishing my resume, adding in my—hopefully—new degree, and proofing and submitting my finals. Later that afternoon, I got a return email with my graded papers. My teacher was lightning fast, and I smiled and internally cheered as I saw that I'd gotten all As. I was set to graduate a week from Friday. I danced around my apartment a bit at that news and wished I had some Martinelli's to celebrate. But I ate another meal of ramen and surprisingly fell asleep with the irritating Draven Leto on my mind.

His ad irritated me, but for no reason at all, I found myself smiling when I thought of him. At least he had a sense of humor.

Little did I know that Draven Leto would frequently bring out those same emotions in me in the days to come.

Irritation.

And laughter.

AFTER CRAWLING out of bed and making an iced coffee to get me started the next morning, I fired my laptop up and checked for any messages I might have gotten overnight.

I'd inquired at a few offices yesterday if they were hiring and wanted to see if they'd gotten back to me.

Instead, I found a message from Draven Leto.

Hmm.

Taking a sip of my iced coffee, I clicked to open the message.

Attn: MiaDurran@credenza.com

Re: My Ad

Dear Ms. Durran,

After reading your email, it occurs to me that there are quite a few things that you don't know about yourself. Please know, Ms. Durran, that I had no intention of taking up valuable ad space with a junk ad. I realize jobs are at a premium these days, and if I had the desire to play a prank such as that on someone in my circle, I certainly wouldn't place it nationwide where every person with an opinion would come out of the woodworks and send zinging emails to my inbox.

Since you don't believe that such an ad can be legit, I offer you proof. Take the ad around to your neighbors and see if they can see the ad. I'm betting they won't be able to. Once finished, email me back, and we'll talk.

Regards, Draven Leto

I ALMOST SPIT out my coffee.

What?

That was a bizarre request. Take it to my neighbors? And, what, like an obedient puppy I was just supposed to go bother my neighbors because some random weirdo asked me to? Just no. Then again... The request might be odd, but it sparked my curiosity. Why did he think that asking other people about the ad would prove something to me? And what point was he trying to prove?

I growled into my coffee, not sure what I wanted to do. I definitely didn't want to disturb my neighbors over something so trivial, but I was also very curious now about what Mr. Draven Leto was hinting at.

As I read over his words again, a smile slowly bloomed on my face. I decided I would play his game, if only to let him know, in no uncertain terms, that I didn't appreciate being the butt of what had to be a joke.

I gulped the rest of my coffee down and slipped the My Spirit Animal is a Tiger mug into the sink, ran some water into it, yanked on some shorts and ran a brush through my hair. I slid into my slip-on tennies, scooped the paper up, grabbed my keys so I wouldn't accidentally get locked out, and knocked on the neighbor's door to the right of mine.

A harried mom with smooth, dark hair pulled back into a quick twist and dark skin answered the door. Her shirt looked like it had been gummed to death, there was spit-up on her shoulder, and she had dark shadows under her bloodshot eyes.

Yikes. Maybe I should offer to babysit her son more often.

I squirmed a little in embarrassment. "Hi, Leona." I smiled half-heartedly. "Really sorry to bother you, but I'm clearing up a bit of a bet." I placed a blue, nail-wrapped fingertip against the Vampire's Assistant ad. "You can see this ad here, right?"

Leona looked at where my finger was pointing, looked back at me, and looked back at my fingertip.

"Mia." Her voice was steady and measured.

"Yes?"

"Can you hear Daniel?"

I could indeed hear her baby Daniel screaming in the other room now that her door was open. I cringed again. Bad timing.

"Yes?"

"Then you can understand that I don't have time for any funny business, right?"

My face fell. My thoughts went a little blank. So... that was a no?

"You really can't see it?"

She glared at me. "There's nothing there, Mia!"

Slam.

Well, okay then. I wasn't really sure what had just happened. Sleep deprived moms were serious heroes, but perhaps Leona wasn't the best person to ask at the moment?

I *did* know that I definitely needed to offer to watch Daniel more often.

Leona clearly needed a break.

Not to be deterred, I systematically hit up every available person on my floor.

Zero people could see the ad.

I slumped into my apartment and dumped the ad and myself onto my ratty, tan couch. I was so confused. There was a possibility that a few needed to put their glasses on, or were preoccupied like Leona. Some could have been lying to me. But the likelihood of *all* of them saying they couldn't see the ad when it was very clearly there was infinitesimal.

I was staring at it. It was in a big, bold type, with a rounded font. It looked to be in sixteen-point type, even. Plenty big for those that might be optically challenged. I was flabbergasted, embarrassed that I had just gone around to all my neighbors who probably thought I was a little crazy now, and irritated that Draven Leto had been right. And still so very confused.

As I took another shower to tame my crazy hair and found some presentable clothes to go looking for a job in, I pondered the puzzle. Draven Leto had hinted heavily that not many people would be able to see the ad. I could see it, but no one else on my floor could. It begged the question...if

I could see it, did that somehow make me different? If so, in what way was I different? Would others outside of my building be able to see it?

And the scary thought, if I could see it, and others couldn't, did that make the crazy ad the slightest bit legit? Vampires belonged in fiction, clearly. At least I hoped so. But what about the other people in the world that I'd never been able to get a strong sense of? Could they be different in the same way that I seemed to be different?

My thoughts ran round and round. Should I email him back? Or would it be better—safer—to just let it go.

The irony of my personality was that I was, by nature, a curious person. I'd learned, because of what I dealt with around others, to stymie that curiosity, but only to a point. I still wanted to love people. Heck, I'd love some friends I didn't feel ick around. And this, this had me wanting to reach out to the irritating Draven Leto for some answers. For curiosity's sake, sure, but also because I sort of feared that Draven Leto was *other*. And that what he'd meant was that I was *other* too.

It should logically make me want to run. I had a very finely tuned run-o-meter. But, strangely, it didn't. I felt drawn into something greater than myself, and insanely curious about what that something might be.

There was something nagging at me, too. Like I'd heard the name Draven Leto before somewhere. As I applied makeup, pulled my hair in a half-up twist, and found some shoes I could walk in but were interview ready, I puzzled over the dilemma.

It was when I was reaching out to grab my coat that it hit me. Sometime back, there had been something in the news about a luxury hotel owned by him in Florence, Italy that had burned to the ground. No lives had been lost, if I remembered correctly. This, at least, legitimatized his claim that he was both a businessman and that he had a company that needed secretarial work. Neither of those meant that he wasn't crazy or dangerous, but I needed a job, didn't I?

I hung my coat back on the coat stand, sighed at what a woman would do for a job and for curiosity's sake, then plopped back onto the couch as I reached again for my laptop.

Attn: DravenLetoIndustries@Excelsior.com

Re: Your Ad

Mr. Leto,

I am unsure why I'm again corresponding with you, except maybe to put this to rest in my mind. I checked with my entire floor. No one could see the ad. Not a single person.

I have no idea what to say to that.

The ad is there. I'm looking at it right now, in fact.

Can you please explain what the heck is going on?

You can reach me at (212) 617-8974

Mia

I sent it and sighed into the couch. My stomach grumbled, and I placed a palm over the ache and tried to figure out my next steps for my day. I needed more groceries, but I didn't have any money. I had some mac and cheese in the cupboard. It wasn't great with just water and no butter, but it would work. I think I also had a jar of pasta sauce and some leftover linguini noodles. I could scrounge around for change and buy a loaf of bread and a jar of peanut butter, and that would have to work for this week. I was just getting up to make the mac and cheese when my phone buzzed. I flipped it over to look at the name. *Draven Leto.*

I gasped and sat up. Even though I'd given him my number—I considered it networking—I hadn't expected him to call me!

I felt a sense of anticipation and excitement as I hit the green button.

"Hello?"

"Ms. Durran, so good to hear from you. Can I assume you gave me your number because you're curious about why you can see the ad and those around you can't?" His voice was wicked-deep and sensuously amused.

"You can. Also, I'm looking for a secretarial job, and you seem to be looking for a secretary." Although, what *kind* of secretary he was looking for, I still wasn't entirely sure of. Personal assistant to a vampire was just crazy talk.

His laughter was potent and heady, filling me with a combustible, effervescent feeling. I tapped a finger on my sensible cotton pants I used for job searching and tried to come up with a sane, polite way of asking my question.

"To answer your question, Ms. Durran, only a small percentage of people would have been able to see the ad."

"But why?" I stood at the window, my breath and the

23

chilled window colliding and creating steamy fog. It was early spring, but Manhattan was still locked in icy weather.

I heard a shuffling of papers, and the *skritch* of an expensive pen-nub on paper. "I'd like the opportunity to explain in person, and I'd like to interview you for the job. Can I send a courier with a plane ticket?"

A beat of silence. My first thought was, *Yay, a job!* My second was astonishment that he was still playing the game of looking for an assistant. And that he apparently was a vampire. Uh-huh.

"You mean the job for a vampire's assistant?" I said, disbelief heavy in my wry tone.

His smile was almost audible. The *skritch* of the pen stopped. "I can prove it over the phone if you'd like."

I almost laughed aloud. He'd like to prove it. Over the phone. That he was a vampire.

Well, game on!

"Of course, Mr. Leto. By all means, please prove that you're a vampire."

I just knew that his smile had become wolfish. How...did I know that?

I shook my head to clear it.

"Where are you standing in your apartment, Mia?"

I frowned. "At my window."

"All right. Thank you."

"You're welcome."

Laughter again. Deep and sensuous. "So polite."

Then his voice changed. The laughter was gone, and in its place was a thick, powerful presence that sent warm chills down my spine. *Warm chills are different,* I thought inanely. "Mia, go to your refrigerator door and open it."

My spine snapped straight, my hands clenched the

phone, and my feet marched to my fridge. And I knew it would sound crazy to others, but I wasn't at all afraid. Even over the phone, I felt such a powerful surge of peace that it almost broke whatever hold Mr. Leto had over me. The peace, in fact, was so strong that tears pricked my eyes. I felt content for the first time in a long time. It was such an alien feeling that I had to blink away more tears. I reached the fridge and yanked on the handle. The light blinked on, somewhat stutteringly, and the cold air hit me with a soothing puff of breeze. "What's in your fridge, Mia?"

I fought the response that sprang to my lips, embarrassment making me cringe. I didn't want to tell a potential employer, and an obviously well-off man, that here was one water bottle in my fridge and nothing else. Not even an open box of baking soda.

His tone turned soft, but still had that zing of command. "Mia, what's in your fridge?"

"Nothing," I sighed. "A water bottle."

He was quiet for a moment. "No food?" His tone had changed into one of concern, and I felt validated in my assessment of that tiny part of him, at least. Mr. Leto seemed to have a bit of a caretaker's personality.

I shook my head and then rolled my eyes. *He can't see you, Mia!* "No food in the fridge, but I have some in the cupboards," I said truthfully, but with the obvious intent that he wouldn't feel sorry for me. Heck, I just might need to go grocery shopping, for all he knew!

As if on command, my stomach snarled loudly. I put a hand over it to soothe it, but Draven apparently had the ears of a fox.

"Was that your stomach?" His voice sounded half

amused and half appalled. What, he'd never been hungry before?

My cheeks burned. "Yes."

He was quiet for another moment, and then that voice of command poured out of my phone speaker again. "Mia, go sit on the couch."

My legs, without me giving them permission, walked themselves over to the couch, and deposited me there.

I still wasn't afraid, but my mind was churning over the fact that he *could* do this. He *was* controlling my body somehow. My mind helpfully-not-helpfully spat out one word: Vampire. I growled in frustration. Leave it up to me to find the supernatural in a world with almost eight billion people in it.

He laughed. "Did you just growl at me? Are you sure you're not part shifter?" I heard a faint tapping on his end. Keys being pressed into a keyboard. After a minute, the tapping stopped.

Time went by, but my butt was still firmly planted on the couch, and my spine was still annoyingly at attention. I couldn't move. And trust me, I tried to break his control. I still had all my own thoughts. I just couldn't break the hold he had over my gross motor functions. I could still do small things on my own power, blink, purse my lips, clench my hands, so I figured his control was only lightly being applied to me.

"What I'm using on you is not generally used on another being," he said, his voice soothing. "It's not illegal, however, and I thought it would make my point nicely." I didn't need the soothing voice. I still wasn't afraid.

"That you're a vampire?" Funny, my question this time didn't sound at all ironic. I think my subconscious was pretty sure this person was legit. I was fighting the thought, because if this was true, then a whole lot of other things might be true. And if those things were true, then what the heck was *I* if I could see them? That thought was both terrifying and exhilarating.

"I'm not afraid. You don't need to pacify me."

The pen tapping sound came again from his end of the phone.

"Interesting."

Interesting? Well, okay, my reaction might be atypical, but that was only because I was getting such a powerful surge of peace from this guy...err, vampire, that I couldn't help but believe that he was a genuinely good person. I trusted my instincts.

Before I could say anything in response, my doorbell rang, and the feeling of being taken over left. I sighed in relief. It was so nice to have my body back under my control. It hadn't been a painful experience, but I didn't think I'd ever take the control I had over my own body for granted again, either.

I ignored Mr. Leto's humming and got up to answer the door. Through the peephole I could see the delivery boy from Michelana's Italian Restaurant with a huge bag in his hands. Puzzled, I opened the door to tell him he had the wrong apartment, and to see if I could direct him to the right one, but he smiled politely before I could get any words out. "Delivery for Mia Durran?"

"I..."

"Just sign here, Miss."

He shoved an electronic signature thing in my hand, and I scribbled my name while hastily trying to explain that I hadn't ordered anything.

"Someone has already paid for it, Miss. Including the tip." And with that, he was off, and I was left standing dumbly in my doorway with the aroma of garlic breadsticks and meaty lasagna tickling my nose.

"I... What the heck just happened?"

Draven's chuckle sounded from my loosely dangling phone. I put the phone back to my ear. "You sounded hungry. Your phone's area code is for Manhattan. I just looked up the best Italian restaurant and took the chance that you'd ordered takeout through them before. Fortunately, they are a rare gem of a business and keep their customer's addresses on file so they don't have to bother customers by asking for them each time they order food there."

Well, I ate there anytime I could scrounge together some money, so his story seemed at least plausible.

"Thank you." I was both humbled by his kindness and embarrassed at the need for it. I hated being embarrassed, and I hated feeling exposed. I was also reeling over the fact that supernaturals existed. It was very cool, but also very sobering.

I set everything down on my kitchen table, put my hot hands up to my cool face, and covered my eyes. It was soothing; very, very soothing. I breathed in deeply, and out deeply, and repeated it several times before I picked my phone up again and said with a voice that wasn't on the verge of a major freak out, "I'll take those tickets, Mr. Leto. But to be completely transparent, I don't have my degree yet. I'm graduating next week. I was just starting the process of polishing my resume with the new information and looking for a secretarial job."

"I understand. I can send the tickets for a flight in two weeks?"

"You'd hold the job until then?" I was flabbergasted. Why would he hold the job that long?

"Ms. Durran, I think you are operating under the mistaken belief that you are not a rare find." He said this as though I knew what he was talking about. My eyebrows scrunched down as I tried to figure out what he meant.

"I'm sorry. I'm not trying to disagree with you; I'm just trying to figure out what you're talking about. It says you're based in Oregon. There should be plenty of people looking for an assistant job there."

He was quiet for a few minutes, and, though I didn't know how, I could feel his surprise over the phone.

"You don't know what you are, do you?" he asked gently.

I clutched the phone tighter. And because I was uncomfortable, I resorted to being a smart aleck. "An Earthling?" I said facetiously.

His genuine laughter made those effervescent bubbles pop in my chest again. I rubbed my chest and smiled at the broken tension. He laughed for quite a while, and I just sat there, grinning like a fool, listening to the sound, and rubbing the part of my chest where the effervescence kept fizzing. This was so new to me. Not just making someone laugh, but the easy way we were talking to one another. The innocent camaraderie.

"Yes, an Earthling." His tone turned gentle. "But Mia, you're also a supernatural. You couldn't have seen the ad otherwise. And I have a strong feeling I know what kind of supernatural you are. If I'm right, with your education, you will be a perfect fit for the position. So, yes, I'll hold the job for you."

I felt elated! A potential new job! And I'd always wanted to move out of the city. I hated the smog and congestion. I could figure out the tiny details—like what I would do for food for the next two weeks, and where I would stay when the apartment manager locked me out of my apartment in a week—later.

As though he could hear my thoughts, Draven asked, "Mia, are you okay where you are for two weeks? I can send a travel bonus that would get you by until you come for your interview. It would also allow you to rent a storage unit and move the things you want to keep in there until you're ready for them again."

"You can't read minds, can you?" I hadn't felt fear about the taking over my body thing, but the idea that he might be able to hear my thoughts made me cringe.

He laughed. "No, Miss Durran. I assure you, I cannot hear your thoughts. It was a passing feeling, nothing more."

A passing feeling my foot. The part about him not being able to hear thoughts rang true, at least.

I couldn't believe I was about to have this conversation with a potential employer. "I had a last payment for my tuition that was overdue. It made me short on my rent. My building manager has already been by and has given me a week's deadline." I tried to state all of this as concisely and succinctly as I could. I had no desire to give him exhaustive details about the deplorable state of my personal finances.

"I'll book a hotel for you under a company card," he said, tapping on his computer again.

My protest died on my lips. He was being kind, yes, but he was also being practical. If it was true that I was a rare find, and that he was eager for me to interview for the position, then it would also be true that he would want me to make it to the interview in one piece.

I received a text with the hotel booking information. "You're clear to arrive as early as today," he said.

I felt a weight leave my shoulders. Sometimes, the sweetest words to an ex-homeless person were, "You have a place to stay." Once you've been homeless, you always had an eternal fear that you'd end up back on the streets.

"Thank you," I said, my throat tight.

"You're welcome, Miss Durran. I look forward to your interview." He clicked off, and I sat at my table with my head in my hands.

My mind was reeling at everything that had just happened, but I knew one thing with absolute certainty: in two weeks I was going to Oregon to meet a possible vampire for a job interview.

I laughed and shook my head.

Life was so weird sometimes.

CHAPTER 2
MIA

"You didn't have to book me into the poshest hotel you could find," I said into the phone later that evening. "The tiles on the bathroom floor are heated, for goodness' sake! There's an actual rainforest setting on the lighting pad I can switch on so I can hear rainforest sounds when I shower. Who does that?"

He laughed. "I disagree that I didn't have to. Is the location disagreeable?" His voice had that wicked sound of playful amusement again. I was so glad that I could keep my potential boss amused by my antics and provincial views of life and money.

"You know it's not," I grumbled.

"How's the view?"

I sighed as I opened the sliding glass door. "It's clear today. I can see the Statue of Liberty from my balcony. The balcony that is ridiculously large, by the way."

It was funny. I hadn't stopped to think about reaching out to him when I got to the hotel and settled in. I somehow knew he'd want to hear from me and know I was safe.

And if that wasn't bizarre enough, this was the second and only time in my life that I could recall feeling such peace when I was interacting with another person, and both times had been with him.

As I spent the afternoon boxing up the things from my apartment that I wanted to keep—mainly clothing and the few personal things I'd acquired over the years—I'd reflected on our phone call. People who weren't...supernaturals felt chaotic to me, but Draven Leto, a self-proclaimed vampire, made my soul feel like it was submerged in warm, lavender-scented water. He felt incredibly peaceful to me, and I was trying to figure out if it was just him, or if it was supernaturals in general.

"Have you had dinner yet?"

I shut the slider, shivering at the cool air that had entered in just the few moments I'd had it open. "No, I haven't." I wasn't planning on it either. To say I was in an affluent area of town would be a vast understatement. There was nothing near me that I felt justified in spending the money he'd wired me on. Besides, I had to save most of it for essentials. I was out of just about everything: shaving cream, razor cartridges, shampoo and conditioner, lotion, toothpaste, and I needed to replace them all before I left in two weeks.

Mr. Leto was quiet, and I marveled again that I'd reached out to him. I'd actually reached out to another person. I had no idea if this was a breakthrough for me, or if my desire to talk stemmed from the fact that Mr. Leto was so thoroughly likable.

The fact that he was potentially a vampire did not go unnoticed by me. I found it ironic. Vampires had such a bad rap in the fictional world. They were written as bloodthirsty savages who had no moral compass and viewed human life, really *any* life, as so beneath them that they felt like they were sullying themselves by being around anything other than their own kind.

Draven didn't give off those vibes at all. From the little I'd interacted with him, I found him to be kind, thoughtful, intelligent, and prone to bouts of what most might consider excessive generosity. His laugh did strange things to my chest, and I felt like I could be around him, day in and day out, without difficulty.

In fact, I was getting the impression from him that he was as lonely as I was. Maybe not to the point that he would welcome a feral cat, like I'd been getting perilously close to doing, but there was a loneliness in his voice that I could hear. I was careful not to indicate that I knew this through any of my actions or conversation. It was a tidbit about him that I kept close to my chest and pondered.

There was a knock at the door, and I wasn't really surprised to find room service on the other side with a rolling tray of covered dishes. They wheeled the rolling tray in and arranged everything on the table in the dining area. I tried to tip them, but was rebuffed. "Mr. Leto has taken care of all gratuities for your stay, Miss," I was again kindly reminded.

Of course he had. I felt a little like a sheep that was being herded by a sheepdog.

"You realize I can choose my own food, yes?" I said into the phone, still connected with Draven.

"You wouldn't have eaten."

It frustrated me that he knew that about me so quickly. Was I that transparent? I sighed in defeat and tried not to grumble at the nice man that just wanted to make sure I wasn't going to starve to death while waiting for my interview with him. I swallowed my pride.

"Thank you."

"You're welcome, Miss Durran. Have a good evening."

"You, too."

We clicked off, and I took the lids off the platters of food on the table, my stomach snarling in anticipation of having yummy food again. Draven seemed to have an uncanny idea of my tastes, or at least what most people liked. I thought this was amusing considering what he potentially was and what vampires ate.

One plate contained pan roasted filet mignon and braised short-rib ravioli with natural jus. I wouldn't have known what it was, but the hotel kindly put a menu card on each silver tray. The other plate contained an assortment of desserts.

My eyes widened. I'd never had filet mignon before, and the braised short-rib ravioli sounded delish too. I grabbed a plate off the warmer and loaded it up with a bit of everything, including the side-salad with house dressing they'd provided. A bevy of drinks was lined up behind the silver platters. I chose a Dr. Pepper and sat down on the couch, turning on some mindless TV so I didn't have to listen to the silence in the room.

I went to bed early that night, and for the first time that I could remember, I felt anticipation at the thought of waking up and doing this all over again the next day. The wonderful hotel room, the yummy food, and the fact that I had nothing more stressful on my to-do list than taking a walk and later getting some essentials for my trip, filled me with such a contented feeling that I laughed out loud.

I hadn't realized the sheer weight of worry and stress I'd

been carrying until it had been lifted. I marveled that I was graduating with my business degree in a week, and that I already had a job interview that sounded incredibly promising. And I marveled yet again at the emergence of supernaturals into my life, and the fact that I was so blasé about it. It was like...I'd somehow known all along.

I fell asleep to that thought with a smile on my face.

TWO WEEKS LATER, I arrived at the Portland, Oregon airport around two-thirty a.m., bleary-eyed and drooping. All caffeinated beverages had failed their one and only job, and my jaw kept cracking open in wide yawns that probably showed the other weary travelers around me all of my teeth fillings and my entire esophagus.

Mr. Leto had called the moment the courier arrived and handed over my tickets, somehow knowing I'd just signed for them, and explained that he'd gotten me a red-eye flight into Oregon because he wanted to be able to meet me the moment I arrived at his estate. And as he slept primarily during the daylight hours, a red-eye flight was best. I'd figured he'd at least have one or two cliché vampire habits, so I'd just thanked him for the tickets, and said I looked forward to the interview.

We hadn't talked much more during my stay, but he'd called about a week ago to let me know that he'd have a driver at the airport waiting for me, and to apologize once again for the flight time. It hadn't really bothered me. It had been a quiet flight, with most of the passengers asleep. But, because I'd been getting regular sleep for the past two weeks, and getting to bed early at that, the change to my schedule and the long flight had made me so dang tired that I was having a hard time keeping my eyes open. I hadn't been able to sleep on the flight in, despite the extra room that those seated in first class were given.

A tall, muscular man with alarming grayish skin held up a sign in front of me that read *Mia Durran*. I looked around me bleary-eyed. No one else was looking at him in alarm. Of course, it was the middle of the night, but still.

"That's me," I said, as I shuffled for my license. He nodded and didn't laugh at my terrible license picture. I thought that took considerable restraint. He showed me his license to verify that he was who Draven had said would meet me, then he held a finger up, asking me to wait for just a moment while he dialed a number, and held his phone out to me.

I took it just as Draven's voice said, "Is she with you?"

"Umm, yes. I'm here in Oregon. I'm assuming he handed me the phone so I could double verify that he's the right person, and not an axe murderer?"

Draven chuckled. "Yes. Mesmer is big on safety."

My tired brain appreciated that Mesmer had thought to reach out to Draven. "I have your word that he's safe?" I cupped my hand around the phone and spoke in a low voice. "He's gray, you realize?" I knew I was being rude, but my curiosity was roused. I couldn't think of what a gray supernatural might be. I looked at him, taking in his immense size, thick thighs and calves, gigantic arms and chest, and oversized head. He had gray eyes, and thick, black, buzz-cut hair.

I knew tiredness might affect my sense of him, but he wasn't really giving off any vibes. He just felt like a quiet, larger-than-life presence to me. Somehow, that was comforting.

"He's safe. And he's gray because he's a gargoyle. Gargoyles are excellent bodyguards, and Mesmer is one of the best. He's also one of the most loyal beings I've ever met." He changed the subject. "You sound tired."

While Draven spoke, Mesmer had grabbed my three huge suitcases like he was merely picking up a fluffy pillow and led me out of the airport and into an idling gray limo.

"I got spoiled at the hotel. The change to my sleep schedule's just thrown me off. I'll be fine tomorrow."

He hummed in thought, and I had the sense that he wanted to apologize again for the lateness of the hour, but refrained. "I'll let you get some sleep then. It's a three-hour drive. That should give you time to get a good nap in."

His thoughtfulness touched me. "Thanks. See you soon."

We hung up, and my phone dinged with a text as I slung my purse onto the bar in front of me and grabbed a bottle of water

A message from a number I was unfamiliar with said:

> Mesmer: It's nice to meet you, Mia. Drinks are in the fridge. On-demand movies are available on the TV. We should arrive at our destination in 3 hours.

> Mia: Thanks, Mesmer. It's nice to meet you too.

> Mesmer: You're welcome.

Mesmer must have handed me his company phone inside the airport, and was now using his personal one to text me with. I put it safely in my purse, took a sip of water, let my body melt into the decadent, cushy seats, and had no more thoughts for the rest of the drive.

Next I was aware, big, gentle hands were persistently shaking my shoulders. I pushed them away, still mostly asleep, and heard a quiet chuckle, and then the gigantic hands were back, nudging my shoulders a little harder.

I suddenly remembered where I was and bolted upright, probably looking like an owl with large, startled eyes and my hair flying all over the place. My glance darted around until I looked up into Mesmer's face.

I slumped in relief.

"Oh, hello again. I must have fallen asleep. Thank you for waking me."

His smile was warm and soft as he patted my hand and went to grab the bags out of the trunk.

I rubbed my face, trying to wake up, digging deep grooves into the sockets of my eyes before I got out of the car to look around. My eyes widened as I took in my surroundings. Had I accidentally flown to Italy?

"That's an Italian villa."

Mesmer nodded, not at all bothered or surprised by my astonishment, and motioned for me to follow. I looked around in befuddled interest. "Well, I always wanted to visit Italy."

Rounded, double entryway steps led to a mahogany door with a huge copper knocker in the shape of a lion. As I stumbled up the steps, my legs refusing to work properly because of weariness, I looked around at the surrounding area. A forest surrounded us, and beyond the villa, white, sandy beach and glistening, deep-blue water shone in the full moonlight.

"Holy shmoley."

Mesmer chuckled.

The door opened and a thin man in an honest-to-goodness tuxedo answered the door. He had thick, gray eyebrows and hair, pale skin, and a hawkish nose. But it was his eyes that were the most arresting. They were aqua blue.

My jaw wanted to sag open at the impossible color, but I refused to let it. I would not gawk at everyone and everything. From the corner of my eye, though, I tried to take in as much as I could. Mesmer took off in a different direction after giving me a pat on my shoulder. And for someone so big, he moved like a panther, silently and gracefully. I wondered if he studied martial arts.

"This way, miss," the butler said, trying to wrest my attention from the lemon trees that sat at either end of the entry hall. They made it smell so bright and yummy right when you walked in, and I wanted to take a picture of the beautiful, glazed pots they were housed in.

The butler moved swiftly, and I tried to take in as much of my surroundings as I could as we passed through an entry hall, a formal dining room, a parlor, a living room, and a billiard room, until finally the servant knocked on a door, then let me into an office of mammoth proportions.

"Mia Durran for you, Master Leto."

"Thank you, Aiwin."

Aiwin bowed me in, and I stiffened my spine for courage before I walked in.

The room was enormous, but felt cozy. A fire blazed merrily in the rock fireplace, various overstuffed couches and chairs sat interspersed throughout the room, and an enormous mahogany desk stood at the far end. Murals covered the walls. Nature scenes, mostly. One wall had green vines and leaves stenciled all over a creamy background with a pale sun and a robin's egg-blue sky. Another had a wall of tinted windows that looked out over the ocean.

I fell in love on the spot.

I knew right there and then that this room would be one of my happy places. I still had an interview to get through, though, and I needed to meet my boss and everyone in the villa to see if I'd be comfortable working here. So far, through my tour with Aiwin, and spotting the scurrying employees in the villa, I'd felt great about being here. All the chaotic feelings that I had become used to weren't present.

I puzzled over this as my eyes finally found the male sitting behind the desk, and my feet instantly turned into useless blocks of concrete. I squeezed my purse in a death-grip and tried in vain not to gape at the beautiful person across from me.

Glorious, chocolate curls adorned a face that looked like it belonged either to a runway model or a Michelangelo statue. Sculpted cheeks, beautifully formed nose and lips, expressive, arched eyebrows, and smooth, café au lait skin all short-circuited my brain from my mouth. I gaped at him. I'd heard the stories, that vampires were beautiful so they could lure their prey in, but it wasn't until right then, standing in that sweet-smelling office, that I came to believe in those stories.

I marveled at my maybe future boss for what must have been a full minute before I pulled myself together and could form sentences that weren't gibberish. Did vampires have a lure?

Draven laughed, that deep sensuous sound, and I felt

those effervescent bubbles popping again in my chest. "To answer your unasked question, Miss Durran, all vampires have a slight lure. It's autonomous. We can't control the base level of the lure. We can, however, turn up the heat, so to speak. What you're feeling is the autonomous lure that I can't control. I would never use the other on you. You're safe here."

"Yeah, that might be a problem," I could finally say. It felt like I literally had to unstick my tongue from the roof of my mouth to say it. "If I can't function, I can't do the job you want me for."

He smiled, and my brain went a little blank. Like the cartoons where they hung up a sign behind their vacant eyes that said Out to lunch. I shook my head to clear it and closed my eyes, breathing deeply and reaching for my sense of inner balance.

Mr. Leto let me; the room descended into quiet. When I opened my eyes, I felt more centered, and more able to tackle Mr. Leto's unearthly beauty and the lure that he couldn't control.

Draven smiled and clasped my hand as he waved me toward a seat on one of the couches.

"Please sit. You needn't worry about the lure. The longer you're in my presence, the weaker the lure will get, until eventually, you won't even notice it anymore."

I nodded as I sank into the decadent couch. If I never moved again, I would consider myself lucky. The couch sucked me in like it had been made of fluffy, supportive clouds. "That's good to know. On the outside looking in, this is a very bizarre job interview, at least for me." I paused, searching my feelings. I didn't feel the same peace I'd felt on the phone with him, but I felt calm and at ease. That was better than ninety percent of my past jobs, so I was pretty happy with it.

"Thank you for coming. I know this is all new to you."

"Thank you for the opportunity to interview with you." I was proud of myself for my poise. I'd only slept the three hours in the car. My brain felt like someone had stuffed it with fuzzy cotton, and even though I was intrigued by the fact that Mr. Leto was a vampire and Moonhaven Cove was full of supernaturals, I tried to let my curiosity and expectations go so I could focus.

Aiwin came in with some peppermint tea. I sipped it and studied him. He looked to be in his mid-to-late eighties. He wore a gray suit, but the white shirt underneath had a lace collar, and an apricot-colored ascot in place of a tie. He felt mischievous to me, though I couldn't see it from my observations of him. My guess was that he was an elf or fae of some kind. His ears were tipped at the ends, and though he had a willowy build, he looked strong and fit.

"Will there be anything else, Master?"

"No, Aiwin, thank you."

Aiwin bowed himself out, and Mr. Leto asked if I wanted chocolate cake.

I peered at him, wondering if this was a trick question.

He shook his head and chuckled, then served me a thick slice of the chocolate cake, along with a linen napkin, a heavy silver fork, and a beautiful plate with red and pink roses around the gilded edges.

I tried to control my ravenous appetite, but the smell of the decadent chocolate threatened to undo me. "Pixie ponies, this cake is amazing. I'd love to take your chef home with me if this doesn't work out." Well, there was nowhere to go if this didn't work out, but I was pointedly ignoring that train of thought at the moment.

"I'm sure his wife would miss him."

I nodded my head, trying in vain to daintily eat the cake instead of shoveling it in my face. Not only was I starving, but I'd never had cake this good. I was tempted to sneak in after the interview and snag the rest of it. "I would miss him too." After sipping a scalding gulp of peppermint tea, all conversation halted as I devoured the cake.

Devoured.

I ate it so fast that if I were watching as an innocent bystander, I think I would have been terrified.

I could feel Draven's eyes on me the whole time. I felt as though he got a lot of satisfaction out of seeing me eat that cake, but I didn't know why, and I was a little too occupied to ask right then. After the cake was gone, I looked at the plate and wondered how impolite it would be if I licked up all the crumbs.

"By all means," Draven said. "Lick it clean. Or you could just have another slice." His humor made me remember our phone conversations the last two weeks. How I'd reached out to him. His humor and kindness on the phone. It made me feel as though I knew him already, which I realized was a dangerous trap. I didn't know him. And I needed to remember that.

"I just might," I mumbled. Sighing, I set the plate on the nice table and sat back.

"You seem comfortable in my presence, Miss Durran." Draven's right eyebrow winged upward. "Can I assume you aren't afraid of me?"

I squinted at him, my tired brain taking in his presence. I really wanted to see his teeth.

In horror, I realized I'd said the knee-jerk thought out loud when he spluttered and laughed.

"I am not a horse."

I went red in embarrassment. I really needed to get some more sleep!

"Of course not!"

Draven studied me, probably trying to see if I'd bolt if he showed me. When I showed no fear, he lifted one corner of his top lip with his index finger. The incisor there lengthened as I watched it. I wanted to get closer and observe it in fascination. By sheer force of will, I forced myself to remain seated.

I canted my head to the side as he released his lip. My fingers tapped on my bottom lip as I stared at him. I wasn't sure what I was feeling at the moment. Definitely calm and ease, but also... curiosity. I was no dummy. Fictional vampires tended to be stabby with their teeth, and sort of murdery. But I was curious because that was not at all what Draven Leto projected. And not at all what I felt around him.

My instincts dismissed his top-of-the-line suit and his thousand-dollar watch, reminding me that pretty packages sometimes held killers. My feelings quietly whispered that he was a genuinely good person, and for the moment, he looked totally at ease and not at all murdery *or* stabby.

Would it be rude of me to assume that he'd already eaten for the evening?

Probably.

After a long silence, I finally answered him. "I'm not afraid, but keep in mind my head is full of cotton at the moment. I reserve the right to be afraid or change my mind in the future. This is not exactly a typical interview for me, no matter how typical it is for you or the people of this town."

He nodded.

I'd missed seeing the town I'd come into, being asleep and all, but I knew from a conversation with Draven that it was a hidden town of supernaturals that mortals couldn't find and couldn't enter.

I refocused and handed him my resume, which I dug out of my handbag.

"Here's my updated resume with my degree listed. I have a generalized degree in business, but I can handle any secretarial or administrative assistant job. I don't have experience, but I graduated at the top of my class."

Draven poured some of my tea into another floral teacup, and sat back with it, sipping it. He looked at the cup a little in surprise, and I could tell he was trying to figure out if he liked it or not.

I could tell that he was picking up on my puzzlement over him making such a fuss over bringing me in for an interview. Not that I was complaining. It would be lovely to work here, but I still didn't understand what made me a good candidate.

"Have you been able to figure out what kind of supernatural you are yet?"

"No, I haven't."

And it hadn't been for lack of trying. I looked fully human when I looked in the mirror. No gray skin or tipped ears. I didn't seem to have any extra strength, and I for sure didn't have wings. I would have noticed those bad boys long before now.

"You're an empath, Miss Durran, and my guess is that you're a strong one." He eyed me over the steam of his cup.

"When I took control of your motor functions, you could still think clearly and move some of your body, yes?"

His question didn't sound like a question at all. It felt like he already knew the answer. "Yes. I could think clearly. I could also move small things on my body." There was no need to mention that the sense of peace I'd felt speaking with him had been so abnormal for me, and so strong that it'd almost snapped me out of his control.

He nodded, as if what I was saying was something he had expected. "Empaths get strength from a sense of equanimity inside of them. Everything in our lives is designed to test our inner balance, and for an empath, that can sometimes be an unsurmountable task. One that many empaths never find. I don't know if it's common for you to have that sense of harmony every day, but on the day of the test, I felt, through my control of your body, that you had an incredibly strong sense of inner balance. As a matter of fact, I felt my control over you slide off for a few brief moments, as though you'd blinked out of existence. There's really only one type of supernatural that can combat a vampire's control, and that's an empath. Empaths of significant strength are a rarity.

"I run a multi-billion-dollar company. A strong empath would be helpful to me in the day-to-day running of my corporation. You can give me insights that I wouldn't otherwise be able to have into the companies and the people I deal with on an everyday basis. From those who work for me at my firm, to the CEOs and staff of other companies that I'm interested in doing business with. That insight would help me know if the company and people are honorable and truthful. or if they're a den of vipers, intent on taking my money without intending to keep their end of the contract. I have my own senses, too, of course, but I would trust yours over my own in most cases. You would also help me with personnel issues at DL Industries. We work from home, but I'm often on video conference with my CFO and COO from our home office, and the hard truth is that in this large of a company, personalities, priorities, and experiences clash, creating a disharmonious workplace. I want to avoid that as much as possible. Part of your job duties will be to take video calls from the various department heads and help them manage our large team."

I blinked, my mind churning with the blast of too much information. An empath? I was an empath? A sudden and intense sense of peace descended upon me. It was so strong that I could only sit there in stillness and let it run its course through my body. An empath. That made...sense. It felt right. It actually explained so much! I wondered if the fact that I'd been raised around non-supernaturals and lived among them had been the reason I'd felt so chaotic. Maybe mortals *always* felt that chaotic? Because, thus far, I was feeling pretty serene, even considering that he'd just basically told me I'd be a babysitter for adults.

Some of what I was feeling, the awe over my being an empath, and the cringiness of having to mediate grown adults, must have shown on my face, because Mr. Leto laughed.

"So, if I'm hearing you correctly, I would need to sit in on your board meetings, and your meetings with other businesses you're auditioning to see if what they want and what you're offering is a good fit. I'd also need to help with whatever personnel problems the heads of departments are having at your main office."

He nodded. "As well as general secretarial things here. This is where we will work from." He indicated his desk.

I assumed I would get a desk too, and I was excited about that. I remembered being a little kid and getting excited when school would start again in the fall, because each kid in the group home got a new binder, pencils, pens, paper, etc. The thought of new erasers had made my nine-year-old self heady with delight. I felt the same delight over having a desk all to myself, and being able to stock it with a pin board, knickknacks, pens, etc.

I almost chortled. I eyed the space on the opposite end of Mr. Leto's desk and thought my desk would go there very nicely. When I glanced back to Draven, I could tell he'd noted my mental wanderings, and by the look on his face, had guessed at them.

Right. Vampire older than dinosaurs.

Draven set his teacup down. "Your face is very expressive. At least to me," he said. His lips twitched, and I grimaced. I usually kept my thoughts under better wraps than that.

"So, back to me being an empath. That actually makes sense, as I think back on my life. But what else does that make me? Does that make me a witch? A wizard?"

He shook his head. "For now, it just makes you a very strong empath. Empaths sometimes get secondary gifts of magic as well, especially if you had magic on both sides of your bloodline. But you don't know your biological parents, am I right?"

I nodded. He and I'd had that conversation the second time we'd talked. He'd been curious about my parents, and I'd had to tell him that they were no longer living.

"Well, that just means you're a wildcard right now,"

Draven continued. "One of your parents might have been an empath, and the other could have been human or another type of paranormal." He scrutinized me. "Any other things in your past that seem out of place or different?"

I mean, where should I start? All joking aside, I tried to remember anything *extra* odd about my past, and came up with nothing.

"No." I shook my head. "Not that I'm aware of."

He nodded. "Okay, we'll get back to that later. Getting back to the position, do you think you might be interested?"

I studied him. Where I was an open book, he was the king of inscrutable. I mean, yes! I was interested! But I also needed to take a look at some paperwork and ask about a million more questions. I yawned, covering my mouth so Mr. Leto wouldn't get the same penny show the other passengers of the plane had gotten.

He chuckled, and the fizzies popped in my chest again. That was getting aggravating. It wasn't painful, it just felt really odd. Was it something to do with vampire laughter? Was it normal?

I inconspicuously massaged my chest.

His chuckle cut off abruptly.

"Are you alright?" He looked...concerned wasn't the word. I guess he looked cautiously optimistic, but like he was fighting the optimism at the same time.

"Is that one of those things vampires can do, the whole champagne bubbles in my chest when you laugh thing?" My energy was starting to sputter and wane. Whatever energy I'd had marching into this office was draining quickly.

He looked down at his lap in thought for a few moments, and I dropped my hand from my chest. Something about my reaction bothered him. And I found myself bothered by *his* reaction to *my* reaction. I wanted to rub my head to soothe the sudden ache.

"No," he murmured. "It's not a vampire gift."

I nodded. Okay, I could get on board with that. Maybe it was because I found him attractive? Moving on, I took a deep breath and looked him in the eye. "I'm interested in the job, and I think I would be a good fit. Do you need to ask me any other questions?"

"I think that was supposed to be my line," he quipped, and I laughed. He got up to retrieve a manilla envelope and handed it to me, gesturing for me to open it.

I pulled a sheaf of papers out, neatly paper-clipped together, and started to read through everything. There was an NDA on top that outlined what I could and could not say about Draven, the business, the town, etc. On another page was a more complete list of what my duties would be, along with a full list of my benefits and salary.

I tried not to wheeze at the salary. "Holy cheese puffs!" I squeaked.

Deep breaths, Mia.

Reading through my basic duties again, I had the distinct thought that I'd earn every penny of my profuse salary. There was a page requiring my signature, giving Mr. Leto the right to have bodyguards outside my room, occasionally *inside* the room I was in, and at least one bodyguard would be with me whenever I left the villa. More would be added if necessary. I reflected on that for a moment. I wasn't looking forward to the loss of some of my privacy, but I was okay with the guards.

Lastly, I looked through a waiver that said there would be times when the job would be dangerous, and so I was being asked to sign away my and my family's rights to sue

Draven Leto Inc. for any pain, suffering or death I might incur on the job.

Okay, that page brought me up short. Pain and suffering? Death?

I rubbed my lips with my fingertips, my eyes scanning those words again and again. From his beautiful home and what I knew of his bio, Draven was a person of abundant means. I understood that to mean that he was a prize to some, but a roadblock and hindrance to others. Also, I was sure his looks did not reflect his age accurately. He'd probably picked up some enemies along the path of his extended lifetime. Enemies that would want to hurt him and the people who worked with him. It made me remember that article in the paper of the boutique hotel in Italy that had burned down. Had someone burned down his hotel?

Carrion birds.

I knew them well.

I looked up at Draven. "May I have a pen, please?"

CHAPTER 3
MIA

I spent the night in a guest room on the main floor. Mr. Leto had explained that he was having my bathroom re-done, but that it should be ready today. I'd gotten a tour this morning by a quiet Mesmer. Whereas most tours actually included words, mine hadn't. And I'd had to bite my lip to keep from laughing as Mesmer had zoomed through the hallways, communal rooms, and grounds of the villa, pointing to things, but not speaking. I hadn't really minded. Most of it was self-explanatory anyway. He'd grunted when we'd gotten to my room, but as I'd went to turn the knob to see what it looked like, he'd shaken his finger and directed me onwards.

"Mesmer, thank you so much for taking me to the bank." We were in the Town Car owned by my new boss; one of many cars the employees could use for villa or personal business. It was nice without being ostentatious, unlike the limo I'd arrived last night in. Mesmer nodded, and I looked out the window. Moonhaven Cove was beautiful. The town itself looked like a seaside European town, with bright colors, cute cafes, coffee shops, and bakeries. There were trees everywhere, some evergreen, others deciduous trees coming into blossom, and flowers bloomed everywhere.

I played spot the supernatural with myself. I saw tall, stately people with tipped ears—maybe elves since they didn't have wings—and more that looked like Mesmer: built like they could cause a landslide single-handedly. I knew these people to be gargoyles. There were a few people milling about in robes, but most wore modern clothing. I guessed those in robes were ancient wizards. Old vampires who didn't care about modern attire I could see wearing period clothing, like from the Renaissance, the Middle Ages, or from possibly before the fall of Rome. I counted myself fortunate that Mr. Leto wore modern clothing. It made him feel more contemporary to me. There were small people—fairies, maybe—who gave off a shimmering, very faint glow. And there were a rare few of an indeterminate species that it was hard to look at because they gave off such an aura of power that it was like trying to look at the sun. If you looked too long, you'd see sunspots.

We'd just passed a cute florist shop, Pushing Daisies, and were going over a bridge, when Mesmer, without warning, wrenched the steering wheel and gunned the accelerator. The engine revved as he changed into solid rock in an instant, growing bigger and taller. He sliced my seatbelt and pulled me to him as he punched out the door and flew straight up.

I tried not to scream as he shot into the sky and hovered in place, using his huge wings to keep us airborne. I looked down below and watched as our Town Car smashed through the bridge's railing and nosedived into the vast lake. Right after it sank fully below the water, a concussive *boom* shook the area, spraying water fifty feet into the air in all directions.

I clutched Mesmer, wrapping my arms around him like I was a boa constrictor and he was my favorite meal. I tried not to hyperventilate as my eyes flitted to everything happening below us. Our car was sinking to the bottom of the lake. Drivers, distracted by the explosion, smashed into each other. A sizable chunk of the bridge railing was in the lake, having been torn off by the impact of the car. People got out of their cars and started shouting to each other. Some shouted at Mesmer, asking him what was happening. It was a madhouse. Sirens began screaming from the far side of the bridge. Mesmer waited until the MHP had swarmed the area and emergency crews were taking care of the mess on the bridge before he flew off and landed on a grassy knoll south of the bridge.

I closed my eyes when we landed, gladder than I could ever remember being that we were on terra firma again. Mesmer patted my back with his huge hands, and I stood in his arms and shook uncontrollably. I leaned against him for support, trying to calm my breathing and my racing thoughts.

I could feel the people's emotions on the bridge. Some were calm, but most of them were scared, frustrated, even a few were angry—I sensed those knew Mesmer personally—and the mix of emotional overload hit me hard. I groaned, trying to shut them out, but couldn't until I remembered Mr. Leto's unintended advice from last night. That an empath's strength came from their equanimity. I wondered if that also meant that I could shut out other people's emotions if I myself were calm? I quickly tested that theory by breathing steadily in and out several times until I found my center and then I tried to put up a shield around what I viewed as my heartcenter, which to all others was the brain, but I viewed it as brain and spirit combined. I huffed a weary laugh when it worked and stood a little more steadily on my own two feet.

A sheriff's car braked, skidding onto the knoll and out of the flow of traffic. I could barely see around me because Mesmer had me cocooned in his thick, leathery wings, so I was out of the public eye and less of a target. Impatiently, I pushed them away from me so I could talk with the cop.

A furious man, wiry and lean with muscle, got out of the car, but stayed by his open door until Mesmer nodded for him to approach us. I couldn't focus. I kept seeing the huge *whoosh* of water that had spewed up after the boom of the bomb in my mind's eye.

There had been a bomb in the car.

There had been a *bomb* in the car!

Under the car, most likely!

Mesmer had saved my life! I wanted to kiss him or strangle him in a hug. I knew he was my chief bodyguard, but my body had never *needed* guarding before, and I'd certainly never lived through an attempted bombing. Adrenaline was still pumping through my system, making me feel weak and shaky.

The officer stayed well away from Mesmer, giving us a ring of space that he didn't cross into. Mesmer felt my hand shake from the dump of adrenaline and wrongly assumed I was afraid of the cop. His wings shot out again like a huge accordion, blocking me from view. "It's okay, Mesmer. We can talk with him." I was feeling calmer now. Not calm, but calmer. I could handle talking with law enforcement.

His eyes, which I noticed were pale yellow in his full

gargoyle form, speared me for a moment before he grunted and pulled his wings back just enough so I could see in front of me.

The Sheriff nodded curtly to both of us in greeting. He had cat's eyes that were yellow and green, and he looked mad enough to punch a polar bear. He pulled off his blue ball cap that had an S with an eight-star compass on it, crushed it in his hands—not standard wear, I was guessing—and glared up at Mesmer. Personally, I would have been terrified of glaring at Mesmer. The guy was *huge!*

"You want to tell me why you almost blew up my bridge, Mesmer!" he yelled. "I've got nineteen accidents out there, a hole in the bridge, a car in the lake, and a mess on my hands! What happened!"

Whoa, his eyes were *glowing.*

Mesmer grunted, not at all impressed with the glowing eyes or the alpha posturing the guy was doing, and kept circling his gaze around us, looking for danger or more crazy people with bombs. I, personally wanted him to keep doing that, so I swallowed my fear and stuck my still shaking hand out. "Hi. I'm Draven Leto's new assistant, Mia Durran. I can give you my statement. Mesmer was just protecting me. He's my bodyguard."

The Sheriff glared up at Mesmer before shaking my hand. "Finn Daranell." His words came out growly, even though he seemed to temper them somewhat for me. I appreciated that. I sensed he was some kind of alpha supernatural. He had what felt like the growl of an alpha. I wondered if he was some kind of cat shifter.

"Is it rude to ask what you are?" I couldn't help it; I was insanely curious, despite the disaster that had just taken place.

"Lion shifter. Now you wanna tell me about this mess?" He jerked a thumb in the bridge's direction.

"Umm, I'm not really sure." I worked to piece together my thoughts. "We'd just made a trip to the bank. We were on our way back to the Leto Villa when Mesmer suddenly twisted the wheel so that it would crash into the side of the bridge, gunned the gas, grabbed me, and smashed out of the driver's side door. He hovered over the lake as the car went through the railing and hit the water. Not ten seconds after it submerged completely, there was an enormous *boom* and water spewed up in every direction."

I looked up at Mesmer's stoic face. "I'm guessing...a bomb had been placed on the car somewhere, maybe after we'd stopped at the bank, and Mesmer heard it or sensed something was wrong."

Sheriff Finn growled and sighed deeply, yanked his hair in frustration, and closed his eyes. He muttered under his breath as he picked up his hat, dusted it off, and smashed it back on his head. Backwards.

If I hadn't just almost gotten blown up, I would have smiled. I liked the sheriff. He had a baseball cap and an attitude, and he seemed like a good guy. I felt safe in his presence; safe and calm. He focused my empathy in a distinct way, like a clarifying agent. I wondered if that was a pull that alphas had? In any case, I felt better knowing that he was sheriff over the town.

"Alright," he sighed. "If you could just send a Leto employee representative to the station later for an official statement, we'll call that good. I'm glad you're safe, ma'am." He smirked. "And welcome to Moonhaven Cove."

I grimaced at him and watched as he got into the police

cruiser and sped off to the scene of the disaster, sirens blazing.

"Mesmer?"

Yellow eyes looked down at me. "Thank you."

He nodded regally. I shrieked in surprise when he launched us into the air again. When we touched down in the villa's courtyard, at least ten bodyguards greeted us. Mesmer nodded at them but ushered me up the stairs and into the foyer without speaking with them. When we crossed the threshold, my eyes had to adjust to the lower light. Spots danced briefly as I tried to focus, and when I did, I drew in a surprised breath.

Draven was there, and he looked furious. Power was rolling off of him, darkening the lights, making the floor tremble, and making my knees wobble. I struggled to stay standing, helped only by Mesmer's grip on my arm.

"Mesmer. My office." Draven's voice punched through the space with a ton of power. Even still, Mesmer hesitated, searching Draven's eyes. After finding whatever he'd been looking for, he nodded, squeezed my arms softly, and strode toward Draven's office.

I vaguely noticed he was in his normal form again, or whatever it was called. His human-looking form.

In a blink, Draven was five inches from my face as his eyes carefully traced over every square inch of skin that was visible. And then he did it again, just to be sure.

"I'm fine," I said. Or tried to say. My throat felt thick as the shock of the afternoon still buzzed through my body. My hands hadn't stopped shaking, and my limbs were tingling. I looked down at the floor. My blue suede Vans were scuffing Draven's nice marble entryway. My legs felt unsteady and shaky, like I needed to sit down before I fell down.

Draven's hands settled on my arms. He tilted my face up to his. "I'm sorry, Mia," he said. There was so much regret in his voice that it made me wince. "You've just arrived and already someone has tried to hurt you."

He stepped away and dropped his hands, making me feel abruptly colder. "I would understand if you wanted to go back to Manhattan."

I peered up at him. His face was closed off, and I wasn't sure what I'd seen in his expression.

Power was still rolling around me in what felt like waves. The waves crashed into me, still threatening to drop me to my knees, but I stiffened my legs and fought to stay upright. Before I could ask him if he could stop flooding the room with zinging power, the surrounding force stopped abruptly and dissipated. Maybe making the new assistant pee in the entryway like a puppy was a faux pas. Something polite vampires tried not to do.

I was extremely grateful.

I did a quick assessment of myself and, realistically, my situation. And the overwhelming consensus was that I wanted to stay. Not for Draven or my new position, but for myself. I'd never known any of this existed. Bomb notwithstanding, I'd never felt so much peace before. Anywhere. As we'd cruised through the medium-sized town, I'd been so impressed that most people felt good to me. Some, like Draven, felt like what I imagined catnip felt like to a cat. Soooo relaxing. It was a new way of living for me, and one I didn't want to give up. Not for any reason. I was so sick of living day-to-day feeling chaotic and anxious. I wouldn't recommend it to anyone.

"I'll stay," I whispered, trying to smile. But I was certain it ended up more grimace than smile when Draven looked at my offering with a troubled look in his eyes. "I think I need a double chocolate chip muffin. If you'll excuse me."

I headed toward the kitchens, but Draven's soft, velvety voice stopped me. "Thank you for staying, Mia. We'll keep you protected."

I made my way to the kitchen on weak legs without looking back at him and pushed through the door.

I needed a whole lot of carbs.

AFTER GRABBING my muffin from the kitchen and meeting the French chef Henri (Ahn-rEE), I tried to find my way back to my suite again. I was still trembling, but it was getting more manageable.

I'd learned on my whirlwind tour with the silent Mesmer that the villa was broken up into four different wings: the Garden Wing, the Ocean Wing, the Forest Wing, and the Galaxy Wing. Even though I'd stayed in another guest room last night as they finished up my bathroom, I knew that I'd been put in the Ocean Wing in the Sunset Suite, so I headed there with my muffin, humming under my breath as I ate my chocolatey Prozac. It was such an unhealthy thing, eating your feelings, but I'd just been almost blown up. If anything, I was rather proud of myself for only reaching for chocolate. Maybe a valium would have been a better choice.

They'd decorated each wing of the house according to its name. Somehow, someone had guessed that I loved the ocean, so I got to traverse these halls, gazing in awe at the murals on the walls that looked like I'd gotten transported to various beaches around the world. Some had underwater themes, and had tons of creatures and ocean plants, but most were just murals of beaches around the world. They *covered* entire walls and were *gorgeous!*

As I finished the chocolaty goodness that is a double chocolate chip muffin, I licked my fingers and entered my suite. Murals of beaches from Borneo, Australia, and Fiji covered my walls. My chandelier was made of seashells, and my walls were painted a soft sand color. My bed was a canopy bed with cool blue sheets and a luxurious baby-blue comforter. Thick, sandy colored carpet covered the floors, with a large seashell themed rug. An enormous fireplace took up part of the wall across from my bed, and a huge curved-in window with a thick, padded bench seat took up the other wall.

I slipped off my shoes and looked around at the knick-knacks that filled the floating shelves and the shelves above my dresser. I'd been told I could make this room my own, but I had brought little from home, and even though Draven had paid someone to ship the things in my storage unit back in Manhattan to me, nothing had arrived yet. When they did, I would put my personal stamp on my room. Coinciden-tally, most of my knickknacks were ocean themed. They would fit in perfectly here.

My hands were sticky from the muffin, so I tried to locate the door to the bathroom. The first doorwas a smallish closet that looked like it was full of linens for my bed. The second was the newly redone bathroom.

My eyes went wide as I looked around. It was *huge!* The bathtub looked to be some high tech, ridiculously comfort-able tub with jets, but the shower seemed to be the focal point of the whole bathroom. It was the size of my kitchen back home. It was a round walk-in with glass enclosing everything from waist up, and tile from waist down. There was an entrance just in front, with a small step that led in. The tile had been done in swirls of differing shades of blue and silver. It had two shower heads, one on each side, three windows set at eye-level that were open to the breeze coming off the coast, and beneath the windows, a curved bench that sat against the wall. It was amazing! Breathtaking!

Also, there was a naked man in it.

I yelped, making some kind of embarrassing noise between indignation and mortification. I had a brief glimpse of paleish skin, short silver hair and tattoos of celestial bodies before I threw my hands over my eyes.

"What are you doing in my shower?" I demanded. Seriously, why was there someone in my shower? For a minute I worried that I'd gotten the wrong room, but nope, I remembered the hallway, and I remembered Mesmer showing me the door I'd just come in perfectly. I *was* in the right room. *He* wasn't!

The man laughed. "It's the best shower in the villa!"

Well...yes, probably. From what little I'd seen of it, it had looked divine. "I don't care if my shower is better than Buckingham Palace, it's not your shower!" I growled. I was suddenly very territorial over my beautiful, perfect bathroom. I'd never seen anything so gorgeous in all of my life, and I didn't want to share. I felt completely justified in this. "Out!"

I twitched one of my fingers a little to the side and looked to see if he was finishing up. Focusing only on his face, I watched as he pumped some conditioner into his hands and worked it through his hair. I growled at him. I wanted him gone, and he was not listening!

Trying to keep my eyes squeezed mostly shut, I stomped into the shower, and blindly felt for the nozzle to turn it off, getting myself soaked in the process. Once I turned it the last bit, my ears picked up the sound of the other shower head spurting out water. Growling, I stomped to that one, and turned it off too.

Then the first one came back on.

"We can do this all day, Starshine. I need to rinse."

"You wouldn't need to rinse the conditioner out if you'd left when I first asked!" The nerve of this guy.

I turned to him and folded my hands across my chest, staring him down. The man was handsome, I reluctantly admitted to myself. He wasn't built like a linebacker, but he wasn't without muscle either. He had more of a toned swimmer's build. His hair was a beautiful silver, and his eyes were dark purple with specks of gold dust in them. He had tattoos on his pecs of stars and moons, and one sleeve tattoo that looked like a swirling galaxy.

"Who are you, and why are you in my shower?"

"I told you. It's the best shower in the villa. Draven lets me shower here." He rinsed the conditioner out of his hair and then reached into a shower caddy and grabbed an anti-fog mirror. Hanging it up on the middle window latch, he did something glowy with his right hand, and used what looked like hardened starlight to shave.

Suddenly, I was just tired. The danger to my life, and then dealing with Draven's power levels being through the roof when we'd returned had exhausted me. I felt like I could barely lift my head. And just that quickly, I wasn't interested in the man in the shower anymore. I needed to lie down. I figured if Draven had let him in, he most likely wasn't an axe murderer. He felt like a jolt of almost electric energy, the slow-moving peace of a river, the mischievous-ness of a five-year-old on their birthday, and the goofiness of all the bad dad jokes in the entire world. In short, I knew him to be safe. Safe enough for me to go lie down in my room. I slowly made my way to the fireplace in my bedroom and slumped down onto the mega beanbag chair in front of it. The chair was the size of a small car and felt like a thick, cloudy heaven.

I lay there, soaked, staring at the ceiling, wondering how my day had turned so completely to crap. Bombs under my car, naked men in my shower... Most people might consider that last one a boon, but I just sighed in frustration and exhaustion.

Someone had tried to kill me today.

From the outside, the town looked and felt so safe. Like a quaint European seaside town with bright colors and cute shops. And they had such cute names: The Laughing Elf, Chocula Chocolates, The Serenading Siren, Midnight Masquerade, Wyld's Wallflowers... In theory I knew they must have some crazies here too, but I guess I'd just wanted it to be idyllic. Like a supernatural Eden. I think it was for most, just maybe not for an ancient vampire and his assistant. I groaned.

I wanted some chocolates from Chocula Chocolates right then. My hands were still shaking, and I knew the chocolate would help. It always did.

Mr. moon tats came in wearing sweats and a tee shirt that said Elves Do It Better. He invaded my space, smelling like citrus and spearmint and something cold and distant like starlight, if starlight had a smell. Which it didn't. I was clearly hallucinating now. Help. Send chocolate.

I was splayed on the beanbag with my arms and legs out

like a starfish, trying to calm my frantic heartbeat by breathing in and out in deep, measured breaths.

I remembered back to just before and after the bomb had gone off, and the emotions that had hit me that hadn't felt like mine. It was hard to refute now that I really was an empath of unknown origins. I mean, it was one thing to know, but now I *knew*. I felt it deep down inside of me. I released a stuttered breath. It was possible I was also something else mixed in, but until I manifested other abilities, I was content to assume I was simply an empath.

I'd mentioned that to Draven last night, and he'd laughed. Apparently, empaths are rare. Like, rarer than four-leaf clovers in the North Pole, rare. I did a few more deep breaths, and finally felt my heart and nervous system calm. I was so very grateful for bodyguards. I was going to ask Henri to make them something fantastic, especially Mesmer.

Speaking of empaths, I could feel Mr. Moon Tats next to me. His emotions were rippling between fascination, attraction, and irritation.

"Why are *you* irritated with *me*?" I squawked in indignation. "You invaded my space, you plunked your naked self in my shower, and I almost died today!" I said, way too dramatically.

My eyes stung with tears, but I ignored them and opened my eyes wide until the liquid dried out.

Ugh.

I picked my head up and glared at the man next to me. "You're done with your shower. Why are you still here?"

His beautiful eyes studied me as he laced his hands on his stomach and leaned against the wall. "You are the new assistant?" His voice was a little bit growl, and a little bit melodic. It was kind of soothing.

I sighed. "I'm sorry. I'm not usually this teenager-moody, or grumpy, but you invaded my space, and someone almost blasted me into tiny pieces today. I'm a little high-strung right now."

He sat up straight, tense as a bowstring. "A bomb in Moonhaven? Is everyone okay?"

I nodded. "Yep. Well, other than the car that exploded, and the huge hole in the bridge railing, but pretty much. Mesmer sensed it from the undercarriage of the car. He forced the car to drive off the bridge and into the water and flew me to safety."

The man was quiet. Though, now that he wasn't naked and I could get a closer look at his ears, I thought he might be an elf. He had slightly pointed ears. Huh, the shirt made sense now. Obviously, he was magical. I mean, his eyes were a dead giveaway. The gold dust in the dark purple *moved*.

The elf drew closer to me, hesitated, then opened his arms, looking very uncertain. I eyed him for a minute, and eyed his arms, and then said heck with it and scooted closer so he could hug me. I sighed into the hug. It felt nice. I didn't have much experience with them. It was also nice to be hugged after a horrible experience. So much so that I sort of mourned the fact that I'd never had hugs after the bad experiences of my youth and early adult years.

He smoothed his hands down my ponytail and rubbed my back a bit. "Not a very great welcome to our town, was it?"

I shook my head and moved away from him. Hugs might feel fantastic, but I still wasn't used to them. He studied me for another moment before he put his hand out. "I'm Rhys Liakis, owner of The Laughing Elf."

I put my icy hand into his. "Mia Durran, future assistant extraordinaire, and very new to the paranormal community."

He smiled cheekily at me. His was the grin of a person who knew he was handsome and fully expected any and all females to worship him. I almost laughed out loud. *Yeah, not going to happen.* I mean, he was really handsome, it was true, but I wasn't attracted to him. And he for sure didn't give me the warm flutteries I felt around Draven. I was determined to ignore those flutteries for multiple, very logical reasons. The most important being that I wanted to keep my job.

"I heard you're an empath?"

I frowned, wondering if rumors about me were circling the town. I didn't like that one bit. "That was private information."

He shrugged. "For everyone but the Pacific Northwest Council, it would be. I'm part of the Council."

I blinked at him. "You must be ancient then. Draven's on the Council and he's at least a thousand years old."

He looked startled for a moment, and then he started laughing uproariously, hunching over and holding his stomach. I pursed my lips at him. It hadn't been that funny.

I ignored him and looked at the chips in my speckled bronze nail wraps and decided I needed to do a new nail wrap soon. I had a sparkly blue one with moons and stars that I thought would be appropriate.

Rhys's laughter died down, and he winked at me. "We're going to be pals, you and I."

"And you know this, how?" I mean, I wasn't *opposed* exactly. I could use a friend.

He smirked. "It's written in the stars."

"Well, okay then. Nice to meet you, friend."

Rhys and I spent all of my exile—resting from my almost death—in in my room getting to know one another. He never once looked at his watch or seemed to lose focus on the conversation that was flowing. By the end of the evening, I felt like I'd known him my entire life. He was funny and charismatic, but also kind of dorky, especially for what I imagined an elf should be. He was a star elf. An elf that could harness the power of the stars and use it magically.

To me, it sounded crazy.

I mean, harness the power of the stars?

Uh-huh. Sure. Even though he'd done something glowy in the shower to shave with, it didn't mean he had the power of the stars at his disposal.

He just smirked at me and let me have my disbelief.

He'd set up a nail station, and was putting my moon and star nail wraps on like a pro.

"Done this for many girlfriends?"

He looked sad for a moment. "I don't really date."

"Ever?"

"Are you interested?" He perked up and paused what he was doing to waggle his eyebrows at me.

"You wish!"

He smirked and went back to filing the excess nail wrap down around my thumb. "I have a broken heart that hasn't mended yet. I'm not ready to date again."

I squeezed his hand with my free one. "Sorry, Geezer. Broken hearts suck, or so I've heard."

He ignored my lack of previous social life and sputtered a laugh, lifting the nail file so he didn't do permanent damage to me. "Geezer?"

I shrugged. "It fits, right? You're like eight hundred and ninety-nine?"

He scowled at me. "One hundred and forty-one, smart aleck. If I were human, I would be in my thirties. Still the prime of my life."

I smiled. "I stand by Geezer. And so you shall be named." I picked up a pen off the table, and tapped both his shoulders, and then the crown of his head like I was knighting him.

He laughed, a goofy grin on his face. "You're a little weird, you know that, right?"

"All the best people are." I was a firm believer in this.

I grabbed the virgin piña colada that Henri had sent me and took a long sip through the curlicue straw. "Did you know they can make anything in the kitchens?"

He nodded. "We're doing a movie after, right? We should order dinner and snacks."

"Henri gave me his cell number earlier. He told me to text him what I wanted for dinner tonight since he knew I'd be resting in my room." I pulled out my cell phone and prepared to text the chef. "What do you want?"

He moved to my index finger, clipping the excess nail wrap and filing the jagged ends. He shrugged. "I can eat just about anything."

"Hmm, how about chicken fettuccine alfredo with garlic bread, and something chocolaty for the movie?"

He smirked. "Comfort food and carbs, huh?"

I refused to feel bad for my carb-laden food order. I shrugged. "I eat like this all the time."

"Like a teenager who's been given a recent emancipation from parents?"

I laughed. "Speaking of teenagers, this feels very teenage-esque. You doing my nails, us watching a movie."

He looked up at me, his boysenberry eyes serious. "Did you get to do things like this when you were a teenager?"

His eyes held mine, and I found it hard to look away. "I, umm, I worked a lot when I was a teenager. I didn't really have time for friends." I didn't want to bother explaining that I'd tried to make friends but couldn't hack the feeling of intense nausea being around non-supernaturals gave me, and the chaotic whirlwind that caused me so much anxiety.

His head canted to one side. "Am I your first friend?"

I was extremely embarrassed and didn't want to answer. Before I could decide on an evasive response, he smacked me with the flat of the nail file again. "No prevaricating!"

"I was going to be vague," I said indignantly, and then sighed. "Yep, my first friend is a geezer. How lame does that make me?"

He scowled at me. "It makes you amazing, considering I don't have friends either."

My mouth fell open. "What?"

He finished my nails and started cleaning up. "I have associates, business and personal. In my long life, I've only had a few friends."

I wanted to hug him, but restrained myself. He wasn't looking for sympathy; he was just being factual.

"What about Draven?"

"What about him?"

"Come on! You shower here!"

He dumped the trash and put the rest of the nail stuff in a container and then shoved it under the bathroom sink. "I'm on the PNW council with him. He feels sorry for me, I think."

I doubted that. Draven didn't seem the type. He probably was making overtures because he was comfortable with Rhys, but Geezer was only willing to let him in so much. Hmm, I felt like Dr. Phil as I analyzed my new friend. What pain had he gone through to make him leery of friendships? And why was I different? The random thought that an empath might be like catnip to supernaturals almost made me laugh out loud. "So, you're a vagrant?"

He scowled at me. "I have a shower at my club. It's just stuffy, is the size of a shoebox, and smells like onion rings."

I soooo wanted to ask why it smelled like onion rings, but felt like that would get things too wildly off track. "Do you not have a home?"

"I don't need one. There's a couch in my office at the club and a shower. I've been using all the income generated to keep my business in the black."

I shook my head. On the one hand, I was amazed at his dedication and business acumen, but on the other, I felt terrible that I had kicked him out of my shower earlier.

"Geezer, if you're using other people's showers," here I glared at him, "and you don't look like you're sleeping very well, then maybe it's time to get a rental? There are shadows under your eyes."

He sighed, picking at the lint on his tee shirt. "I hate house hunting."

"Okay, well, what about an apartment, or a townhome?"

"Maybe a townhome. They have some over on Schooner

that look nice. They have wood-burning fireplaces, and a pool. And some of them are ocean front."

I stole his phone and sent myself a text so I had his number. "Text me this week with a time, and I'll come with you. No one should have to go house hunting alone."

His silver eyebrows winged upward. "I'm a big elf, fully grown and everything. I can do it on my own."

Wow, he really did push away friendly overtures. "Text me." I growled at him, narrowing my eyes. It was odd to me that I was so protective of this elf this quickly. But I didn't want him to be lonely while looking for a place to live. He was already doing this on my recommendation. The least I could do was keep him company.

He answered the knock at the door, grumbling at me under his breath.

Henri had provided a huge feast for us with a plate each of the fettuccine alfredo, along with a tray of breadsticks with marinara dipping sauce, chocolate cheesecake, six-layer cake, and berry cobbler.

"I think I'm in heaven."

Rhys laughed and picked up the remote. "Action or rom-com?"

I piled my plate high with creamy pasta goodness, grabbed some bread and a little of each dessert, and settled into the overstuffed cushions of my sofa. "How about something sci-fi?"

We chose something that looked good, and soon got sucked into the compelling story. Before the movie was half over, my eyelids got droopy, and Rhys threw a blanket over me. I fell asleep before the movie ended.

CHAPTER 4
MIA

I arrived to work bright and early, before the sun was even up, because I wanted to get a good start on things. I had a lot to learn about Draven's business, and I didn't want to take up his valuable time taking too long to learn it. It was a good thing I picked up on things quickly.

When I opened the door to the study, I found my boss sitting across the room, studying his phone like it held the mysteries of the universe and nodding at it. I found this funny for about three and a half seconds until what sounded like Portuguese flowed smoothly from the phone's speaker. He was on a conference call this early?

I blinked in surprise and started internally panicking. Was I late? What time was I supposed to have come in? Before I could get too far into my spiral of panic, Draven ended the call and smiled at me. "You're fine. You don't have to be in until nine. I just had an early morning conference call with one of the boutique hotels I've invested in overseas."

I nodded, relieved I hadn't been late on my first day, then put my purse away and looked at the desk that had been moved into the study for me. It was a beautiful desk with a cherry lacquered top and lots of cubbies and drawers to put all of my stuff in.

I loved it. My very first desk. I grabbed my phone and snapped a photo, and captioned it, *Woohoo! And best* of all, it had a rollie chair that dwarfed me when I sat down. I laughed in delight, rolling it back and forth.

Draven laughed at me as I took a few more spins in my chair. "They are fun. Down at the main building, my staff has an annual Office Olympics. One of the events is a Roller Chair Derby. You should join them next time. There are great vacation prizes for the winners."

"I would love to do that! That sounds like so much fun!" I was getting the feeling that Draven was an amazing boss. I felt like I had been so blessed by this job. Words couldn't even describe the kind of hopelessness that I'd felt recently. With that thought in mind, I wanted to prove that I could do a competent job here. Not just to my boss, but to myself. I checked the drawers for all the little things I'd need over the course of my first day and noted that I didn't have everything.

"If you're missing anything, there's a room down the hall that I use as an office supply room. I'll show you where it is later. It should have anything you could possibly need in there."

I made a mental note to check it out later.

Draven nodded at the spread in the middle of the room on a high table. "Help yourself to something to break your fast. I'm sure you haven't eaten yet."

I palmed my grumbling tummy. Just the thought of the

delicious food that came out of the kitchens here had me salivating. "Thanks." I blushed, certain he could hear my stomach, even from across the room. I'd gotten the sense that the books had gotten that part about vampires right: they had amazing hearing.

Henri had set the tray up with what looked like croissants, coffee, peppermint tea, and butter. I opened up a steaming croissant and slathered some of the butter inside. It smelled heavenly!

"Oh my gosh, this is good. Is that honey butter? Yum."

I tried not to shove the whole croissant in my face and eat like a lady, but it was a very near thing. Honey butter was awesome stuff. I poured some peppermint tea, served myself another loaded croissant, and scooted back to my desk. Seeing that I needed a few things still before I could even get started, I had Draven show me the office supply room, and just stared at the cornucopia in awe. Draven chuckled from behind me and gently nudged me inside. "Go on. It won't bite," he said with that trademark wicked amusement of his.

I shook my head. If a person had never gone into an office supply store, and almost gotten kicked out because they wanted to smell, taste, touch, and *hoard* all the pretties, this would not make sense to them. But I was *exactly* such a person. I had a weakness for crazy and cute erasers, like penguins and sparkly lions. I loved colored pencils and pens, colorful binders and paperclips, reams of different packets of papers in the colors of the rainbow. There were coffee mugs! Draven, with a curl of his lip, handed me one that said World's Best Boss.

I handed him one back that said World's Best Assistant. He laughed while I loaded up a shopping bag's worth of beautiful stuff and logged out what I'd taken in the open logbook on the counter.

I had a feeling I was going to love my job.

ONCE WE GOT BACK to the office, he showed me on the computer how to log in to his private network and walked me through what he needed from me week to week, and I got started. I input his schedule into an app that I then shared to his phone so he would have his schedule handy if he needed it. I also printed a copy and pegged it on my new seafoam colored corkboard behind me.

I worked on catching up his account books for his private office and started inputting all the numbers into the computer. When I finished that, I mailed off all of his correspondence and sent off emails. My to-do pile was still enormous, but my ta-da-done pile was slowly growing.

By late afternoon, my stomach snarling interrupted the quiet of the office.

Draven laughed and made a call to the kitchens. When the food arrived, I almost jumped the boy with the tray, I was so hungry. He took one look at my feral eyes and decided to put the tray down and make a run for it. Only Henri, with his pursed lips and haughty air, stayed.

I plopped myself onto the couch gracelessly and dug into the Chinese chicken salad and the amazing loaded-potato chowder that went with it. I poured some sweet tea, an addiction of mine, and closed my eyes in bliss.

"Henri, are you sure you're married? I'd marry you in a heartbeat."

Henri unfolded a linen napkin and placed it over my lap. "Yes. My wife adores me."

I laughed. "I'm sure she does. Do you cook for her as well? Does she live close by? I would love to meet her." I was curious about the fussy Henri and his home life. What was his wife like?

Henri pursed his lips again. "You are a constant stream of questions. Yes, miss, she lives close by. We have a suite in The Garden Wing. As for if you will meet or not?" He shrugged elegantly. "Probably soon. She is one of the keepers of the gardens. She's very busy."

"Vegetable gardens?"

Henri nodded, fidgeting.

"Well, please ask her, okay?" We had vegetable gardens? I really wanted to see those. Mesmer hadn't included them on the tour.

"Of course, miss. Will there be anything else you need?" He brushed nonexistent lint off of his white chef's smock, and speared me with his piercing gray eyes.

"Umm." I hesitated to ask...

"Yes?" He sounded like a man being led to the gallows, and I knew it was because he could sense what my request was going to be. I wanted to laugh, but didn't dare.

"Can I have a double chocolate chip muffin, please?"

He sighed. "Miss, I can see that I will need to make a double batch of those each week."

I tried to smile angelically. I'm not sure it worked because he harrumphed at me, and then sped out the door muttering under his breath that he didn't know where I put it all. I smiled. I was very blessed with a fast metabolism. I could eat all day and not gain anything. It was wonderful. I took full advantage of it by eating like a teenager denied junk food their entire life.

I dipped my spoon into the creamy potato soup, hummed in delight, and looked at Draven. "I feel like I'm making friends."

Draven laughed.

"Do you have any new information on the car bomb?"

Draven wiped his fingers and nodded. "We don't have much. Finn and his team dragged the lake and salvaged what remained of the car and the bomb." He grabbed something from his desk and handed it to me. "As you can see, there were no prints on the bomb casing. They pulled the outside camera footage from the bank, and all they found was a person of indeterminate age, weight, and gender around the Town Car for a brief moment before they flashed away. The speed that they left the frame of the camera suggests a supernatural that can use flash speed, like a vampire. Finn has pulled a few people in for questioning, but he's not all that confidant, based on the evidence, that he'll be able to nail this guy."

"Or girl," I said.

Draven nodded. "Or girl."

"So, what, we just wait for them to attack again? And why was it Mesmer and I that were attacked if they were after you?"

Draven steepled his fingers and leaned back on the couch. "I did say, Miss Durran, that my enemies might become your enemies as well. By getting to you, they get to me. You are under my protection. Not only as my employee, but also you have become a part of House Leto."

The spoon clinked in the bowl as I dropped it. I was no

longer hungry. "Had anything happened recently? Before I came?"

Draven shook his head. "No. It's been many years since there was an attack on me or mine. And those people have long been dealt with. This is something, or *someone* new, and for a purpose that I can only guess at."

I swallowed thickly. Yeah. That sounded about right. There was a supernatural killer on the loose, and it seemed I'd somehow ticked them off by accepting a job with Mr. Leto.

Crushing crackers!

WEEKS WENT by without any new attacks. I spent my days, and some of my evenings closeted in the study with Draven as we worked on a stack of businesses that he'd invested in that were in trouble. He met virtually with various department heads, pinpointing problem areas, and suggesting various rescue companies that, with some work, could pull their businesses back into the black.

He invested in a ton of diverse businesses and enterprises. And even though it wasn't his place as the investor to help these companies out if they were struggling, he still seemed to care, and worked hard to help them. He wanted them to succeed.

He also financed individuals who had what he called "grand ideas." Some inventions that he had financed over the years made me giggle, and some of them boggled my mind. There were a lot of clever people out there.

Some of the tech he financed was only in the developmental stage and looked like something you'd see on *Star*

Trek or *Star Wars*. I pored over those schematics, fascinated with all of them, but not really understanding much of what I saw. They were interesting to look at, though.

I urged him to find someone that could invent biological matter to matter transport, like the transporters in *Star Trek*. He laughed quite a bit at that one while I kept a dignified silence. It could happen! And when it did, I promised myself I wouldn't gloat. Much.

As the weeks went by, I squirreled away all the observations I'd gleaned about Draven.

One, he was a very driven person.

I'd imagined vampires would have a sort of languid energy because they'd been around so long and seen so much, but Draven wasn't like that at all. He was very focused, intent, and intense.

I thought at first that his intensity would bother me. Being an empath, I was really sensitive to other's emotions. Intense emotions were especially hard for me to bear. But I found it wasn't like that with Draven. His emotions weren't barbed. They didn't hurt me. In fact, in a very real way, his intensity brought me comfort. He was intense about the things that he cared about. As time went by, I was starting to hope that I would someday be one of the things that Draven was intense about.

Two, he was wicked smart. Like genius level smart.

If someone handed him a schematic, he seemed to instantly be able to tell if it was going to work. He would talk me through why it would work, or why it would fail. I understood little of what he said at first, but he loved to teach, I'd found, and as time went by, I started being able to pick up certain things, and could see for myself what he was talking about for the simplified blueprints.

For those inventors who showed him schematics that were close to being functional, he worked with them until he thought they had a good chance of making it work, and then gave it back over into their hands. So, in that way, he was also a specialized consultant in a field that didn't really have that. I could actually verify that on the front end, he made little being a consultant. But on the back end, when the inventors finished their product, and sales started rolling in, Draven got a percentage of those sales according to their contract, and *that* was where he made a ton of money. Obscene amounts of money, because over his long lifetime, he'd consulted on hundreds, maybe thousands of products.

Three, he was quiet.

I wasn't sure if it was because I was new and he wasn't really sure about me, or if he was just quiet in general. My impression was that he was quieter than the average person, but that his mind was constantly active, thinking, ruminating, calculating. Like I said, insanely intelligent. I was beginning to see the downside of intelligence. I don't think his brain was ever just quiet or at peace. After understanding this, I could completely understand why he didn't feel the need to fill every silence with words.

ONE MORNING, I was taking my daily walk along the shore. Mesmer was behind us, trying to give me and Rhys privacy. Not that we needed it, but it was still sweet of him. It was fully spring now. The weather in Moonhaven Cove still had a bite to it, but the sun was glorious and warm on my fair skin. Rhys was in board shorts and a tee shirt and looked like an elf surfer. I imagined Legolas from *Lord of the Rings* on a surfboard saying, *Righteous, dude,* and had to bite back a laugh. My imagination sometimes came up with the most random things.

"Has that big block of rock told you what kind of gargoyle he is yet?"

I made a grab for my hair, trying to wrangle it up into a messy bun so that it wouldn't fly in my face. I tied it with an elastic, hoping for the best. "Nope. I just figure he'll tell me when he wants to."

Rhys's eyebrow shot up. "He *talks* to you? Like, actually talks, with words and everything."

I smirked, feeling special. Word around town was that Mesmer didn't like to talk to most people. He spoke to Draven and me, and maybe a few others. I wasn't sure why. I had an empathic sense it was because Mesmer gave off a brute vibe, and people expected him to be dumb as a rock. But inside, Mesmer was actually really sensitive. People's words hurt him, maybe more than the average person/supernatural, and he was afraid of getting hurt. It'd amazed me when I'd put that together. Mesmer was so huge he could snap a tree trunk in half with his bare hands. It melted my heart that inside he was so tender and sensitive, and it infuriated me that people could be so cold and cruel to someone that would literally give the shirt off his back for a stranger.

"Of course he talks to me. I'm wonderful." I batted my lashes at Rhys and he laughed.

He hooked my arm through his. "You are one lucky, lucky girl."

I nodded. I felt lucky. Blessed in my job, and my new friends. Blessed that I didn't live in poverty anymore, and that I was in a town where I was starting to feel at home. I looked back at Mesmer, who was continuously scanning our surroundings, keeping me safe.

"I know. He just started talking to me one day in the car." My eyes went a little glossy. "I think he knew how hard it was for me to get back into a vehicle." I looked at Rhys. "Whenever I tried, I would nearly hyperventilate. I would get shaky and sick, and for a few weeks I just couldn't do it. Mesmer worked with me on it. We'd sit in the driveway with the car in park but with the engine running, and he'd just talk to me. He'd talk about inane things, just creating this comforting rumble of noise in the background that calmed me. We did that for a while. He would stop by the office, and we'd go sit in the car, and he'd just talk. After a few weeks, he took me just down the street to get ice cream, and we sat on a park bench eating our ice cream, and enjoyed the peace of the outdoors. I think he wanted to show me that we could make a trip in a car without it ending in a disaster. Little by little, he helped me become less afraid. Now, I can get in the car with only the bad memory, but none of the paralyzing fear."

That had endeared Mesmer to me, and I felt that through those experiences, we'd become friends. I also think he was aware that I knew he was a sensitive soul, and because of that, he felt more comfortable around me. I also think he just thought I was cool.

"So, he didn't say, 'Stop sniveling, human. You're embarrassing yourself?'"

I laughed and poked him hard in the ribs. "Of course not! Mesmer is actually *nice* to me!"

Rhys looked insulted. "I'm nice to you!"

I shook my head. "Yeah, no."

"I took you out to dinner just last week! It was a nice restaurant, too! You are not a cheap date, by the way."

"And then ditched me because someone called from the club." I reminded him.

Rhys looked sheepish; his purple eyes glowed. "Yeah, sorry about that."

"It's okay. You can make it up to me by taking me to that new tea place, The Tea Hobbit."

His expression turned mulish. "Not going to happen."

"What? Why not?"

"They only employ pixies there."

"Okaaayyyy?"

He turned away from me and gazed out at the ocean, hiding his face.

"Oh my gosh, are you blushing?" I was blown away. Rhys didn't seem like the type of person who would blush. From what I'd seen, he had almost zero inhibitions. "What gives!"

He mashed his lips together and refused to answer me. I looked behind me and found that Mesmer had halved his previous distance between us. "What gives, Mesmer? Why are pixies a problem?" Inside, I was doing a happy dance. Pixies! I had watched the *Tinker Bell* movies soooo many times. They never failed on the days where I just needed some extra comfort and warmth at the end of a crummy day. I was half in love with pixies already, and I hadn't even met any in person. I couldn't wait to meet one!

Mesmer kept scanning around us as he answered. "Pixies view star elves like teenagers view rockstars."

My jaw dropped. "Seriously?" I whispered in abject delight, a great big smile blooming on my face.

Mesmer nodded. "Some of them thrive off of the adoration, but Mr. Rhys seems to be a different breed of star elf."

"Oh. My. Gosh." I swung around and poked Rhys again. "You're like a rockstar to pixies!" My voice went up an octave, and I tried not to bust up laughing. "I have to see this. We have to go."

Rhys shook his head. "I've been avoiding that place like the plague. There is no way you're going to get me in there."

I grinned. "Not even if I come up with something you really want?"

He scowled down at me. "There's nothing I want that badly."

I held up a finger. "Not even a meeting with Draven Leto where his genius brain looks at your business and helps you take it to the next level?"

Rhys stopped and wrapped his hands around my arms, squeezing gently. "Could you do that?" Draven was well known in the supernatural business community, and I took full advantage of that fact by waving him like a dangling carrot in front of my best friend's nose.

I shrugged nonchalantly. "Everyone knows Draven is a genius with businesses. He can look at all your financials, and the full spectrum of your business, and help you make it better." I looked at my glittery pink nailwraps with a bored air. "I already asked him, and he said it wouldn't be a problem." Trying to be inconspicuous, I peeked at him from the corner of my lashes.

Rhys scooped me up and attacked my mouth with a kiss. Then he dropped me and whooped and hollered as he danced in the damp sand while I spluttered and spit his disgusting germs off of me. I thought, and not for the first time, that Rhys was a dork. All of those books about elves who were polished and dignified *lied!* Exhibit A was still dancing in front of me, carrying on like he'd just won the lottery.

"No kissing!" I yelled at him. I mean, the guy wasn't disgusting or anything, but it was like kissing my brother! Gross!

With no warning at all, Mesmer's enormous body was right behind me, and his rocky arm banded around my waist in a steel clamp. Rhys, picking up on the suddenly serious vibes, stopped making a fool of himself and went still.

"What is it?"

"Look ahead," Mesmer whispered softly. "And don't. Move."

Rhys made starlight blades as he scanned with me. We both saw the huge tiger at the same time.

Holey shmoley!

My heart took off in an all-out sprint, and I trembled, sandwiched between Rhys and Mesmer. "What do we do?"

"I can fly you out of here?"

"We can't leave Rhys."

"Guys, look," Rhys interrupted. "He's not attacking or anything. It looks like he's waiting for us."

Rhys clued into that a lot sooner than I did. The tiger really *did* look like it was waiting for something or someone.

"Do you think it's tame?" I asked.

"There's only one way to find out," Mesmer said. "Stay!" His eyes speared me, and he sent me a look that said he meant business.

I nodded, wide eyed. *Of course* I wasn't going near the huge cat! What was I, crazy?

Mesmer slowly walked toward the cat, his rock body the only thing that kept me from being terrified he'd become kitty chow. If the cat *did* attack, I was pretty confident Mesmer would be fine. I didn't even think a tiger's claws could scratch him. His rock skin could literally repel bullets.

He got a few feet away and stopped. I could tell he was talking to the cat in a low, soothing tone, but I couldn't hear what he was saying.

"That's not a normal cat," Rhys whispered, grabbing my hand. "There's a magical aura coming off of it."

I squeezed his hand. "Could it be a shifter?" Tiger shifters were a thing, right? And if they were, I really wanted to meet one.

He shook his head. "Different aura. I think," he paused. "I think it's a witch's familiar."

I was close enough to the cat to see when it made eye contact with me, ignoring Mesmer. My insides tried to make a break for it to my outsides, and my whole body flushed warmly. Like the cozy warmth I felt in front of a fire with the soft sound of a rainstorm outside. Oh. My. Gosh.

"I think, could it be *my* familiar?"

"But you're an empath!" Rhys protested. "Empaths don't get familiars. You're not a witch, wizard, or mage."

"Umm." I cleared my suddenly dry throat. "Draven said I might have more to my bloodline? He knew I was an empath, but he didn't know if I would have another source of paranormal, because we don't know who my parents are. I could get my empath abilities from one side of the family, and something different from the other side, or even the same side, for that matter. Genetics can be a confusing mess."

Rhys scanned me from head to toe, obviously looking for clues to what other sort of supernatural I could be, but I had no patience for this. Not when I might get my very own tiger! I wanted to get closer. I tried to drop Rhys's hand and catch up with Mesmer, but Rhys refused to let go, obviously trying to protect me. I ended up dragging him through the sand, towing him toward the tiger. Mesmer was still speaking to the cat in low tones when I came level with him.

He held a rock arm out, preventing me from getting closer, and gave me the stink eye for not listening and staying put where he'd left me. I shrugged sheepishly, and his face softened. Aww, the big guy always forgave me. Even when I made it difficult for him to protect me. I patted his hand and squeezed his bicep as I poked my head around his huge body and looked at the kitty cat.

The tiger was black and white, but not like the white tigers I'd seen before. This one looked like it had a black body with white stripes. Even then, it looked like his black fur was sprinkled liberally with white fur. His ears—or hers?—were black but tipped with white. His huge paws were black with tufts of white in patches sprinkled in, and his tail was all black. The markings on his face were beautiful. Right above his eyebrows were white stripes that ran up in zigzags. And other than the tufts of whiskers which had some white on them, the rest of his face was black. His eyes were a medium amber color. He was gorgeous!

"I don't think he means you harm, Miss Mia. He seems very calm to me, and very intelligent." Mesmer glanced at me. "I get the feeling he was waiting for you."

"Umm." Deep breaths. In. Out. "Okay." I nodded. I stayed behind Mesmer at first as I tried to speak to the huge animal. My body trembled, both from excitement—tiger!—and fear.

"Hey kitty. Are you looking for someone?" I asked, my

voice as high and squeaky as a chipmunk. If I was trying to prove how brave I was, I was failing epically.

I suddenly felt a warm body flatten itself against my back and I shrieked in surprise. Rhys and Mesmer were on either side of me. That meant someone I didn't know was behind me, holding me close to them.

"It's just me," said a voice that made my stomach flutter.

Draven.

Wait, Draven!

I turned to push him away, back toward the villa. "Draven, the sun is up! You can't be out here!"

He stilled my pushing hands with his own. "Don't worry," he said softly. "I'm old enough now that only full sun can do anything to me. It shocks me a bit like an electric charge. Anything less, and it just feels like a soft scraping against my skin."

"Shocks you?" That didn't sound pleasant.

He cupped his hand over my elbow and nodded. "Sticking your tongue to a nine-volt battery is the closest I can describe it, except all over your skin, and stronger."

I shivered. Eww. That would be a heeby-jeeby feeling.

Draven nodded at the big cat. "I sense this guy belongs to you, Miss Durran. Mesmer and I will be here if we're wrong, but I'd like you to get closer so we can know for sure. If he is, it's an enormous indicator as to the depths of your talents. Only the very gifted mages and witches need a familiar to help ground them. We may not know what else you are yet, but if he's yours, we'll know that you'll likely be very powerful."

I took all of that in, but still saw one glaring problem with his suggestion. I folded my arms over my chest and scowled at him. "You know tigers hunt by snapping down on the carotid artery, right? I'd be dead in moments."

Draven flashed me a wicked smile. "I'm faster than I look."

Ignoring the flutters in my stomach from his smile, I grumbled at him, but did as he suggested. I kneeled down in front of the tiger, and the rest of the guys backed up to give us some space.

"Hi, guy. You're really beautiful, but I guess you probably want me to say handsome. The consensus seems to be that you're a guy, and guys hate it when you call them beautiful."

There were a few snickers behind me, but I studiously ignored them.

"Umm," I thumbed behind me toward Draven, "he seems to believe that you're my familiar. Are you?"

The big cat rubbed his face against my cheek and made a weird sound. I tried not to fall over onto my butt in surprise.

"He's chuffing," Draven explained. "That's a sound tigers make to say hello or to just let others know they're happy or content."

My mind was whirling. It was strange. There was still some fear there, there was a huge cat in front of me after all, but I could also feel the tiger's emotions, and he felt calm. So much so that it was calming *me* down. That had never happened to me before. For one, I'd never been able to feel another animal's emotions this strongly before. I'd gotten brief glimpses now and again, but with the tiger in front of me, it was like what he was feeling was a broadcasting satellite. It was that strong. And two, even though I reacted to other's emotions, they'd never been able to *directly* influence me. Being around this guy was chilling me out so much that

I suddenly felt like taking a nap. And I wanted grilled fish? Eww. I hated fish.

"Hilarious," I told the tiger.

He chuffed and gave me tiger kisses. I giggled and pushed his head away, wiping the slobber from my face with my sleeve. "Yeah, it's official," I said. "He's my familiar." I turned to the guys. "Unless other animals can influence my emotions like he can?" I made it a question because I genuinely wanted to know. I'd not been around many animals in the city.

"Only a familiar would help balance your emotions," Draven said. "An especially helpful tool for an empath." He helped me up from the sand and squeezed my arm softly. "Congratulations, Mia. A familiar is a partner and friend for life. He'll live as long as you do, and he'll help you to develop your empathy. And if you have another gift? He'll help with that as well." Draven dusted the sand from his hands and squatted down next to the tiger's head.

"Hello handsome fellow." The tiger allowed him to rub his neck and chest, but then batted his hand aside with his paw, and nuzzled closer to me. "I think he's been alone quite a while, looking for you. He's not in as good of shape as he should be in. He needs to gain some weight, and his fur is beautiful but matted in places." He stood up and turned to me. "I'll call a vet. Our vet is a brownie and brownies are fantastic with animals. He'll have your tiger fixed up in no time."

I was so touched that Draven wanted to help, and so ecstatic that I had a tiger familiar, that I hugged my boss impulsively. He stiffened for a minute, and then melted into the hug, hugging me back tightly.

"Thank you," I said. And I meant it from the bottom of my heart.

THE VET DROPPED by the villa a few hours later.

My tiger—yet to be named—and I met him in the den/office that Draven and I worked out of. Once the tiger had come into the office, he sniffed around and then followed his nose to the den. Apparently, it was where my smell on this floor was the strongest. To my embarrassment, he'd gone to the kitchens first. I chose to ignore that jab at my eating habits.

Just about every member of the Leto Villa had dropped by to gawk at my tiger as we'd waited. I'd felt a little like Vanna White from *Wheel of Fortune* as I'd pointed out how calm and chill he was being, and that he wouldn't hurt them.

When the brownie walked in, I blinked in surprise. I'd heard of what brownies looked like in folklore and fairytales, and this brownie looked nothing like that. He was about five feet tall, brown skin, slender, and completely hairless, including the top of his head. He had longish, delicate looking fingers, large, ocean blue eyes without scleras or pupils, a hawkish nose, pronounced cheekbones, no eyebrows, and very long eyelashes. He was wearing dark blue-jeans and a gray hoodie that said Ben's Beasts Veterinary. He was carrying an old-fashioned black satchel.

"Thank you for coming," Draven said, leading him to my tiger, who was lounging in front of the fire. He'd sat by the fireplace, looking at Draven in expectation until Draven had relented and lit the fire. It wasn't chilly, really, being that it was mid-spring, but my tiger wanted a fire, so a fire was what he got. I could see already that he would be spoiled. And, as I observed how the tiger interacted with Draven, I puzzled over the level of communication they already seemed to have with each other, and the ease. Rhys had tried to pet him, and he'd bumped him so hard he'd shoved Rhys onto his butt. Hmm, something to think about.

I shook the brownie's hand but kept out of his way as he kneeled next to the tiger and looked into his eyes for a good minute, before he hummed to himself and started his examination. "He's got good stamina and strength, although his diet has been lacking for a few months," the brownie said. He turned to me. "I'm Ben, by the way. It's nice to meet you. And congratulations on your new familiar!"

I smiled shyly. "Thank you. I need to name him. I keep calling him the tiger in my head."

The brownie bobbed his head. "The naming of a familiar is linked with the bond between mage and familiar. You see, your familiar already has a name, and once you discover it, the bond will be complete."

My eyes widened. I had so much to learn, both about familiars and tigers. I knew I would be researching like crazy until I was confident that I could be a good mage to my familiar and a good big-cat companion. I hesitated to say owner because I had the distinct feeling that he would own me rather than the other way around.

Ben stood. "He needs a good bath." He pulled a few things from his bag and started handing them to me with instructions. "This is for the bath. Use warm water, and gentle soap. Mix this in and have him stay in the water for at least half an hour. He needs to absorb all of it. It's an emergency stop-gap to help replenish some vitamins he's lost.

It's kind of like a big animal IV without the needles." He chuckled, and my lips twitched. Vet humor.

He handed me a bottle of vitamins that looked like horse pills, they were so large. I could see them through the clear bottle. "These he won't like as much. Mix them with his food, and he should eat them readily enough." He turned and looked down at the tiger. "You need these," he said in a firm voice. "Don't make your mage's life difficult by refusing them."

I was amused to see my tiger hunch in on himself a little, as though the diminutive brownie intimidated him. Either this was one tough brownie, or my tiger was a big baby.

Ben turned back to me and handed me a large paddle brush. "Use this on his fur after the bath and after he's dry." He looked back at the cat. "You've been eating junk food, haven't you?"

My cat, to everyone's amusement, hid his eyes with his huge paws. Well, that answered that question. Ben shook his finger at him. "No more junk food! It's bad for you!"

"I'll make sure he only eats the right foods," I said dryly. So, my tiger was a big baby, and a junk food addict. I wanted to laugh so badly, but didn't dare. It would undermine the scolding Ben was giving. It probably wasn't fair to say that my tiger was a baby, because Ben looked like he could scare a T. Rex into being a vegetarian with that stare, but the fact that my tiger was a junk food addict like me cracked me up.

Ben turned back to Draven and I. "Otherwise, he's fine. Make sure he gets extra food for the next few months. He's only about half grown right now. He'll get added bulk and height as he matures. Once he hits maturity, you can taper down to an adult tiger's normal feed." He handed me a paper with some websites on it. "Here are some reputable websites that will give you all you need to know to take care of him. Don't use others. They're not accurate for a tiger familiar."

Ben bent over to pet the tiger, and the tiger chuffed at him, nuzzling him. I was amazed. He'd only done that with me so far. Ben was like an animal whisperer. I was curious. I knew it was bad form, but Ben was right there!

I cleared my throat. "Hey, Ben? Umm, I hope this isn't rude, but I thought brownies were fixers? That they fixed household things?" I shifted my stance. "I'm new to supernaturals, you see. I don't know a lot about the different species."

Ben chuckled. "I *am* a fixer. I just fix living animals instead of inanimate objects." He patted my hand. "I take no offense. It's natural for you to be curious." He grabbed his bag. "Well, let me know if you have any further questions or problems with him." He saluted. "Good luck, Leto Villa!"

Aiwin opened the door for him, and showed him out and I looked at my cat, who was grooming himself nonchalantly.

"Hmm," I said.

Draven laughed. "This is going to be a fun pairing. I can already tell."

"We live to amuse," I said drolly.

CHAPTER 5
MIA

I t would not be an understatement to say that during the next week I put in just as many hours researching everything there was to know about my familiar as I did in my vampire assistant duties.

In fact, I'd researched tigers so much that I was now dreaming of tigers and could recite how to care for and feed them in my sleep. I learned everything I could get my hands on regarding a tiger familiar's growth, physiology, and psychology.

For example, I knew he needed to eat lots of meat and a little bit of grasses. I knew where he liked to sleep—he'd taken over my beanbag, the scamp—and I knew that he would just about die for belly rubs. I knew how much sleep he needed, and I also learned, quite by accident, that swimming with my tiger was not conducive to my health.

One warm spring day, I'd decided the sunshine was too amazing to stay inside. I'd already finished my work for the day, and I was itching to try the pool I'd not tried yet, so I put on my turquoise tankini, grabbed a towel, sunscreen, snack and hat, and shoved it all in my I Love Beaches bag.

My familiar, somehow knowing we were going to the pool, politely nudged me out of the way with his big, scruffy head so he could exit our room first, and led the way out of the villa to the backyard.

The pool had huge rock formations and waterfalls that dripped into a gigantic, deep blue pool. The bottom was a darker color than I was used to seeing in pools, almost black. It had stairs that led down and looked like something you'd see on a front page, full color shot in *Better Homes and Gardens.*

There were tons of lounge chairs and tables set up around the pool, with large, colorful umbrellas. There was also a little pool room that had a bathroom and outdoor shower, a small kitchen, an outdoor grill and a full fridge loaded with sugary snacks and all kinds of drinks.

I put my stuff down onto a table, switched my water bottle out with a colder one from the fridge, and took a long drink. The day was really warm, but the sun felt good on my skin. Draven kept the temperature in the villa at a balmy sixty-five degrees. Penguins would be quite happy here.

My tiger, meanwhile, was following me with his eyes like I was his sun and moon. He'd been doing that for days, and I still couldn't get over the fact that I had a familiar.

A familiar that was a tiger.

I kept expecting to wake up in my old apartment, having dreamed the last few months. My life now was so different from what it had been a mere two months ago that I sometimes felt like an imposter.

My tiger's beautiful black, white, and gray fur rippled a

little with the slight breeze we were getting from the ocean, and he kept staring at me.

"I need to figure out your name. I can't keep calling you *my tiger*."

He snorted and made that chuffing sound.

Aww. So cute. He was happy. I went over to give him hugs. Except, he thought this meant that I was ready to swim, because he bumped me with his huge head right over the edge and into the pool.

"Ack!"

Splash!

I spit water out of my mouth, having taken in a whole lake-full because I had been screaming as I'd gone in. My familiar looked at me with big, amber, kitty eyes in apology as I scowled at him.

"Ugh. Not fair that you already know how to use those."

And then he jumped in, swam over, and tried to sit in my lap.

"You don't fit!" I squeaked, trying to shove him off me. "What are you doing? There's an entire pool to swim in!" I kept trying to push him away, but he was like taffy in the warm sun, impossible to separate from my person.

And that was how my boss found me.

Me, trying not to drown with a two hundred-pound, not fully-grown tiger on my lap. And my kitty cat mewling in distress every time I tried to push him off of me.

Draven chuckled as he sat down and put his feet in. "I think he needs some swimming pointers."

Holy shmoley!

Draven was in board shorts and nothing else.

I about had a heart attack.

In my inattentiveness to what I was doing, my tiger's

weight shoved me underwater. I took on water like a ship that was capsizing as I tried really hard not to ogle the beautiful man with washboard abs, a chest that probably made grown women weep, and skin a burnished bronze, and swim at the same time.

I shook my head, getting the water out of my ears and nose, and swam to the pool ledge so I could avoid drowning. I cleared my throat. "A little help?"

He smiled and pushed off the edge into the water.

My tiger watched him carefully, looking like he was learning some pointers. When Draven got close enough, he got off my lap and went swimming with the vampire.

And man, could that vampire swim! I guess he technically didn't need to breathe, so coming up for air was unnecessary, which meant that he could spend hours under the water, swimming from one end to the other. After we swam ourselves out, we got a good game of pool volleyball going, the only volleyball I could actually play. I had my familiar on my team, though I didn't really want him because he was a ball hog. In the end, he just ended up popping the ball with his four-inch canines and long claws, and we had to stop.

Note to self, buy Draven a new ball.

I had been trying for the last several weeks to ignore the feelings I was developing for my boss.

There were so many reasons why my attraction to him was a no-no. At the top of that list was that I loved my new job. It was actually my dream job. And if we dated and then broke up, I didn't know what I would do. Probably go beg Rhys for a job.

And second, I was a little damaged from my past. More than I'd realized, because the idea of opening up to someone made me feel like I was about to get up in front of ten thousand people and give a speech: sweaty hands, racing heart, the feeling that I needed to lie down, general nausea. My brain knew that supernaturals were different. That they felt different to my empathic senses. That they didn't over-whelm or hurt me. Draven *especially* felt really peaceful to me. So my brain knew this, had actually experienced it for the last several months, but my heart, I'd found, was still leery. It wanted reassurances and more data.

It seemed so much easier in books and movies. I mean, sure, there was always something keeping the couple from just diving right into a relationship right off the bat, but usually, those things seemed doable.

This. This did not seem doable.

And besides, I'd had zero indications that Draven even found me attractive. The guy was locked up tighter than Fort Knox.

We got out, and Draven immediately went to sit in a huge lounge chair under a very wide, very UV-protecting umbrella. My tiger got out using the steps, shook himself off, then laid down next to me in the shade, yawning and obviously tuckered out. It was so hard being a big cat. Play, eat, sleep. Repeat.

"Did you want something from the fridge?" I asked, as I looked over my sunglasses at Draven.

He gave me a look, and then nodded. "I'll get it. You rest."

I slipped my sunglasses back up and laid back. Draven came back with what looked like an old-fashioned Coke bottle with dark-red fluid inside. Yeah, that was blood. I was icked out, but I refused to show it. Draven was testing me. He hadn't yet shown any real signs of vampiness around me, and I'd been waiting for him to so I could show him I was cool with it. I wanted him to trust me. It was really important to me. Also, I wanted him to be able to fully relax around me, and so far, he'd been unable to. This was an important step for him. As an empath, I had things about me that were not convenient. I got burned out by being around people too much. I needed frequent breaks and alone time so I could detox from all the emotions swimming around me all the time. With Draven, he needed blood. End of story. And he couldn't change that any more than I could change my need for frequent solitude.

He popped the cap on the bottle, and plopped a straw in the liquid, before he started slurping it up like it was a soda.

"Yummy?" I asked with an eyebrow arched.

He gave me a look, and then he laughed, his shoulders settling as the tension drained out of him.

Yep. I passed.

I mentally high-fived myself.

Way to go, Mia!

I could be cool. I could be chill.

Totally. Chill.

"Yes." And then his smile turned wicked. "Want some?" he asked, holding the bottle out to me.

My nose scrunched up. "I'm going to pass on that one, big guy. But you go to town on it."

His wolfish smile disappeared, and he stared at me intently with his lovely brown eyes.

Yikes. I needed a fan or a water mister for a look that intense.

"You're different than I imagined."

"Oh yeah? How so?"

He took another drink. "When you first emailed me, I knew right then that I wanted to talk to you and feel you out about the job. Here you were, this woman that had no idea that she could see the ad because she was supernatural, and yet you still had the gumption to email me and chew me out for using premium ad space for something farcical. I could tell you were a spitfire, and to be honest, the job required someone of that bent."

"Someone tough?"

He nodded. "You've seen what the job is like, Miss Durran. It requires someone of courage." He grinned. "Not to mention someone of patience who will put up with me."

I laughed. "Putting up with you is the easy part. I love this job, and you've been incredibly patient and gone above and beyond teaching me the finer points of your company. You've even taught me some engineering principles, which I was *not* expecting. But I've found...I love all of it." I smirked. "Even the midnight conference calls with Tokyo that you need me alert enough to take notes in."

He winced. "Sorry about getting you out of bed and dragging you to a meeting."

I couldn't help but laugh. "Well, it was my first ever conference call in my pajamas!"

He grinned. "And Hiroshuki said that he loved the polar bear on your pajama top."

I blushed. "I didn't mean to get in the camera's range. I just thought it would be fine if I sat behind the camera and took notes."

Draven slurped from his bottle, and I tried not to shudder. It would take me a little while to get used to that. "As far as I'm concerned," he said, "you can come to work every day in pajamas."

I eyed him, trying to see if he was serious. He looked like he was. "Let's do pajama day on Fridays. Just me?" I asked.

He thought about it. "All the staff?"

I laughed. "Is that a question? You're the boss."

"All the staff," he said definitively.

"Including you?" I grinned a villainous grin, and he eyed my smile with some misgiving.

"I don't wear pajamas, but to get into the spirit of things, I'll go inside after this and purchase some so they're here before Friday."

I rubbed my hands together in excitement. "Mesmer, did you hear that?"

I heard the longest sigh ever, and I giggled. "Come on, big guy, we can go shopping for some pj's for you. We'll make sure they're martial arts adaptable, so you can still kick butt if you need to."

"Yes, Mia," Mesmer said with the same tone of voice that someone would use going to a funeral.

"Aww, it won't be that bad!"

Draven chuckled. "Poor Mesmer. Before you came, he was a respectable bodyguard. Now all the other bodyguards will laugh at him."

There was another sigh from behind the planter, and I grinned. What a fun day this was turning out to be!

My tiger made some growly noises, and I looked down and realized he was asleep and dreaming. Huh, do tigers dream? I guess I should research more and see.

I rubbed his head and he quieted down.

"He's a remarkable animal," Draven said.

I nodded. I was a very blessed girl. I stood up to grab my cover-up and throw it on. I didn't know how Draven stood it out here. It must be flaying his skin.

I eyed him. "Are you okay out here? Isn't the sun stinging?"

He shrugged, finishing his blood bottle. "A little, but I wanted to come swimming with you."

My hurt twinged at his words, but I tried not to take them to mean anything other than he wanted to hang out outside of work to get to know me better.

"Forgive me for asking—it's unbearably rude—but are you and Rhys...?"

I sputtered and sprayed my sip of water on my familiar's head. He wuffed at me, woken from a dead sleep. "I'm so sorry!" I used my towel to clean his head off. He licked my hand, blinked a long, slow blink, and went back to sleep. "No!" I said to Draven. "We're friends. He's like a brother to me."

Draven nodded, dropping the subject. From his chair, he tossed his bottle into a huge, black trash can, and the bottle clinked loudly as it hit the bottom.

I put my hands up in the air like a dork and shouted, "Score!"

Draven smirked.

"Speaking of Rhys, I've been trying to get him to go to the new tea shop in town, The Tea Hobbit, but he's apparently terrified of pixies."

"Understandable."

"Don't take his side! I really want to go!"

"What if I go with and I give him business advice while we're there? You were just asking me about that the other day. Something that will take his mind off the pixies."

"You don't think my sparkling wit will keep him occupied?"

He bit his lip and a dimple popped out.

Oh, heavens! Seriously, just stop getting cuter!

"I'm old enough not to walk into that one," he said with

a laugh, then he looked down at his shorts. "Well, looks like I'm dry." His eyes found mine. "Ready for lunch?"

I got up, gathered my stuff, and shoved it in my beach bag. "I'm starving!"

I turned around and gasped. Draven had moved behind me without a sound. And he moved very, very fast.

"Can I carry that for you?" he asked, holding out a hand, being a gentleman.

I was dumfounded for a minute. Had anyone ever asked to carry my bag for me? The fact that it was very light and I could easily carry it wasn't even on my radar.

"You have old world values that I appreciate very much," I said to him, completely serious.

Somehow, he'd moved closer, and I was now getting a close-up view of his beautiful eyes and long, full eyelashes.

I tried not to breathe him in, because I knew his scent was kind of my kryptonite. He smelled like pine trees, rain, and limes. Three things that you wouldn't think to put together, but on him, it hit me like a gut punch.

He smelled *so* good.

He didn't move, just stood there and gazed down at me. I tried to reach out empathically and get a sense of what he was feeling, but he was locked down tight, and there were only questions simmering in his eyes.

The air got heavy, and it felt sultry. Like the thick air before a lightning storm or a tornado. I wanted so badly to lean into him and just adore his mouth with mine, or maybe nibble on his chin, but I held myself back.

My heart was racing, and I knew he could hear it. His eyes grew very intense. My breath grew heavy.

Seriously, someone, throw me a life raft!

Intervention needed!

I can't fall for my boss!

My tiger nudged between us and nosed Draven a step back from me. I swayed. Maybe I had heatstroke? I felt my warm face. I'd read about this online. I think I needed ice, and maybe ice cream? I needed something. And I really needed my heart to slow down.

Draven squatted down until he was level with my familiar. "I won't hurt her, boy," he said, rubbing the cat's ears.

That was yet to be seen.

My head was screaming, *Danger! Danger, Will Robinson!* And my heart was trying to eat all the other organs, like some kind of carnivore heart on steroids.

I rubbed my chest. This crush stuff was painful.

CHAPTER 6
MIA

On Thursday, I finally convinced Rhys to go to The Tea Hobbit with me. I had to *promise* that Draven would come to talk to him about his business so that he could increase his customer base.

It didn't really bother me that I had to bribe my best friend to hang out with me. I would likely do it again in the course of our friendship. I knew it had nothing to do with me, anyway, and everything to do with the wait staff at The Tea Hobbit. Rhys was probably exaggerating how pixies acted around star elves. Though, he didn't seem prone to exaggeration...

The pixies were gorgeous. I knew pixies had wings, but I couldn't see them. Maybe they could make them visible/invisible at will? There were two of them working when we stepped in. Both of them were shorter than me. One had platinum blonde, short, spiky hair, ripped jeans, and a black tee shirt that said, No, you're right. Let's do this the dumbest way possible to make it easier for you. Her lips were a gorgeous red and pouty. She didn't seem bothered in the least that a star elf had showed up at the tea shop.

But the other one...

Let's just say I now knew someone that could make such a high-pitched noise that only certain animals could hear it. Well, animals and paranormals. Both Rhys and Draven winced in pain when we stepped into the shop as the other pixie, Falista, as we found her name out to be later, screeched and dropped a tray, scattering broken shards of what looked like previously beautiful china.

An old hobbit woman came out in a frilly, fifties style of dress and bare feet. "Falista, what's all the ruckus?" She glowered at Falista while Rhys, Draven, and I seated ourselves, watching the drama unfold. Me with glee, Rhys with a sense of doom, and Draven with politeness. Hopefully, we were in the other pixie's grouping of tables, and it would be her that took our order. I wasn't sure Rhys was ever going to forgive me for this.

When Falista fainted dead to the floor after babbling about Rhys for a solid minute to the hobbit owner, the blonde pixie rolled her eyes and came over to our table with an order tablet and stylus. "What can I get everyone?"

She didn't appear to be fan-girling over Rhys, and she seemed as calm as a cucumber. I admired this. If a star elf was a species that pixies revered, she was handling meeting Rhys with grace and poise. Either that or she didn't really care that Rhys was a star elf. As I focused on my empath senses, I could tell it was the latter. She didn't care what he was; she just wanted to do her job and go home.

I liked her already.

I smiled at her. "First, thank you so much for being chill around my friend here." I nodded toward Rhys, who was avoiding eye contact with me. Huh. Hurtful. "Second, I *love* that shirt!"

Draven laughed, and Rhys said something derogatory about me under his breath. I ignored him.

The waitress nodded politely at me and allowed a small smile to grace her ruby lips. "Thank you."

"What do you recommend?" I asked.

She looked at each of us, studying us for a minute. "For the vampire, I would recommend our sweet Nightingale tea. It's made from a blend of valerian root, peppermint, and lemon." She nodded at Rhys. "For the star elf, I'd recommend our Luscious Berries, which has strawberries and cream, black tea, and an extra rosehips shot. And for you, miss, I'd recommend our Candy Cane Lane herbal tea with a shot of hazelnut chocolate."

"How did you do that?" Rhys demanded, eying her. He was giving off unnerved vibes.

Draven's attention was occupied with the hobbit woman patting the cheeks of the other pixie to rouse her. When that didn't work, the hobbit dumped water on the pixie's face. The pixie shrieked and started babbling again to the woman, who dragged her up to her feet, and gently and kindly pushed her back through the swinging doors to the back area, keeping her away from our table. She had my gratitude. And I'd thought Rhys had been exaggerating. Turned out, he hadn't been.

Our server never even looked back to check to see what was going on. She was very focused and very professional.

Rhys was looking at her with squinty, suspicious eyes. I kicked him lightly under the table.

She's being nice! Don't antagonize the nice pixie!

When he ignored my subtle hints, I cleared my throat until I had his attention and glared at him.

"What? Do you know what she did?"

"She gave the recommendations that I asked her for? Could you not be weird?"

The pixie waited calmly for us. I peeked up at her, and her cheeks were pink, but her expression was both calm and patient.

Wow. I was really impressed with her.

Draven spoke up, distracting Rhys. "You were looking for feedback from me for The Laughing Elf?"

Rhys sat up and nodded. He pulled out a mini notebook and pen and looked adorably ready to learn all the things.

Draven flicked his eyes toward the pixie. "Hire her to run your bar, and pay her at least double what she's making here, plus tips."

The pixie shifted, looking interested. Heck, I would be too if I were in her position. She clearly didn't fit in with the business she currently worked for. Maybe Rhys' club would be a better fit for her?

"What's your name, angel?" Rhys asked, eying her speculatively now, like she was a rare piece of chocolate that must be acquired at all costs. I could see it in his eyes. Draven, the business guru, had spoken, and thus it was. I held in an inappropriate snicker. It was just so adorable.

"Paradise, but I go by Dice."

"Dice is such a cool name! Wanna hang out sometime? I'm new in town and have no friends." I said, butting into their conversation. I pointedly ignored Rhys' protests at my 'no friends' comment.

Dice had really cool vibes. She was kinda like a biker pixie? At least that was the vibe she gave off. I wanted to hang out with her for that reason alone, and because she was so chill with Rhys and just in general. But I was worried about the level of fear I was getting off of her. I didn't know why she was afraid—I sensed it wasn't us or anyone in the shop—but my protective instincts were kicking into high gear, and I wanted to make sure she stayed safe.

Draven and Rhys laughed at my abruptness, but Dice nodded. Her eyes warmed, and I sensed she was grateful for my invitation. She seemed lonely. "I would love to. I'll give you my number on your receipt."

I formed a heart with my fingers and held it up to my chest. She laughed, and I grinned in victory. I loved making people laugh. It was one more thing that was new to me in this town. I couldn't remember ever making someone laugh before. How sad was that? It was like I'd been bound by invisible chains before, and now I'd been set free.

"Are you interested?" Rhys asked again, getting back to his earlier question.

She pondered him for a few minutes. "You're the owner of The Laughing Elf?"

He nodded, clasping his hands together on the table and leaning back in his seat. "I'd love to hire you, if you're interested. I'll at least double your salary from here, and it comes with benefits."

Dice glanced at all of us, and then back at Rhys. "I've never been to the club. Can I come and see it before I decide?"

Rhys nodded. "Of course, angel." He reached into his leather jacket and pulled out a card. "Call me when you want to come in. I'll set it up."

Dice nodded and tucked the card away. "I'll just go put your orders in."

"Thanks," I said brightly.

She smiled and left.

I looked at the guys. "She and I are going to be besties," I announced. I knew I sounded like I was twelve, but I couldn't help it. I liked Dice. She was my kind of people, and I felt the teensiest bit protective of her since I'd realized that she was afraid of someone.

They busted up laughing, and I leaned back in my chair. Sadly, they thought I was joking. As I'd discovered with Rhys, Mesmer, and from my perspective, Draven, having friends was all kinds of amazing. I was still me, the empath with a serious social problem, but I was learning that friendship with people who didn't give off chaotic vibes, and who were fun and easy for me to be around, was something I could do. In fact, I was starting to cherish the friendships I had. They made me laugh and got me through the tough days where nothing seemed to go right. And they were there on the good days as well. And best of all, I wasn't alone anymore. I'd been so lonely before that I was ready to take in a feral cat or a rabid wolf. And bonus! I got to drag them with me to new and interesting places!

Exhibit A: Dragging them to the tea shop with me. So far, it had been both fun *and* educational!

Draven grew serious, getting back to his recommendation. "She has to have some sort of connection with the needs of people."

I paused, trying to find the right words. "She feels...a little like me? She's not really an empath, though. It's like she can discern what someone needs physically? She's not tapped into emotions, that I can tell."

Draven nodded. "She gave us recommendations based on what's going on with each of us physically."

Dice came and delivered our orders and then disappeared into the back, leaving The Tea Hobbit mostly empty. It was just us and one other customer over along the back wall.

Draven nodded at his tea. "Mine has valerian root. I've been...struggling with stress lately." He looked at me almost guiltily, and I sat up straight. Wait. Was the stress because of me? Why? Before I could go back mentally over our interactions for the last few weeks, Draven continued. "She picked up on that and gave me not only something to help with that, but made sure it was coupled with other flavors that I'd like as well."

Rhys stirred his tea, taking a sip. "And she knew I was getting a cold, hence the extra shot of rosehips in mine."

I sipped mine and hummed in enjoyment. It was amazing! "And she knew I loved chocolate and peppermint," I added, and the guys nodded. "And we all know a girl *needs* her chocolate. Huh, that's really impressive. So, her magical gift is being able to read people physically? Wait, does that mean she can see things like more serious illnesses in someone? Like cancer?"

Draven pursed his lips and blew on his valerian blend. "Unfortunately, my guess is that she does see all of that. It must be difficult."

I stared at the swinging door she'd disappeared behind in horror. It was hard enough for me to deal with people's emotions. I could sense battery victims, hurt children, grief over the loss of a loved one, greed, lust, anger, etc. But to feel the physicality of all of those? To physically feel people suffering from various illnesses and diseases? Wow, she really needed a friend! I wasn't naive enough to believe that I would be the perfect friend to her, but I could at least empathize with what she was going through. And I didn't know why she was afraid, but I'd also been afraid in my life, and in hiding. I could empathize with that as well.

I busied myself with my tea and looking around the pretty shop while the guys talked about The Laughing Elf. Draven dove right into a small, but detailed, list of things that he recommended Rhys implement. Among those was to have regular theme nights, a half off night for ladies, and utilize social media ads when he was going to have big headliners come in for the laughing hour.

Rhys nodded, making notes on his phone. "I have a wall of screens that I rarely get to put to good use. We could use that to put up, for instance, the Eiffel Tower for a themed Paris night."

"Count me in for that, if you have it," I said. "That sounds like a ton of fun. And it would give me the kick in the butt I need to find a date." Which I very much needed. I'd tried dating before. To say it had epically failed would be a vast understatement. It didn't help to feel your date's every feeling. I'd given up. I was in my late twenties and I'd never kissed someone, or had a good date, for that matter. It was time. Also, I really wanted to get rid of my growing interest in my boss. Dating other people was a surefire way to do that.

Draven was staring at me intently when I glanced up at him. I tilted my head to the side, asking him with my eyes what he was thinking about. His eyes became hooded as he stared at me, and I wanted to gulp, but instead stayed very still. I'd read before that people in the wild could feel when they were in the sights of a predator. I could verify that. Yes. Yes, you could.

Draven turned to Rhys. "You can do whatever you want

with the themes, but after checking out your club, I'd recommend going with the classier themes. Like a Paris night, or a Roaring Twenties night. The interior of your club lends itself more to those than, say, eighties grunge night."

I widened my eyes and turned to Rhys, Draven's weirdness momentarily forgotten. "How classy is this club of yours, Geezer?"

Rhys scowled at the nickname, and Draven laughed before he said with an amused drawl, "Very classy."

"But the bathroom smells like onion rings?" I asked, confused. I could see a concession stand bathroom smelling like onion rings, but not a posh club.

"My shower is just off the break room. One of my employees orders onion rings *every time* he takes his lunch break. It makes my office and personal bathroom smell like a deep fryer."

I laughed and patted his hand. "Poor baby."

The silver bells above the door caught my attention as someone came in. A blonde bombshell walked into the tea shop, and I tried not to gape at her. I must not have been very successful because Rhys and Draven looked up to see what had caught my attention. Rhys's eyebrow went up while Draven leaned further back into the seats, giving off a very faux-relaxed vibe. He wasn't relaxed at all, though. His emotions had tightened down, like battening down the hatches before a storm.

I lowered my feet back to the floor and sat up straight as the woman came to our table and put a flirty, dripping-with-rings hand on Draven's shoulder. "Darling, I haven't seen you in a while!" She looked at me with a raised eyebrow like I was dog chow, and then leaned in and kissed Draven's cheek, leaving a berry-pink stain on it. Why didn't she just pee on him? It would have left the same keep-your-grubby-hands-off-him vibes. "Dinner tonight?"

It was taking everything I had not to *accidentally* stab her hand with a fork.

Rhys grabbed the hand not holding my tea as though he could read my mind. He shook his head at me, and I could read the silent warning: *Proceed with caution. Stabbing the blonde viper would be frowned upon by society at large.* Also, it would inconvenience Draven.

My eyes conveyed to him that there were some things that needed to be dealt with swiftly. Like they used to do in the wild west. Shoot 'em up. Bang. Bang.

His eyes conveyed that stabbing is a crime punishable by the law, and that we weren't living in the wild west. That we weren't even living in the right century, for that matter.

Draven, either ignoring Rhys' and my silent byplay, or completely oblivious, said goodbye to the blonde bombshell, and she left, sashaying out the door like a woman on the runway instead of a simple tea shop.

I hated her and wanted her gone from the earth. I thought it was possible she deserved to be thrown into the pit of Mordor. What a vile character! And her vibe was ick. She felt so fake to me, with a greedy under-base that blazed like a greasy lightning rod.

"Who was she?" I tapped my teacup with my purple nailwrap and tried to keep my disgust for Draven's friend out of my voice.

I must have failed epically because Draven gave me a curious look before he answered. "A dining partner. I," he paused, "don't have many friends, and I hate to try new places alone." He seemed a little embarrassed to admit to this, but I thought it was a totally valid thing. I hated it as well. In fact, I thought most people probably hated it. It was no fun trying new places all by yourself.

"So, she's not a friend?" Or more, my nosy mind added.

Rhys started choking on his tea, his eyes watering like crazy. I reached across to help him with that problem by patting his back. That I patted it a little harder than necessary was a cathartic service my best friend was offering me. "You okay?" I asked.

My expression must have convinced him to keep his thoughts to himself, because he nodded and winced at my tender ministrations.

"No, she's not." He looked uncomfortable. "She sought me out a year or so ago and asked me out. I made it clear to her I would be happy to attend as an acquaintance, but that I wasn't ready to date. She agreed, and we've been out as acquaintances a few times to restaurant openings."

"Oh." I knew I shouldn't say anything, but...

I sighed. "She's not a good person, Draven. You know that, right?"

He stared at me, then finally said, "I did sense a falseness in her. It occasionally made me uncomfortable."

I nodded. "Yeah, she's about as false as fool's gold. I'm sorry. But if it's any consolation, I'll go to new places with you! I dragged you both here, after all. Or, if you prefer to go with a guy, Rhys will go with you!"

Rhys actually nodded, not bothered at all that I'd just volunteered him. Aww, the sweetie. "I would actually love to hang out, Draven." He rubbed the back of his neck, looking uncomfortable. "I need to apologize. Mia made me realize that you've been extending a friendly hand my way, and I was unintentionally rebuffing you. I hope you know it's not because of you. I'm just leery of people in general."

I squinted at him. "You weren't with *me?*"

He smiled and took a sip of his blend. "You are a special case," he said ruefully.

I preened. Of course I was. I hesitated to delve into someone's past, but maybe it was time for Rhys and I to have a heart-to-heart about why he was so afraid of opening the friendship/relationship door.

"It's not a problem," Draven said. "I knew you were going through a rough patch. We're all entitled to those."

My heart melted a little. Draven was so considerate of other's feelings. However, his abundant good qualities reinforced the many reasons *why* having a crush on him was so hard to move past. Since our first meeting, he'd treated me with care, consideration, and respect. As time had gone on, his consideration had morphed into doing little things for me that went above and beyond a boss/employee relationship, and veered more into friendship territory. I felt like we were friends, but I wasn't sure about him. He was so hard to read sometimes!

I breathed out slowly, letting my frustrations go. And then...the emotions from outside the tea shop hit me like a ton of bricks, and I screamed as I jumped across the table in a flying tackle, knocking both Rhys and Draven to the floor, with me on top of them. "Everyone get down!" I shouted in panic at the people in the shop.

Pop pop pop pop, crash!

The glass window that had been just to the left of our table shattered into a million pieces. It blew outward with a whoosh of purple magic and *exploded* into the tea shop.

My grip on the guys was so tight that I couldn't feel my hands. I winced as the force of the magical explosion of glass speared me in so many places that I felt like a pincushion. I whimpered in pain.

Draven immediately flipped us over so that he was on top, and I was protected underneath him, while Rhys put up a shield of hardened moonlight that bulged around us like a thick, silvery-clear dome.

The employees in the back screamed in terror, but Dice was already out in the dining area and crawling toward us in an Army crawl over the glass-strewn floor. She had thick towels protecting her arms from the glass. Her eyes were laser focused on the blood running down my bare legs.

I was trying hard not to whimper, but I was in so much pain that I couldn't hold the tears at bay.

Rhys kept his dome up with one hand and held my hand with his other, while Draven rushed out of the shop faster than I could follow with my eyes. All I felt was the *whoosh* of air as he left.

Dice finally got to us and took instant control. "Help me get her behind the counter where it's safer."

Rhys nodded, and carried me, keeping both of us low to the ground. Dice laid down a towel and propped me onto my side. "I'm going to pull the glass out, okay?"

Her calm soothed me, and I nodded jerkily, not letting go of my death-grip on Rhys' hand. "The employees in the back called the sheriff. Finn should be here soon."

Dice's hands were steady as she poured alcohol over tweezers that she'd grabbed from her purse, and carefully started pulling glass out of my skin and plunking it into a crystal pitcher.

I kept my eyes closed, not wanting to watch the grue-some process. Rhys used his other hand to dab at the blood that ran down my legs and arms with a white towel. "Where did Draven go?"

Rhys squeezed my hand. "He went after them."

I opened my eyes because he sounded worried. The smell of the rubbing alcohol mixed with the blood and the scent of the various teas was making my stomach churn. I looked up at him. "What is that tone in your voice?"

Rhys hesitated.

"Just tell me," I demanded.

"I think if he finds whoever did this, he's going to kill them, without waiting for due process of the law." He shrugged. "Not that I blame him. I would do the same thing."

I bit down on my lip as Dice pulled a long, thin shard of glass out of my calf. Death to whomever had done this to me didn't sound half bad right then. But...vigilante justice wasn't the right way to go, no matter how much I wanted the idiot to pay. "Go after him."

Rhys shook his head. "He'll kill *me* if I leave you, Starshine. Stars, I'd kill myself if I left you alone right now! Besides, the laws are slightly different here, and Draven Leto is a founding member. I can't imagine they would prosecute him for taking down someone that has been hunting his employees."

"I hope you're right."

SHERIFF FINN THANKED us and left after getting our statements. I was sitting up in my hospital bed, trying not to wince as the sheet kept rubbing the cuts on my legs. I couldn't find a comfortable position, and I ached everywhere. Draven shifted, hovering behind me. I knew he was just about to ask me for the third time if he could get me anything when the doctor came in.

He was a thin man with a balding head, long, thin fingers, and an amiable smile. "Hello, Mia." He patted my hand. "We're real sorry you were attacked, hun."

I didn't really know what to say to that. What did you say when you were the target of a deadly paranormal who apparently wanted to wipe your existence from the face of the earth? I just wanted to go home and snuggle with my tiger. "Can I be discharged now?"

Draven was so close I could feel his breath billowing the hair on the top of my head. His hand was on my shoulder, and the warmth of his body comforted my jittery feelings. He hadn't let go of me since he'd come back into The Tea Hobbit with empty hands and a feral, cold fury blackening his expression.

I shivered, remembering his eyes, and the promise of death in them.

The doctor nodded at me, re-wrapping the dressing on my arm. "We've sealed the worst of the gashes with liquid stitches. Some just needed to be dressed cleanly and medicated. The liquid stitches will hold until the wounds heal. The rest just needs to be kept clean and re-dressed once a day. Put some antibiotic ointment on the wounds and give them some air every day so they can heal. Sunshine wouldn't hurt them, either."

I guess I was lounging by the pool for the next few days. What a sacrifice.

The doctor left and a nurse came in with the discharge papers. Draven gave them my healthcare cards, which he'd stolen from my purse, and the nurse went to make copies while I signed or initialed where there was highlighter to prompt me to do so. When she came back, Draven took my cards, and then he and Rhys wheeled me out of the hospital in a wheelchair against my futile, protesting wishes that I could walk.

"We need to pick up your pain meds at the pharmacy," Draven said, loading me into the back of the limo. Mesmer was looking at us in the rearview mirror with a sad, guilty expression on his face. I knew he was beating himself up for not catching the paranormal that kept trying to kill me. He'd been stationed outside of the tea shop and had searched the area after the blast with Draven, but they hadn't found anything.

"I'm okay, Mesmer," I assured him, winking. "Remember, I'm tough. It'll take a lot more than this to keep me down. And it wasn't your fault!" I told him sternly.

He nodded, but still looked soulfully at the bandages on my arms, neck, and legs. At least my face had been smashed up against the guys' bodies and had escaped any damage.

I sighed. He was such a softie, and I loved him for it. I got out of the car against the protests of everyone and opened Mesmer's door to give him a big hug. "I'm okay," I whispered into his chest.

He was infinitely gentle as he hugged me back. "I'm very happy about that, Miss Mia. We'll get the dastard."

"Ooooh, old timey word!" I praised.

He attempted a smile, and I squeezed his hand, then got in the backseat again.

"I'll get a Ryde and pick up her meds from Dax's Drugs," Rhys said, leaning down to kiss my forehead. I didn't protest the kiss. I was happy to receive forehead kisses. I just didn't really want to lock lips with him.

"Thanks, Rhys," Draven said with a grateful look.

Rhys left, and Draven got into the back of the limo with me. He ignored our seatbelts and pulled me carefully against his chest, wrapping his arms around me.

I leaned against him, relaxing completely and letting my full weight settle against him. Draven grabbed a remote to turn the heated seats on, and I sighed in bliss, falling fast asleep against his chest within minutes.

I WOKE up in my bed to my tiger growling quietly. His gigantic head was over my hand, nuzzling it, and his full body was on the bed with me. A mean feat considering his size. I ran my fingers through his thick fur. "Sorry, boy." He licked my arm with his rough tongue and carefully put his head on my stomach.

"I don't think he's going to let you go anywhere without him ever again," a voice that made my heart flitter said from my lounge chair.

I looked over and found Draven sitting next to me, leaning forward, with his elbows on his knees.

"Someone is targeting me," I said, without any preliminaries. I wanted information.

Draven nodded. "I'm sorry, cara. They're targeting me as well. In the last month, I've dealt with numerous attempts on my life. We've thwarted each attack, but have been unable to track down who's behind it."

I laid my head back down and sighed, staring up at my canopy. "What do we do?"

He sat back in the chair. "Well, for one, I think you stick

close to the villa for a while. I'll send someone else to do the in-town errands that you have."

"Are they going to buy my tampons for me, too?"

He smiled. "I'll buy them for you, if you need."

I scrunched up my nose in protest. Then I laughed at a sudden thought. "Send Mesmer."

The idea of huge, bulky Mesmer in the pad and tampon aisle, trying to find the right kind, being horrified at the infinite options... It made me giggle. "And send someone along to get video!" Because I seriously needed to see that.

Draven laughed, then sighed again. "Get some rest. Rhys left your meds beside you." He nodded at my bedside table where a white pharmacy bag labeled Dax's Drugs waited for me.

"I'll thank him when I see him again."

"Dice came by the villa to check on you."

That gave me warm fuzzies. Dice! "Well, at least we can rule out you, Dice, and Rhys as suspects."

Draven stood and leaned over to kiss my forehead. "Feel better, cara. I don't want to see you in the office for at least two days."

I pouted, ignoring the buzz tingling through my body from his lips on my skin. "But I'll be so bored! I need something to do!"

Draven hesitated and then sat on the bed next to my familiar. It amazed me there was room, considering the tiger took up most of the space. I was wedged into an itty-bitty corner, and my familiar's enormous body covered the rest.

Draven smirked at me. "Do you want to play Scrabble?"

Ooooh, Scrabble! "Yes! And when I win, I get a double chocolate chip muffin." He was going down!

LATER, I was relaxing in bed and very tired of being there. My familiar and I were about to get in the shower, so I could scrub the hospital off of me, and my tiger could play in the water. The shower was hardly big enough for both of us, even though it was an enormous walk-in that could possibly fit a football team.

I turned on the spray on both sides—my tiger got one and I got one—and sighed as the warm water enveloped me, laughing at his antics. He had a very tried-and-true method of showering. First, he tested the water with his paws. I knew for a fact he was testing the temperature because if it wasn't the right temperature, he would look at me until I fixed it. He did that now, and I chuckled at him as I added a little more heat.

Second, he would stick only his head under the spray, and let the water run down the top of his head and neck. He would usually pause there for up to several minutes, just enjoying the water on his face. Then, he would get his whole body in, and with his head down, would just let the spray drench him. Usually, but not every time because I didn't want to dry out his skin or beautiful coat, I would soap him up with a special scrub brush, and he'd rinse off as fastidiously as someone trying to get something sticky off of them.

We went through that same routine today because today was a shampoo and conditioner day for him. Ben had given me a great shampoo and conditioner for big cats that smelled like lemons. It was the only brand that my familiar liked. We'd tried the one that smelled like peppermint, and he'd sneezed for days.

I hurried through my routine as my tiger was rinsing off and shut off the water. He sat in the shower waiting for me, and I chuckled again, moving gingerly because of the pain. My cuts had already scabbed over. It turned out that all elves could make healing draughts keyed into someone's DNA. Aiwin made me one earlier—while apologizing that it was shamefully weak; he blamed it on his mother's side—that had made all of my cuts scab over. Rhys promised to make me a powerful one that would heal me more deeply, but I had to wait, because it would take a while.

I was just happy to be able to shower.

After getting dressed in the softest leggings and over-sized shirt possible, I pulled my hair up into a messy bun and got out the hair dryer. My tiger, used to this routine, shook off any excess water from his coat, and then stepped out onto the towel that I'd laid down for him.

"You're spoiled, you know that?"

He chuffed at me, rubbing his wet head against my hip. I kissed his head, and turned the dryer on full blast, aiming the warm air at my prima donna tiger. It took a long time to get a tiger dry. They just had so much fur! Whenever I felt like it was good enough, I'd move to another section. The whole time my familiar kept his eyes closed with the most blissful expression known to man or beast on his face.

I knew they had warm air full-body dryers for bathrooms. I was considering getting one. That way Zian could...

I stopped, stunned, and turned the dryer off.

"Zian?"

He opened his eyes. Instead of being miffed that I'd stopped his beauty treatment, he went still. I could sense something happening, and I kneeled in front of him.

"Your name is Zian," I breathed.

127

I was absolutely certain of this. As certain as I knew my own name.

Zian chuffed at me and tucked his gigantic head under my arm. I pulled him to me, and we stayed like that for a few minutes. Still. Quiet. Inside, I could feel a connection forming with him. Draven hadn't given me a lot of details about what would happen once Zian and I bonded. He'd said it was something that was different for each familiar and mage.

The connection finished forming, and I knew that Zian could now feel me, wherever I was, and would know if I needed him. And because of the connection, he could now find me anywhere in the world. If I was lost, he'd come and find me. It was as though a weight that I hadn't known was on my shoulders lifted. I got a little misty eyed and laughed when Zian backed up back to his towel, and sat, waiting for me to turn the dryer on again and finish drying His Highness's fur.

"Sappy moment over with, huh?" I chuckled. "I'm so glad I can stop calling you generic names in my head. Saying 'my tiger' or 'my familiar' was getting a little old."

He eyed me.

"Yeah, yeah, less talk, more drying."

Inevitably, when I finished drying him, I would crack up laughing.

"You look like a big fluffball!" I said, giggling. I led him to the full body mirror on my wall so he could get a look at himself. His fur was sticking out everywhere. And I mean *everywhere*. It was so full and fluffy I could barely see his amber eyes.

"Well, Zian, what do you say we bust out of this joint?"

CHAPTER 7
DRAVEN

I was sitting up in my bed with a tumbler of brandy when I had a vision of Mia. The tumbler fell from my hands as the vision consumed my senses.

I knew from hearing others speak of my appearance during a vision that my eyes go pearl white, and my face slackens like I'm having an absence seizure. The muscles in my hands also go slack. Thankfully, I'm still able to remain upright whenever it catches me unaware.

The vision ran its course like a runaway train that you can't stop or slow down. When the final scene played out, and the sound of screams cleared from my brain, my vision returned, and I was up and moving for my clothes as quickly as possible, leaving the mess of brandy and broken glass on the floor.

I needed to check on Mia.

That was the first vision I'd had about her that was violent. The only other vision I'd had about her dealt with her seeing the ad in the newspaper and replying back to me

—something that had already played out. It was what had made me send out the ad in the first place.

I'd mistakenly thought, at the time, that I'd had the vision to find Mia, and find a brilliant assistant and an empath. But, after the way she'd reacted to me when she and I'd first met, the way she'd felt me in her chest, I wasn't sure of anything anymore.

I curled my power tightly around me and shoved it down deep, knowing it was strong enough to bring down an elephant because my emotions were currently so raw. Even as late—or early—as it was, some of my people were still up and working. The villa was always busy. My elven butler, Aiwin, never seemed to sleep, and my chef, Henri, had insomnia worse than anyone I'd ever met. He was a perfectionist, so nothing was ever finished to him. He'd nitpick everything until his under-chefs took it from his clutching hands and served it. This, in turn, made him irritable and difficult. He had a fantastic team that were well used to his ways, thankfully. He'd yet to poison me or my guests, and his dishes were delicious, so I kept him on.

After a while, those that worked for me became like family at the villa. And I treated them as family. Most of my employees made so much money it was ridiculous. Aiwin had been able to retire in luxury for more than a hundred years, and Henri could open a whole chain of restaurants with what he currently made. You treated family well. Always.

It always amused me that in the vampire romance novels of our age that vampires were written as beings who could not eat solid food. In truth, our senses were much more acute than the average human, and therefore we were food snobs. Because if the food didn't have the best and freshest ingredients, we suffered. It would be like humans eating dog food. Not something they typically tried to include in their diet.

As I approached Mia's bedroom, I lightly tapped on her door. She should still be sleeping at three o'clock in the morning, but with her, I was learning not to expect what was typical. When she didn't answer, I thought she might be sleeping too deeply to hear my knock. I hated to intrude upon her privacy, but I *needed* to make sure she was alright.

Mesmer was stationed by her door as her current guard. I knew he took on more shifts than the others guarding her. One, because he was excellent at what he did, and two, because he cared about her. I made a mental note to give him a bonus.

"Sir? Is there something wrong?" Mesmer's voice always had a gravelly sound to it, but it had a lilt of worry just now.

I shook my head. "I'm not sure. I had a vision, but I don't know the timing of it. I just wanted to check on her."

Mesmer nodded. "She should be asleep, sir. But here." He pulled out his master key and unlocked the door for me.

We both peeked in. Pale moonlight washed over her room and bed, and made it very easy to see that her bed was empty. The sheets and blankets were mussed, and looked like she'd tried to sleep, but had been unsuccessful.

Mesmer swore a blue streak, and pushed the button on his earpiece that radioed the rest of his team, while I cursed her Houdini ways and tried to think of where she could be at this witching hour.

Zian was also gone, so at least she had the protection of the tiger, which was no small thing.

Closing my eyes, I tried to listen for her, and smell her jasmine vanilla scent. When I couldn't smell or hear her, I took a guess and moved toward the first floor where our office was. Mesmer moved with me, still talking to the other guards stationed around the villa. So far, no one had spotted her, and they were currently fanning out throughout the villa in search, but I had a feeling she was sneaking in some work even though I'd asked her to take it easy for a few days.

The woman didn't know the meaning of easy. And trying to keep her in bed when she was recovering was akin to trying to herd an entire room full of feral cats.

As I approached the door, I could hear the faint but rapid tap of keyboard keys. I could also hear Zian yawning, and Mia taking a sip of something. I sighed in relief, then took a deep breath and tried to calm myself. My heart hadn't stopped racing from the vision. But she was here, and she was safe.

Mesmer growled and told his team to stand down. I knew that he would have words with his charge the next time he had a moment alone with her.

I was once again amazed that a small, scrappy woman had infiltrated my carefully controlled world and left it in such chaos with so much ease. Chaos that I gladly took on because I'd begun to care about her as more than an assistant.

I went back to my room to grab the healing potion that Rhys had dropped off for her when she'd been asleep and knocked before entering our office so I didn't startle her.

She looked up from her desk with a guilty expression. Her hair was up in a messy bun, and she was wearing what looked like a blue lounge set. The long-sleeve shirt said MONDAY CALLED. I HUNG UP.

My lips twitched. She seemed to favor the same snarky

types of shirts that Dice did, although Mia's were a bit more polite.

"Don't kick me out! I've been kicking paperwork's butt! Look at my ta-da-done pile!" She indicated a pile that was a paperback-book thick. "And my to-do pile is almost gone." She tilted her head at the few stray papers in her to-do pile.

I leaned against the desk, tucking the healing potion under my arms. "The point was for you to rest so that you can heal. You're like a child with too much energy. I played Scrabble with you. Was that not enough?"

I smirked when she frowned. She was still mad that I'd won.

She glared up at me. "I've never lost at Scrabble. I'm convinced you cheated."

I shrugged. "Cheating is one answer. Another could be that the longer you live, the greater your vocabulary. We checked the dictionary. They were all there."

She muttered under her breath about me—a habit that I found humorous—and went back to her papers and rapid tapping on the keyboard.

"I brought you something." I held out the misty blue potion and set it down on her desk. "It should heal everything to about eighty percent. I didn't want you to be so uncomfortable. I know it's hard for you to sleep." I put my hands in my pockets. "We're lucky Rhys can make such powerful healing potions. They're incredibly difficult."

She pursed her lips and looked at the smokey, light-blue liquid. "Aiwin's was clear. Since Rhys keyed this to my DNA, it shouldn't, like, turn me blue like a Smurf, right?"

I laughed. "With any luck."

She pondered the potion some more. "Although, if I do turn blue, I'd be dang cute as a Smurf." So saying, she twisted the cap off, then tilted the bottle up at me in cheers before she upended it in her mouth and swallowed it down. She shivered after she'd swallowed the last of it, and her eyes flashed pale blue before they returned to her normal copper color—a sign that the potion was working.

She squirmed a bit in her chair, and I knew the sensation she fought. It felt like bugs skittering over your skin. A less-than-pleasant feeling. But it was part of the healing process from a potion.

She finally settled back and gave a huge sigh. "Much better," she said. "It tasted like root beer."

I palmed the empty bottle and tucked it into my coat pocket. "Rhys must be fond of you. I've had ones that tasted like toenail fungus."

"Have you actually *had* toenail fungus to compare the two?" she asked me with a kick of sass.

I laughed. "No, Miss Sass. I haven't. But I can imagine."

Mia was peeling off bandages and examining the skin underneath. Nothing was the slightest bit open anymore. The wounds were all shiny pink scabs. She went to scratch at one, and I held her hand.

"If you scratch them, they might scar. Now, let's see if you can sleep."

"But my ta-da-done pile!" she groaned.

I snickered at the title. "It will still be there after you get some sleep. Where did you come up with the name ta-da-done?"

She smiled. "Because if that pile is ever full, and my to-do pile empty, it will have to have been because of magic!"

I laughed and escorted her to her room despite her feeble protests and attempts to escape. Zian followed behind us lazily. It was difficult, even as a vampire, to turn my back to a predator like Zian, but over the last several weeks, I had come to understand something of his devotion to Mia. Those that Mia loved and cared about, Zian would never harm. But those that attacked Mia?

If Zian ever came across them, he would gut them.

And he wasn't the only one.

This...person or organization was frustratingly difficult to track. I had a team of shifters and gargoyles on it, as well as a few vampire associates, and still nothing could be found.

Because of my most recent vision, I knew that whoever they were, they were circling closer, like sharks to chum. And one of the most frustrating things was the fact that I couldn't figure out *why* someone was coming after us; especially after Mia, who was an innocent.

I had to figure out a way to stop them before they hurt her. Or before they breached my defenses and killed me, leaving her defenseless.

We reached her door, and she and Zian went in. Zian went to the small kiddy pool that stored his drinking water and started lapping it up. I smiled a little at the ingenuity of that.

Mia sank onto her bed, but she still looked tense. I put my hand on her shoulder. "I can make you some tea or something," I offered. In the short time that I'd known her, I'd noted that she loved both herbal peppermint tea, and Deep-South sweet tea.

She shook her head and crawled up to her pillow, resting her head on the downy softness. "Would you...can you stay with me tonight? Every time I close my eyes, I see the glass explode. I feel the shards slam into me. I can't sleep, and I just want to feel safe for a while."

I hesitated. It was not a stretch to say that Mia was beautiful. She did not have the unearthly beauty of the fae or vampires, but she was beautiful nonetheless. Even worse was my attraction to her. An attraction that grew day by day and was rooted in far more than just her beautiful figure and face.

I had been fighting it for weeks now, determined to keep her at arm's length. After all, Mia was under my protection. As a being under my care, it was my duty to protect her with all the resources at my disposal. Even if protecting her included protection from myself.

As a vampire, I had a lengthy and bloody past. A past which included my vampire youth, which was filled with horrendous vampire wars where vampire fought against vampire for the right to survive. I did not want to tarnish her innocence with my stained hands, and she *was* innocent. Innocent in the ways of love and lust. And innocent in the ways of paranormals. She didn't know what it was for a vampire to be vulnerable with someone, to sleep with someone near them. Most vampires, even married, slept alone.

But she looked up at me with such a disarming mix of hope and trust that I swallowed my protests, toed off my shoes, and untucked my shirt. I put the dagger and pistol that I carried on the bedside table nearest me and climbed into bed. Zian snuffled my side and hiss-chuffed, clearly put out with me because I'd taken his favorite spot.

"Sorry, boy. Your mistress commands and I obey."

Mia laughed softly at that and snuggled down into the baby-blue blankets. She grabbed a remote from her bedside table and fussed with it for a moment before a fan across the room came on, circulating air into the room.

"You sleep with a fan on?"

"Always," she said. "I can't sleep without one. I need the noise and the cool air, even if it's the dead of winter." She turned on her side. "Will you be cold?"

I slid a lock of her hair away from her damp cheek and ghosted my hand down the warmth there before I removed my hand. "No. Vampires are pretty temperature regulated. It would take extreme temperatures for me to either be hot or cold."

She reached for my hand, and I didn't protest as she laced our fingers together. I could feel the pulse of her heartbeat through her fingers. It was comforting to me, and my heart settled.

"Thanks, Draven," she whispered. "Sleep well."

She fell asleep within minutes, while I—I didn't sleep at all.

CHAPTER 8
MIA

I was sore for basically another week or so, and then Rhys keyed in another potion to my DNA and I healed completely after that. It had been a painful process. As I'd drank the last potion, I'd looked at my eyes changing blue in the mirror and almost spit the potion into my sink. I hadn't seen that happen before, and no one had told me it was common when drinking potions, so I thought I truly was turning into a Smurf. That Rhys had decided to play a practical joke on me. When I remained human, I sighed in relief. Rhys thought it would up his cool factor with me that he could brew potions like an elven warlock, but he already had so many cool points just because he was a star elf. I didn't tell him that, though. I thanked him, but played it off like potion brewing and connecting it to someone's DNA was the most mundane thing on the planet. He was currently disgruntled with me.

I smirked as I applied my makeup. I usually went light on makeup. Just a light mineral powder foundation, some blush, some brown and bronze eyeshadow, mascara to make my eyes pop, and some vanilla mint lip gloss. I curled my hair next, glossed it with my favorite citrus smelling frizz reducer, and added a final spray of hairspray to set the curls. Then I slid into the white, bohemian beachy dress and flats I'd picked out for tonight and gave Zian a scratch under his chin.

"Well, Zian, what do you think?"

He chuffed at me and rubbed his nose along my hip.

"I think that's approval. I'll be late getting in tonight. You can go swimming if you want. Draven had a ramp built into the pool for you to get in and out by yourself."

Zian looked at me as though he understood every word, and I just proceeded through our conversations like he actually could. I knew he was smarter than the average tiger; I just didn't know *how* smart. He really seemed to follow all of my conversations with him. Obviously, he couldn't speak back, but he acted like he understood.

I drew in a deep breath.

"Okay, Zian. Show time."

I made my way down to the main floor just as the doorbell rang. Aiwin answered the door, and let in my date.

I'd finally been able to go to Daygood Goblin Groceries last week, and as I'd been shopping in the tampon aisle—I hadn't ended up asking Mesmer—a cute guy with scruffy blonde hair and mesmerizing golden eyes bumped into me. We'd started talking, and he'd asked me to a luau on a small island that was still in the boundaries the original witch clan had set up for Moonhaven Cove. The boundaries that were protected by a net of spells that rebuffed non-paranormals.

As we left the villa, I saw Draven in an upstairs window, looking down at us. I smiled and waved goodbye, but he just continued to stare and didn't wave back. I shrugged it off, and we zoomed away in Montblanc's red sports car.

I looked over at him as he drove. He was a good-looking guy. His arms were corded with muscle, and he had a nice smile and warm eyes.

"So, what kind of name is Montblanc?"

He chuckled, and pursed his lips as he downshifted to hug the twisty curves we'd just hit leading out of town, and to the bridge that would take us to the island. "My wolf is huge and has white fur, and my parents hail from France, where Mont Blanc Mountain is the second highest mountain in Europe. Mont is French for mountain, and Blanc for white, hence the name."

"That's pretty awesome. I've never met a Montblanc before."

He grinned. "Neither have I. It's just oddball enough to be original."

I laughed and on a tight, zippy turn grabbed the *I'm Going to Die!* bar above my head to keep from sliding around in my seat. Montblanc drove like a NASCAR driver with about a hundred cups of coffee percolating in his veins.

He smirked at me out of the corners of his eyes, but thankfully kept his mostly full attention on the winding roads. "Did you know I had to submit a full DNA sample and a background check before I could take you out?"

His question was asked super casually, but I winced anyway. "Yeah, umm, I'm sorry? Draven, my boss, is a little protective of me at the moment."

His expression turned serious. "I heard about what happened at The Tea Hobbit. I'm sorry that happened to you." He casually looked over my arms and the bit of really pale leg I was showing. "It looks like you're all healed up. Did they catch whoever shot the magic bullets?"

I slumped into my seat. "No. Draven and Mesmer both searched, but they couldn't find anyone. Draven's guys are still working on it." I nodded at the car behind me where Mesmer was handling the curves in the town car even better than Montblanc. "And you can see that I have security. Everything will be fine."

Montblanc nodded, looking preoccupied.

We crossed the bridge over the cove and the air outside changed to balmy and tropical.

My hand trailed outside my window collecting humidity, and the vista changed to a tropical paradise. "Oh my gosh! It's like a tropical island! I thought it was a little strange to be doing a luau in the cool Pacific Northwest temperatures!"

Montblanc nodded. "Yep. Witches spelled the island for one of the original members of the town who settled here. Not much is known about him, but he obviously favored the tropical heat and wanted a more lush landscape."

"Does it get tropical rains here too?"

"Yes. Monsoon season is from mid-July through September, and it can get fifteen inches of rain a day in some places on the island."

I was completely fascinated as I stared out the window. We drove down a quiet, well-maintained road that had banana and papaya trees, birds of paradise, ferns, and tons of orchids. It smelled incredible, and the warmth soothed my chilled skin.

I saw monkeys playing in the trees, eating bananas, and macaws, kingfishers, and toucans swooping and fluttering through the lush foilage.

We made a turn and drove down a less maintained road that truncated at a lazy river, and what I assumed was the place for the luau. It had a stage to one side with a bunch of tables set up for the dinner. A long bench to the other side was being attended to by numerous employees, setting out a ton of what looked like both sweet and savory dishes. I could smell pork roasting, but couldn't see where it was coming from. I'd read online that they had an underground oven called an imu that they roasted the pig in.

It smelled *soooo* good!

Montblanc grabbed my hand as we exited his car and we were set upon by a couple of pretty ladies with lovely brown skin and long, dark hair. They each wore a long, tropical skirt and a bikini top, and one of them smiled at Montblanc like he was a dessert that she was just dying to try. They placed real flower leis over our heads and gave us a cheerful and bubbly welcome as we moved past them.

My eyes tried to take everything in. There were a ton of what looked like traditional island arts and crafts set up in booths around the area. I was at a booth that featured wide precious metal bracelets with beautiful scrollwork and flowers etched into them when I heard Mesmer's car pull up.

I looked over just as the women with the leis accosted him. He looked uncomfortable and blushed as he ducked down so they could place the lei around his wide neck.

I snickered and shook my head. Poor Mesmer. He didn't know what to do with attention from females.

I went back to my shopping but turned back around as a motorcycle pulled up behind Mesmer. My jaw nearly dropped when the person riding it took off their helmet.

My boss was getting off the bright blue motorcycle that

WANTED: VAMPIRE'S ASSISTANT

looked like it could drive straight up a mountain and had probably cost a few million dollars and did something with a wave of his hand so the ladies with the leis didn't see him. They looked around in confusion for a moment, but then shrugged and moved on to the new arrivals.

I glared at him, wondering what the heck he was doing on my date, and then squinted as it became quickly clear that in addition to the ladies not being able to see him, no one else could see him either.

Vampire mojo.

I excused myself from Montblanc for a moment and hurried over to Draven as he checked out a booth selling authentic island grandfather clocks with beautiful teak wood and intricate carvings.

"What are you doing here?" I hissed, hunching my shoulders as the people surrounding us glared at me. I knew what it looked like. Like I was hissing at them. But it couldn't be helped. My boss was crashing my date!

He looked up at me, startled. "You can see me?"

Obviously I could. "Of course I can see you!"

He looked at me for maybe a solid minute before he shook his head. "You shouldn't be able to."

I gestured to the group of people still glaring daggers at me. "I mean, obviously not everyone can, but I saw you pull up just now. What are you doing here?"

He nibbled on his lip as he, no doubt, tried to contrive a brilliant reason for crashing my date on the spot.

Finally, he sighed. "I wasn't comfortable with you leaving the villa without me here. Even with Mesmer."

I felt a rising sense of panic. I was dating, in part, to stymie my feelings for my boss. There was no way to do that if he insisted on crashing all my dates. "Are you telling me you will be coming on all my future dates as well? But you vetted him. Extensively! He passed. And even *that* was extremely intrusive. If this keeps up, I'll never go on another date again. No one's going to want to pass the background check!"

I knew, deep down, that my safety was more important than a solid social life, but the supernaturals of Moonhaven Cove were so much easier for my empathic senses to be around. I had never been able to date before. I hadn't wanted to because of how non-paranormals felt to me— chaotic and painful. But now I could date! And I *needed* to date so I could get over my boss and keep my job!

Draven drew in a deep, slow breath. "It's more important for you to remain safe than for you to date."

I squinted up at him. "So, until we catch this person or persons, I'm going to be locked up at the villa?"

"Either that or I come with you." He smiled at me hopefully. "You can always choose not to date until we find out who's trying to kill us." I eyed him, trying to discern why he seemed happy at that thought, and why he felt it was necessary to be here, even though he'd told me himself that Mesmer was an excellent bodyguard.

I narrowed my eyes at him. "Can you at least sit at another table tonight?" I thought this was a very reasonable request, but Draven shook his head, and I wanted to thump my head against a wall in frustration.

"Our killer has used magic bullets in the past," Draven said quietly. "I need to be close enough to you to stop them if I hear them coming." I didn't know what my face looked like—devastated that he would use his own body to stop bullets aimed for me, probably—so he quickly said, "I just want you to be safe. I promise to stay quiet."

Uh-huh.

I crossed my arms, studying him. He seemed...fragile right then. I wasn't entirely sure of the reasons, but I knew that I had come to matter to Draven. His fragility was a mystery that I would look into later, but for now, he wasn't my boss. He was just a male standing here, not wanting to hurt or frustrate me, but also adamant that he could protect me best. So, I could either fight him all night, or give in gracefully. I chose to give in gracefully. But first, I really needed to clarify some things.

I sighed, dropping my arms. "I know. But I can't be locked away to keep me that way." I pointed at his shoulder, which had been shot clear through as he'd looked out a window the other day at the villa. Only his lightning-fast reflexes had prevented the bullet from lodging in his heart. His enemy had hired snipers now. To say I was terrified, both for him and myself, would be an understatement.

He'd assured me the bullets hadn't been gold tipped. Which meant they would slow him down some, but not outright kill him. Gold, I learned, acted as a slow-moving poison in vampires unless they can get blood fresh from another source to counteract it. Draven kept people on his payroll who served as blood suppliers for just those kinds of emergencies.

As Draven and I stood there, me not knowing how I was going to explain to Montblanc that my boss was crashing our date, and him not willing to move a muscle from my side, they started the pre-meal show on the stage.

Brightly dressed women and men came out, doing a traditional and sinuous dance. It mesmerized me for a few moments before I shook my head, sighed, and pulled Draven by his belt loop, hauling him to the table that Montblanc had secured for us.

Montblanc looked up as I approached, and I introduced my boss to my date. Draven must have done something to allow Montblanc to see him, because my date didn't look at me like I was a crazy person talking to ghosts. Wait...were ghosts a thing here? I didn't know, but I wanted to find out. I'd ask Mesmer later.

Montblanc, far from being irate or frustrated that I had not one, but two men crashing our date now, looked at me like a man who likes a woman does. His gaze made me squirmy and I couldn't figure out why until I turned my head and saw Draven was looking at me. too. Montblanc's gaze was the gaze a guy gives to a woman he's attracted to, but Draven's gaze was as deep as still waters. And just as mysterious.

Now Draven had been alive for a long time. He'd already told me that. But he adamantly refused to tell me how long; when I'd guessed three thousand years out of pure orneriness, he'd looked like he wanted to throw an eraser at me.

So, Draven the vampire, who'd had many, *many* years to perfect his go- ahead-and-level-whatever-at-me-because-I-am-an-ocean-of-calm look, looked about three seconds from leaping across the table and taking a chunk out of Montblanc's neck because of the way Montblanc was staring at me.

Montblanc turned, and his face went tight in surprise before his eyes started to glow gold. I'd only seen that once so far in shifters, so I knew it was them preparing to shift, or being close to a shift because of heightened emotion or a sense of danger. I was trying to figure out what the heck was going on! Why was Draven so mad?

And where the suffering Sasquatch was Mesmer when I needed him?

S.O.S!

How did I get into this mess?

I kicked Draven in his shins underneath the table—he didn't even flinch—and tried to smile charmingly at my date. "I'm really sorry about this. Draven apparently wanted to go to the luau tonight as well."

Montblanc nodded, his eyes still glowing gold. "Also, he doesn't think I can protect you."

Draven looked away, thankfully de-escalating whatever had been going on, and I put my face in my hands in relief. What else could go wrong?

A throat cleared at the opposite end of the table, and I peeked through my fingers.

"Hi, Mesmer." Yay, Mesmer was here!

He nodded at me. His expression seemed to ask if I was okay, and I shook my head. Nope. Not really. He sighed and sat down in a too-small chair that groaned at his prodigious weight.

We all focused on the show, and I let out a silent sigh of relief. The show was epic. I swayed to the rhythm of the dance in my seat and tapped my fingers. When Montblanc scooted his chair closer to me and took my hand, I smiled at him. Happy that he was what I considered my first real date. My attempted dating in Manhattan, I no longer counted. Montblanc was a good guy. I'd been getting that vibe from him all evening. And he was trying really hard to be cool with Draven being with us, and Mesmer sitting at our table. I appreciated that about him.

Later, as we had dinner, I tried my best to focus my conversation on Montblanc. Draven, for the most part, stayed quiet, just eating and observing our surroundings, and I was really grateful for that.

I was sorry I'd been such a pill about him being with us tonight, but to be fair, I was really trying to bury my growing feelings for him, and that was really difficult to do if I was around him twenty-four-seven.

The food was excellent: roasted pulled pork, macaroni salad, pineapple coleslaw, roasted vegetable skewers, and an electric blue mocktail that was sweet, but not too sweet. But what I literally had three helpings of, and couldn't stay away from, was the piña colada triple-layer cake. Oh my gosh, it was amazing! Light, fluffy, and stuffed with my favorite piña colada flavoring. It literally melted on my tongue.

The hula dancers were finishing and the fire dancers were taking the stage. The evening was winding down, and the sun was setting. As the fire dancers started dancing to a deep, bass beat, they asked for members from the audience to come up on stage with them and help them finish their show.

I really, honestly, couldn't dance, but I was feeling the beat so much that I raised my hand.

The guy at the mic picked me and one other woman to come up, and the fire dancers shuffled to one side of the stage as the Kahool dancers came back out. The gourd drum started, and the men around me chanted as they started moving their hands and body in explosive bursts of energy. At the end of each movement, they would shout, '*Hah!*' all in sync. The woman and I watched for a few beats and then joined in. I found the precise movements coupled with the flow of the dance and the *hah* as the punctuation point to each major movement to be strangely energizing. There wasn't a lot of hip shaking. It was just one series of flowing movements after another, ending in a powerful push that we used both hands, feet, body, and voice for. Like we were pushing out all our frustrations, or bad energy, and then using our next hand movements to scoop up the good energy. It was seriously addicting.

When the dance ended, after the applause died down, I noticed Mesmer was waiting for me beside the stage. He walked me back to my seat, and I thanked him with a smile. The regular island dancing was cuing up now, and I grabbed Montblanc's hand to get him to dance with me. I still felt electrified by the previous dance.

What really cracked me up was Mesmer and Draven.

"Are your boss and bodyguard...dancing together?"

I giggled. "Yep."

Montblanc watched them for a few more seconds. "Surprisingly, your bodyguard is an excellent dancer. Gargoyles are not usually so light on their feet."

I shook my head. "Mesmer is a constant surprise to me. I think he practices Aikido. He's really quite graceful."

Draven spun Mesmer out and then reeled him back in again. I giggled because Mesmer had to duck to do it. They stayed close to where Montblanc and I were dancing, but I didn't mind this so much. Free entertainment.

Montblanc looked at me. "This really wasn't the date you were hoping for, was it?"

"What do you mean?"

He looked like he wanted to say something more, but the man on the mic was thanking everyone for coming, and people were starting to leave.

We said goodbye to the guys and headed for Montblanc's sports car.

It was quiet for a bit until Montblanc started laughing. And then once he started, he couldn't seem to stop. He had to pull over to the side of the road.

I smiled at him. "What are you guffawing over?"

He laid his head back against the seat rest, still smirking to himself. "Take your pick. How uncomfortable Master Leto looked crashing your date. How Mesmer looked like he'd rather have spikes shoved under his fingernails than sit at the table with us. Or the dance at the end, where Draven twirled Mesmer around like Mesmer was a prima ballerina. And Mesmer's hands as he twirled out?"

He mimicked Mesmer's hand movements and started cracking up again, and I laughed with him. "I'm so glad they didn't ruin your night. I was worried that I was stacking up to be a terrible date."

Montblanc shook his head. "I'm a really laid-back person. I don't let stuff like that bother me." He turned his head to me, the back of it still resting against his headrest. "I'm really glad you went out with me. This was fun."

I blushed. I could feel how much he meant what he said. That he truly enjoyed being around me, and that he wasn't just telling me what he thought I wanted to hear. "Thank you."

I decided to be brutally honest. "Actually, this is my first real date. I tried dating when I lived in Manhattan, but...non-paranormals...they feel chaotic to me. It actually hurt being around them. I tried once, and it ended in disaster. Like, literal disaster. We got in a car wreck when I asked him to take me home."

He winced. "I'm sorry about that, but I'm so honored to be your first real date."

In for a penny..."It also means I've never kissed anyone before."

He looked dumfounded. "Wait, really!"

I nodded my head. "It wasn't even a temptation, trust me."

Montblanc's eyes were golden as he gazed back at me. Then he got out of the car, came around to my side, and plucked me out too. He sat me on the bonnet of his car and kissed my socks off. Metaphorically.

At first, he started off sweet and slow, like little nibbles on my lips, and then the kissing grew deeper and more charged with electricity. I swear I was starting to give off sparks.

Holy moly, could Montblanc *kiss*! He was going to make some lucky girl very, very happy someday.

Montblanc and I broke apart as a motorcycle screeched to a stop next to us, kicking up dirt and itty-bitty pebbles that pinged off of Montblanc's glorious car. "Whoa," I said, looking at Montblanc in a daze. "You're *awesome* at that!" I mean, I didn't know for sure, but that had seemed to be one amazing kiss! That it wasn't with Draven made my insides twinge, but I steadily ignored that.

He gave me a partly shy, partly smirking grin, kissed the tip of my nose, and said, "I had a lot of fun tonight." Then he moved in close and whispered in my ear. "I wish you and Draven all the happiness in the world. If he breaks your heart, come find me." He pulled back enough to see my eyes, nodded once at my questioning gaze, and then hugged me. "I mean it."

I clasped his hands. "Thank you. I had fun, too." I kissed his cheek, and he helped me get settled on the motorcycle behind a silent Draven, got my helmet on, helped me strap my purse around my middle, and waved us off as Draven peeled away, showering Montblanc's car with pebbles again.

"Are you guys going out again?" Draven's voice in my helmet shocked me so much that I jumped and almost fell off the bike. He laughed at my antics but encouraged my arms around him to grip tighter so I didn't fall. "There's a mic and receiver in your helmet. It's connected to mine. You can just talk normally, and I'll hear you."

I nodded, though of course he couldn't see me. "If we go out again, I think it will just be as friends."

Draven nodded.

We drove home in silence while I silently, and in a very ladylike way without any whoops or additional loud screeches, fell in love with my boss' motorcycle.

"No, you can't borrow my motorcycle," Draven said over the mic, with laughter in his voice.

I sighed. Where was the love?

LATER THAT NIGHT I snuck down to the office to get in more work, Zian following at my heels, and stopped short to see that Draven was sitting moodily before the fire. It looked like he was attempting to read a book but having very little luck at it.

Zian went in and laid his big body on the plush rug before the fire and dropped immediately into sleep.

"I envy him that," Draven said.

"What? Sleeping?"

He nodded. "I don't sleep well, if at all."

"Why?"

He shrugged, and I let the subject drop. Apparently the *why* was a sticky subject.

"I can always try a sledgehammer," I suggested facetiously. I blinked an innocent expression at him, and his lip curled, revealing a sharp incisor.

I stared at it for a moment, captivated. What did it feel like to be bitten by a vampire? Did a vampire's bite turn you instantly? I had so many questions. Whatever questions I'd asked, he'd patiently answered, but some of them, I felt, might veer into being rude.

I was direct, but I didn't like to be rude.

Still, he *had* asked me to come to him with any questions I might have, so I sat next to him on the overstuffed, velveteen sofa, and curled my legs underneath me. My toenails glinted a bright berry color, and I had a tan line where my flip-flops covered my feet when I was out at the pool.

"What does it feel like to be bitten?"

Draven stared at me, and I could tell he was contemplating not answering. "Why, are you interested?"

"In getting bitten?"

He nodded.

I pursed my lips and thought about it. I *did* normally like to experience new things. And as I'd become a recent resident at Moonhaven Cove, I knew there was so much to experience.

I mean, I was sitting here all cozy in my I'm going to take over the world. Just after this cup of coffee, pajamas, talking to a vampire. I was best friends with a star elf who'd yet to reveal all the really cool things he could do. I had a gargoyle bodyguard, a shifter was the town sheriff, Zian's vet was a brownie...the list went on and on. There was so much to learn, and so many new cool things to experience. So, did I want to get bitten by a vampire? Heck yeah! As long as it didn't turn me. I wasn't quite ready for that yet.

I turned back to Draven, who'd very quietly and patiently left me to my thoughts.

"Yes, I would. As long as it doesn't change me into a vampire right now. Not saying that I wouldn't change at another time, but I'm good being...whatever I am at present."

His inky eyebrow winged upward, and I smiled. Those dang expressive eyebrows of his.

"So, we're going to do this?" I said, putting down my cup of tea that I'd carried into the study with me. I splayed my hands on my thighs and sat up, ready to get bitten. "Where do you want me?"

Draven lounged deeper into the sofa and studied me for a long moment. There was a liquid haze of power surrounding him that gave me the good kind of chills. But it was a power that was banked, like you would bank a fire for the evening. He patted the seat next to him.

Zian pushed his head up when I changed seats but went back to sleep when I sat next to Draven. He seemed to have no worries that Draven would drain and kill me.

I didn't really either, but the thought of someone biting me and drinking my blood made me feel weird. Added to that was the fact that it would be *Draven* who was going to bite me and drink my blood, made me feel like goblins were trying to hula dance in my stomach.

Draven was going to have his teeth on me, and his *lips!* I had to admit that I was far more excited about his lips than I was about his teeth.

Draven grabbed my hand and lightly touched the veins

on the top of my hand with his fingertips. "You don't become a vampire with just a bite, Mia," he murmured, focusing intently on my hands. "There's a changing serum that I can secrete with my fangs, but I can also choose not to secrete it, and keep all your lovely blood human."

Goosebumps broke out on my arms, and a hot-cold sensation started from the crown of my head and continued downward to the tips of my toes, melting like a molten river. It felt like pure relaxation. The relaxation you might feel if someone were to take every scrap of worry, fear, and pain away from you in one big swoop. It felt like I was floating. Like I was flying.

Draven looked into my eyes. His were a deep red, and I knew that he was giving me this feeling. I also knew, in a very chill part of myself that wasn't really concerned, but knew I ought to be, that Draven's eyes changing from brown to red meant he was about to feed. This fascinated me. His eyes hadn't changed by the pool when he'd drank blood from a bottle, but they did now. My guess was that actually biting a person required his teeth to be in play, and required all of a vampire's abilities to turn on, like the ability to calm prey so that it didn't run from you. I felt no concern, though. I simply noted the depth of the crimson and the refracting firelight in his irises and waited.

And then I saw the pain in his eyes, and that woke me up like someone had jolted me with a taser while in the bathtub. I sat up straight, my languidness gone in an instant.

"Do you still want me to continue?"

I looked at him for what felt like a very long time. The grandfather clocked ticked, and the fire crackled. I tried to peer into his face, his eyes, his *soul* if I could, because I wanted to discern the secrets behind those eyes. I wanted to discern the reasons behind that pain. What I was coming to realize I wanted, more than anything, was to be someone he turned to. Someone he could rely on. If that meant only as a friend, then I would deal.

Since discovering that I was an empath, I hadn't really tried to tune into the ability much. I just used it in a passive state, never an active state. It felt like a live wire when it was active, and I didn't much like the feeling. But right then, I pushed myself to tune in deeply. I could feel a hum of power in my chest that felt like it was fisted tighter than a vault. It felt jagged and thorny and a lot like someone had shoved a molten lava-ball of glass inside my chest. It hurt to touch, and it hurt to use with intention, to twist around and latch onto people. But I didn't care about that at the moment because someone I was starting to care about very much was hurting.

His red eyes were studying my face carefully, as if he were looking for acceptance and permission to continue to be written on the planes of my cheekbones and across the lines of my forehead.

The hum of power grew stronger, and the jagged edges of the molten ball stabbed me as I tried to reach in with non-physical hands and pry the ball open.

I put my hand on Draven's cheek and felt the stubble of recent growth there. It was soft, unlike what I'd imagined most guys' facial hair to feel. I focused on the warmth of his skin and the soft tickle of hair as I tried to sense inside of him. My power was reluctant and stabby, but I unfurled one petal from the lava-ball, and something blossomed inside of me that felt like Draven's past.

Images flitted through my mind rapidly and with crystal clarity and sound. I flinched at the violence in them, trying to slow them down so I could study them and see them better. But they refused to slow, flickering through my head like a high-speed slideshow: vampires slaughtering one another, a man with a crown on his head shouting to an army behind him, dark gray eyes that glinted with seething hatred, a naked woman with her throat ripped out, her eyes wide open. I felt my breathing stop as Draven covered her body with his, holding her to him, sobbing.

I didn't realize that I was crying until the images abruptly stopped. My breathing was loud, shallow, and fast. So much so that I had to focus on not hyperventilating.

My life had been so...*small* compared to his.

I'd never in my life felt small next to someone.

Until right then.

It was like finding a dragon from a fairy tale, and listening to him tell you the stories from the thousand years he'd lived, and being stuck with the knowledge that you're just this simple milkmaid from the tiny village down the hill. Poor. Easily exchanged for another milkmaid. The knowledge that your life has neither the length nor the breadth to befriend the dragon.

He'd loved the woman. Deeply. He was still mourning her, and I could sense that several hundred years had passed since her death.

I looked away from Draven and used my sleeve to dry my eyes, feeling foolish. I got up intending to get out of the study and head to my room, even though I knew I'd lie awake and miserable in my bed. But Draven, who hadn't said a word to me, but must have felt what had just happened, grabbed my hand and tugged me back down.

I was still reeling, and I wanted nothing more than to disappear somewhere where I could hide and think. I was trembling, and couldn't account for why. Was it the influx of emotions that had come with the scenes? Was it because I felt cold after being separated from Draven's—I didn't know what to call it—his memories? His psyche?

I didn't know what I had done just now. I'd been trying to connect with him empathically, and instead I'd sucked memories out of his head. Not. Cool. And if it felt like this every time, I was never doing it again.

I didn't know how to tell him I'd just majorly violated his privacy, and I was feeling faintly nauseous, so I just sat on the couch, unable to talk, shaking like a leaf in a storm.

Draven drew me onto his lap and wrapped his arms and a blanket around me that had been warming by the fire. He made soothing sounds as he held me.

I felt like an idiot for being this shaken. I was definitely tougher than this, but I was trying to cut myself a little slack. I hadn't known that this was going to happen. From my understanding, empaths could only feel what others felt. There'd been no mention of being able to see into someone's past. I felt like there should be an owner's manual for these things. One that they handed out when people discovered their gifts. *Oh, you're the new empath? Here! Take this owner's manual. It should help a ton!*

My ear was positioned over Draven's chest, and I expected there to be silence because of his vampiness, but there wasn't. There was a *glub-glub* sound as his heart pumped, and his chest rose and fell with each breath and release.

I closed my eyes and focused on that sound, trying to align my breathing to rise and fall with his, and then realized that he was syncing his breath with mine.

"I'm sorry," I finally said.

"For what?"

The sound of his voice echoed in the cavern of his chest, and I could hear the depth of it from my close position pressed up against him. Draven was cuddling with me. Why couldn't I enjoy the moment more? I tried, I really did, but I was still too shaken.

"For...whatever I just did. I'm still not sure, but it felt like a terrible invasion of privacy."

"Your gift is new to you, Mia. I expected there would be some growing pains as you learned to use it, and I'm not angry that you used it on me. As a matter of fact, I feel honored."

Honored? Uh-huh. "Did you see what I saw?"

He shook his head. "No. It's not really like that. It's not like a television broadcasting to everyone. It's more like your magic takes from my thoughts those memories that are the most pertinent to you. So, if I were just a random person on the street, what you just did probably wouldn't work very well on them, because you'd have no intimate connection to them. You'd still be able to read their feelings, just not their memories."

I nodded my head. I *had* been just trying to read his emotions, but had ended up with way more information than I'd asked for. Selfishly, I was glad he didn't know what I'd seen. Most of it had been jumbled and had gone by super-fast, but that last scene had been very private between him and someone else. And if all of that somehow pertained to me personally? I didn't know what to do with that information. I'd have to think about it.

"I don't want to know what you saw, Mia," Draven murmured. "At least...not yet." He pulled away from me and looked down at me. "Is that alright with you?"

I nodded gratefully. I didn't know how to articulate what I'd seen just yet. Given time, I might be able to.

"Now," he continued, "I need some nourishment, and you asked what a vampire's bite feels like. It seems to me that we can help each other."

I laughed dully. "Ok, but I'm not sitting on your lap while you bite me."

He smiled wickedly, making my stomach flutter. "But Mia, I'm comfortable, and you seem comfortable?"

Was Draven...flirting with me?

I looked up at him suspiciously. He looked very, very serious.

"Are you flirting with me?"

My bluntness didn't take him by surprise, as it did most people, and I really liked that about him. He brought two fingers up and mimicked a tiny amount of space between them to show me he was flirting with me a little bit.

"Boss," I said, thunking him on the chest with my hand, "employee," I pointed at myself.

His eyes just glinted more mischievously, and I laughed at him. I really liked this side of him. This mischievous, playful side.

"Ok, *fine*! I'll sit here!" *Argh.* It wasn't really like it was a *sacrifice* to sit on my gorgeous boss's lap, now was it?

He laughed and set me beside him. I wanted to howl in protest, but kept it to myself, and then his crimson eyes made their appearance again, and that heady feeling of absolute contentment and complete lack of pain started from the crown of my head, and moved like a river down to my feet, touching every part of me until I felt like I could just curl up and have the best nap of my life.

Draven brought up my hand and turned it over so my

wrist showed. He traced the blue-green veins that delicately made their way from the crook of my elbow down to my palm, and then he brought my wrist up and, without warning, bit down.

I watched in fascination. The prick of his teeth entering my flesh had been minimal and very, very quick. It felt a bit like a quick sting, there and gone again so fast you barely had the time to recognize that it was there.

He watched me watching him the whole time. Which made the whole thing feel a lot more personal. I'd thought it would feel like a weird dining experience. Instead, it felt intimate, like he was taking something that was very vital to my being, like my genetic code, and making it a part of himself. As if the blood from me was filling the gaps in him. Like what I imagined donating a kidney or another organ to someone might feel like.

It was a heady experience. My intuition said that if he and I were a couple that the sharing of blood between us would be much more intimate. But we weren't, and this felt personal enough.

Even though he was just taking the blood from my wrist, the moment became so intimate that I had an intense urge to look away from his focused gaze. But I couldn't. I felt so locked into his gaze that I didn't think I was even daring to *breathe.*

After a few minutes, he withdrew his fangs, and licked the wound on my wrist, closing the punctures. He licked his lips to get the drop of blood he'd missed and rested my hand with his in his lap.

I was feeling lethargic and full. As if *I* had been the one to drink blood for nourishment.

Empathic. I still forgot about that sometimes.

"I know what you are now." His eyes were a brighter red, and he looked happy and content. I'd done that for him. *Prancing pixies, I think I'm addicted to this now! When could we do this again?*

I re-focused on what Draven was saying. "What I am?"

He nodded. "As well as being an empath, you're a rainmaker."

I knew my expression spoke utter confusion because he chuckled and continued playing with my hand. "Have you ever had a terrible day and found that a storm followed you home? Or, a fantastic day, and found the weather to be exactly what you wanted it to be?"

"Draven, I hate to tell you this, but no sane person in Manhattan thinks that their moods are controlling the weather," I said drolly.

He laughed, and I smiled in reflex. It was good to see, after all the terrible things I'd seen in his past, that his laughter could still come so easily. It gave credence to my theory that Draven was just exceptionally easygoing and happy. He was quiet a lot, but he always felt content to me. Like Zian did when he was lazing out in the sun.

"Well, you do. Not control, per se. But the weather for miles around you definitely reacts to your moods. It's something like a pet to you. When you're happy, it's happy. When you're in danger, it growls and bites. When you're angry, it's angry."

"That could be fun." I waggled my eyebrows. The weather was like my pet, huh? I'd have to make use of that.

He chuckled. "I'll definitely always know when you're mad at me."

Hmm, this new rainmaker thing had promise. I sighed, feeling beat. "Well, I'd better get Zian and me to bed." I leaned in and kissed Draven's scruffy cheek. "Thanks, Draven."

He stilled for a moment, then squeezed my hand before he released me. "Pleasant dreams, Mia."

"You too, Boss."

"Draven," he corrected.

"You too, Boss Draven."

His warm chuckle followed me as I left the study.

CHAPTER 9
MIA

Saturday night was my date with Rhys, whom Draven acknowledged had enough power to protect me for the night. He'd acknowledged it grudgingly, but still. Mesmer was my bodyguard for the night. I looked behind me and saw one of the villa's cars taking the curve we'd just sped past.

Rhys was driving, and the elf did *not* know the meaning of a peaceful joy ride. He drove like flaming tongues of fire were licking at our wheels. What was it with the guys in my life driving like NASCAR racers!

"Slow down, Geezer. I think you left your dentures back at that last turn." Cool as a cucumber, Rhys looked over at me and smirked. It was a gorgeous night. The top was down on his convertible, and the stars were shining above us. The moon was full and gleaming.

"You look great, by the way."

I glanced down at my dress. It was a silver, cold shoulder, fringed, beaded dress that went down to just above my knee. A single, thin strap to kept the dress up.

The cold shoulder had fringed beading, and then from there the fringe fell in layers down to my knees. I was wearing starlight-blue high heels with it, and a bracelet that connected with a ring. I wore glittering opal earrings and my hair fell in soft curls down my back. My eyelids were smoked to perfection, and I had on my signature lip gloss.

I felt like a million bucks tonight.

"You're not getting to go home with me tonight, you know," I told my best friend. "No matter how much you sweet-talk me."

Rhys's celestial purple eyes sparkled at me. "How's about a kiss?" he asked in a leering voice.

"Eww, no. Best friend, not lover. You can hold my hand a little, but that's it. Is Dice working tonight?" I asked, just to get a rise out of him. He flinched, and I smiled evilly. Poor Rhys. He was all kinds of mixed up about that pixie.

"Yeah, she's working the bar." He threw a quick scowl in my direction. Quickly, because he was approaching mach eight with his convertible, and he had to focus because I was very, very breakable. "I know what you're doing. Stop bringing her up."

"I know you have a crush on her. It's okay to admit it, Geezer."

Rhys grew quiet. "I don't know what I feel about her," he finally admitted quietly. "She's scared, Mia. Like, *really* scared. There's nothing at all in her body language to suggest it, but I can feel it."

"I know," I admitted quietly as Rhys pushed the button to bring the top up. As the wind died down and I released my death grip on my hair, I patted the hand that was closest to me. "She feels strong to me. She'll work through it. And we've got her back. Whatever she's running from, we'll help."

Rhys's fingers whitened on the steering wheel, and a vein popped in his neck. "It's wrong what people do to other people sometimes."

"Whoever she's running from isn't a paranormal, right? Cause then they could just get through the barrier?" I asked, suddenly afraid for my friend.

He sighed. "Whoever they are. I hope she's safe here."

"Yeah." We were quiet for a few minutes, and then I changed the subject. "So, tell me about your theme tonight at The Laughing Elf."

Rhys's eyes sparkled again as he handed me something from his breast pocket.

"What's this?" I was holding a small black book with a shiny cover that read *Passport* in rose gold on the cover. I opened it, but the pages were all blank.

Rhys shrugged. "We're handing that out as swag tonight to all the guests. Basically, you bring that each time we have a theme night, and you'll get a stamp. Five stamps, and you get a free night. It's a memento."

"That's really cool. I've never had a passport, so this is going to be amazing." I put the passport book in my beaded clutch until we got to the club.

"That's only the start of it." Rhys grabbed my hand. Now, people could say that I was leading him on, but I knew —and I could tell—that after that first greeting where there was a wave of attraction, Rhys only felt a warm friendship for me now. He loved me as a friend. And I wasn't sure if people in general knew this, but star elves are insanely affectionate. Even though Rhys wasn't into me, he still kissed me on the mouth sometimes, and I squawked like a chicken being chased by ten roosters whenever he did that. He just laughed at me. But I could feel this deep sense of affection toward me as he grabbed my hand and held it. It comforted him and brought him joy, so I tried not to squawk about it.

Too much.

"I commissioned a local metal worker to make the Eiffel Tower. And the metal worker works with a girl just out of town who does glass work, and she put some finishing touches on it. It looks amazing." He looked at me for a moment, and his face was so animated and excited that I smiled in return. It was so nice having friends. "And the menu! We're having a full Parisian themed menu and cocktails."

I squeezed his hand. "It sounds insane. What's the cover tonight?"

He frowned. "You always get in free."

"Aww, you like me, Geezer?" I teased.

He blew me a kiss.

RHYS WAS A GENIUS.

I was expecting The Laughing Elf to be a typical club, but it wasn't *at all*. There were chandeliers above my head, giving off a soft, rosy glow. The stage was empty at the far corner of the room, but the band was just taking a break. Earlier, there had been some lovely Parisian instrumental music happening over there that had managed to be both divine and swingy enough to dance to.

The Eiffel Tower stood in the center of the room, and it

was *gorgeous*. They had filled the metal work in with blue glass, and it glittered under the chandeliers.

All the tables had three peach roses, sans stems, in a glass bowl as the centerpiece. Couples were dancing with their sweethearts or their dates and eating the amazing food. There were pastry bites with feta and caramelized onions for the appetizer, and then an endive blue cheese salad, a vegetable quiche, a fig and goat cheese tartine, and a yummy soup.

I was extremely full, and just enjoying watching the people swirl around me as they laughed and talked and drank. Rhys was up at the bar, trying to chat with Dice, and was also handling a few snags that had come up over the course of the evening, so I was sitting by myself, swirling my finger in my mocktail.

"May I have this dance?"

I nearly jumped out of my skin, I was so surprised. Where had he come from? He'd just...appeared at my table out of thin air!

I blinked at him stupidly for a moment, cataloging his swarthy features and inky hair before I stood hesitantly. I was here with Rhys, but he was busy. Mesmer was holding up a corner wall keeping an eye on me, so I felt a sense of safety saying yes and putting my hand in his as I followed him to the dance floor.

The man's skin was so cold that I felt like a sauna next to him. He moved me into position, and we starting dancing. And I mean fancy dancing! Before we'd gone two steps, I knew we were waltzing. I used to watch *Dancing with The Stars* all the time on my crummy TV in Manhattan, so I knew what a waltz *looked* like, but I didn't know how to *do* one! It didn't seem to matter, as Mr. Tall Dark and Swarthy led me so expertly that I only flubbed a time or two before I felt like I got the dance. His face was impassive, and he made no pleasant conversation. He didn't even ask what my name was, which I thought was kinda rude.

I didn't get a shy vibe from him. As a matter of fact...I stumbled a little. I wasn't feeling *anything* from him. Where he was before me was a blank wall. I focused, trying to get the smallest, teensiest bit from him, but it was as though he weren't standing in front of me at all. I was getting really creeped out. And strangely, my palms were starting to burn.

When the dance was finished, I excused myself to the ladies' room, waiting until Mesmer was trailing me from a discreet distance before I went in.

I splashed cold water on my neck and brow, and looked at myself in the mirror. My skin was strangely flushed on my cheeks and forehead, and I felt hot. Like, *boiling* hot. When I went to turn off the water, I swayed, almost losing my balance. The world tilted crazily, nearly making me lose my lovely dinner.

I clutched the countertop and closed my eyes. "What...?"

I felt eyes looking at me in the dark of my mind. With my eyes closed, it felt like the eyes were staring right at me. And they were cold. So very cold.

Oh startled starlings, what was happening to me?

With my eyes squinted a little to reduce the glare from the lights, I fumbled in my beaded clutch for my cell phone.

It would have been the smartest to call Rhys or even Dice, but I was terrified, and all I wanted was Draven. He was my first speed-dial number for a reason. I hit the two buttons to call him with shaky hands and stumblingly made my way to the couch in the corner.

"What's wrong?" he barked into the phone without bothering with a little thing like *hello* first.

"Hey," I whispered. I put a hand to my stomach. It was roiling so much that I eyed one of the stalls in case I needed to make a break for the toilet.

"Talk to me," Draven said in a calmer voice. "What's going on?"

"I'm not sure," I admitted. Just then, Rhys came into the ladies' room with a murderous look of rage on his face. I blinked, wondering if I was so sick that I was imagining the stars swirling around him in what looked like a dark purple aura. I blinked again and saw a night sky with a swirling nebula. "I think I'm sick," I said shakily. "Rhys looks like the night sky."

"He's brought out his night powers?" If anything, Draven sounded more panicked about that.

What in the heck was going on!

Rhys sat next to me on the couch and moved my head tenderly to his lap without saying anything. He closed his eyes as he ran a star-swirled hand over my forehead and then held it at the crown of my head for a while. Mesmer was in the doorway, standing like an immovable mountain with his arms crossed over his chest, glaring at anyone who dared come near with a full bladder.

Draven was still talking to me on the phone. "I'm on my way." I could hear that. The sound of tires peeling away in the background made that extremely clear. "Talk to me. What is Rhys doing?"

"Umm." I dared to open my eyes again and peek at Rhys, even though the room tilted like I was on a tilt-o-whirl. "He's all swirly with the night, and he's got a hand over my head. His eyes are closed," I whispered.

"He's checking your body for signs of something," Draven explained.

"'K."

Draven's breathing next to my ear helped me to calm down, even though I was starting to feel a lot worse physically. Mesmer moved closer and extracted a bottle of golden powder from his coat pocket. "Here." He tried to hand the powder to Rhys, but Rhys shook his head.

"You do it," he said stiffly, clenching his teeth. "I have to focus to mutate it into something benign."

I whimpered when the pain hit. Flames felt like they were licking my body with huge, blistering tongues. Rhys was shaking with rage and fatigue, Mesmer was coating my hands in the gold powder, and Draven was breathing harshly on the phone as he listened to my cries.

Man, I sucked at this paranormal stuff! And what the heck was going on!?

I asked Draven.

His tires squealed again, and I heard his door slam shut. "It sounds like someone poisoned you with something."

I groaned. "Why do they keep taking pot-shots at *me*?" I mean, I didn't want them to go after Draven either, but seriously, why me?

My eyes widened when my hands glowed hot pink. Oh, crud. That couldn't be good.

"My hands are pink," I whispered into the phone, and then pulled the phone away from my ear when Draven blistered it with curses. He came charging into the bathroom at a run and slipped his phone into his pocket. He took mine too and put it in the same pocket.

"Do you have the blue powder?" he asked Mesmer.

Mesmer nodded and handed it to him. Mesmer was

looking a little chalky, like his body was trying to go full gargoyle, but there was too little space for him to change in here.

I eyed him a little worriedly. "You okay there, Mesmer?" I asked weakly. "No Hulk Smash, okay?"

He nodded and went to stand by the door again as Draven dumped the blue powder onto my hands and rubbed it in. Then he grabbed a basin from a side table and filled it with fresh water and tenderly dipped my hands into the water and washed them.

I hissed. Ouch-a-mommy, that hurt!

He took my hands out and dried them gently with a towel. I looked at them in dismay. There were blisters all over my palms. The back of my hands were fine, but my palms were scorched and blistering.

Dancing doxies! Ouch, that hurt. I whimpered and closed my eyes.

Rhys spoke from above me. "I'm almost finished," he grunted. I squinted at him. Sweat was pouring down his face, and his mouth was about as tense as someone who was being asked to pee in a cup for a sample.

I tried to send him grateful vibes, hoping he'd pick them up. In my current predicament, it was the best I could do. He winked and kissed my forehead.

Message received then.

Rhys finally sat back in exhaustion and looked at me with concern. I was just glad he'd downgraded from murderous rage to concern. My bestie was scary when he was ticked! "Go home. I'll key in a healing draught for you and bring it by in the morning."

I nodded my head weakly. "'K. Give us a kiss?" I tried to tease.

He laughed and kissed me full on the mouth.

"Sneaky elf."

He winked again and carefully stood with me, then handed me to Draven, who clutched me tenderly to his chest.

We went out a back entrance that bypassed the crowd. The night air was chilly, and I shivered as I tried to snuggle closer to Draven for warmth. Draven climbed into the back seat of the Lincoln Town Car with me and situated me carefully across his lap. He pulled a blanket from a hidden compartment and covered me with it.

"What happened?" I asked sleepily. I was still unsure of how I'd suddenly gotten sick. I'd been dancing with Mr. Tall Dark and Swarthy, and then I'd used the ladies' room, and then I'd gotten sick. It made no sense.

"My enemy showed himself today." He looked down at me. In the dim light coming from the windows, I could see that he looked both troubled and furious. "I'm sorry you're getting caught up in this." I could see the regret in his eyes, but more than that, I could feel it radiate out to me.

"Was it the guy I danced with?" That was the only thing that made sense to me. Maybe he had somehow stuck me with a tiny needle and I hadn't noticed?

Draven nodded. "He used a virulent viral agent that transfers from skin to skin, from his hands to your hands. He's immune as a vampire, but you, as a mostly human, are not." He looked regretful at these words, like it was his fault that I was a mostly human.

I hummed in thought, keeping my eyes closed. It seemed safest when the world was so insistent on spinning like a top.

I felt a little floaty. I wasn't afraid, though, because

Draven was with me. I scrunched my brows in thought. "Draven?"

"Hmm?" His hands traced careful paths down my neck, trying to soothe me.

"Are you *ever* going to kiss me?"

I felt him still beneath me and I took my chances and squinted up at him. His eyes were very warm and focused on me. "Just curious what it would feel like for a vampire to kiss you?"

His face was going blurry and wavy, and I was having a hard time focusing on him. "No," I answered honestly, bravely. "Just because I want *you* to kiss me."

"You're not yourself," he dismissed. "You don't really know what you're saying."

I whimpered when he adjusted his legs slightly. He stilled them immediately. "I do," I whispered, trying to keep my breathing even and calm.

"I," he hesitated. "I don't know that I will ever love again, cara mia. And whom I kiss, I love."

"Oh." I internally cringed. Old world values. I kept forgetting that about him.

As if he could sense my thoughts, Draven chuckled low. "I do not judge you for not having the same sentiments as me when it comes to a kiss."

Well, after his declaration, maybe I judged *myself* a little. Just a little, though. My heart broke a bit at his words. I'd grown to care about Draven over the past months we'd worked and spent time together. Caring about him just felt so natural to me.

But not to him, and I needed to remember to respect that.

He shifted carefully, and I held my breath, but there was no pain this time.

"I..." he hesitated again. "I could use a friend, if that sounds amenable to you?"

Without tapping into his emotions, I sensed the difficulty behind that request, and I felt a piercing empathy for him. He must have loved the woman in that vision very much. So much so that he'd barricaded his heart behind a bastion of walls since her murder.

I swallowed, touched and honored that he would open up that much to me and offer his friendship. According to Rhys, Draven wasn't friends with *anyone*. "Yes," I said simply, squeezing his hand. I closed my eyes, and we rode out the rest of the car ride in silence.

CHAPTER 10
MIA

"I've drunk my potion, I've R & R'd, I've Scrabbled, I've bothered Henri so much that he came after me with a spatula. What does a girl have to do around here to escape?"

Draven looked up at me briefly from where he was lounging behind his desk, arched an eyebrow at me, and then hid his face behind the paper again. "You have not rested and relaxed, you threatened to throw the Scrabble board at me when I won again, and you can't leave until we catch the vampire that's after you."

He sounded so *reasonable* when he said it that way.

"Then let me work!" My feet were up on his desk as I sat in my spinny chair across from him. I gave him puppy-dog beseeching eyes.

He didn't even look at me. "No."

"But I feel fine now!"

Draven calmly set his paper down onto his desk, folded his hands together on his flat stomach, and stared at me with cool, calculating eyes.

176

"Stand."

I sprang out of my chair like a jack-in-the-box. It was only after I'd gotten all the way up that I forgot my body currently hated me. I sucked in a breath and tried to swallow my groan. Ouch and double ouch. Being mostly human sucked very much, thank you! Vampires had all the cool resistance to poisons.

I gently sat in my chair again, and sighed as I looked at the ceiling, only now realizing that it was another mural. I very much wanted to meet the person who'd painted this villa. They were a genius.

"I can donate blood again."

Draven smiled. "Desperate, are we?"

"Please, Draven. I think I'm losing my marbles. I could swear Zian spoke to me today."

Draven contemplated Zian across the room, lying in front of the fire as per his usual. "Hmmm."

He picked up his phone and tapped a few buttons, then put it on speaker. Rhys picked up with a hesitant, "Hello?"

"Would you and Dice be available this evening?"

Huge, awkward pause, and then, "Let me check with her."

I gawped at my boss. "Did you just call my best friend and invite him over for a play date?" I asked, part affronted, part excited. *Yay!* I cheered internally. *Play date!*

Draven nodded. "I did."

Well, okay then.

Rhys came back on the phone. "We are available tonight. Meet at the villa?"

"That would be agreeable. Thank you."

Pause. "No problem, man. See you soon."

I jumped up, gasped at the pain, and hobbled my way to the door.

"Where are you going?"

"I have to find cute pajamas! Friends are coming over!"

Draven's laughter echoed behind me.

"W_HY_," I said in a very squished sort of way, "are we all packed in *my* bedroom? There is a whole villa out there!" I flung my hand out to encompass the enormous villa outside of my room and accidentally smacked Draven in the face.

"Sorry, my bad." I settled the offending digits onto my lap again.

Dice, wearing an I USED TO BE A PEOPLE PERSON, BUT PEOPLE RUINED THAT FOR ME tee shirt, sighed. "It's a more defensible room. There's a guard at each door, and one leading out to your balcony, and no one in this room is trying to kill you."

I contemplated my new friend Dice. Her whole body usually gave off an alert vibe, but right now she seemed totally chill. Like she could finally set aside her worries here in my room, and just enjoy. I thought it more likely that those same bodyguards keeping me safe, Dice also felt were keeping *her* safe.

I determined to talk to Draven about getting her a guard later. Maybe I could hire one for her? I made a ton of money now, and I wasn't really racking up any living expenses...

When the food arrived—cheese-stuffed Hawaiian pizza with cheesy bread and marinara sauce to dip it in, as well as chocolatey chocolate-chip cheesecake, and root beer floats —I made a plate and offered it to the guards first. They all thanked me politely but declined. I'd thought they might. I shrugged my shoulders. Well, I would set some aside for them for later.

I dragged my beanbag over, kicking Zian off of it because a girl needs her space, and practically canon-balled into it, wincing as my body twinged with remnants of pain.

Rhys had brought another potion, so my twinges were far less than they were, but I was still sore. I had a best friend that *rocked*. Rhys tried to sit with me, but I held him at bay with a foot. "Uh uh. Girls only. Come on, Dice. Come share before Rhys gets any ideas."

"Too late," he grumbled, plunking his butt down next to Draven. Zian came over to my side and sighed as he plopped down next to me, his enormous head resting on a tiny patch of the beanbag. He looked scandalized that I'd taken his bed.

"Sorry boy. A girl needs her space."

Dice was fighting with the cheese on her gigantic slice of pizza. It kept stretching endlessly, but never breaking apart. I laughed and dug in too, flicking my eyes up to watch Draven eat.

It always amused me to watch him eat, but I tried to be sneaky about it. I didn't want him to feel like he was an animal in a zoo. He ate so precisely. His napkin covered his lap, and he reacted, just a tiny bit, to almost *every* bite. It turned out that vampires were food snobs. And they *loved* excellent cuisine. Draven's eyes lit up as he dipped the cheesy bread into the sauce and took a bite.

I looked down at my pizza and smirked. I had a few things I wanted to introduce him to. He'd never had a double chocolate chip muffin before, after all, and they were one of my favorite food groups. I considered them a class all their own.

Rhys picked out the movie, an action sci-fi with a

romantic bent, and we all settled in to watch. Halfway through the movie, Dice fell asleep. She seemed utterly exhausted. Rhys came over and tucked a blanket around her, and I swapped seats with him, wanting to sit with Draven for a bit.

I plated some cheesecake and curled my legs under me. "I like this movie, Rhys. Good choice."

He smirked. "I have good taste."

"Yep." I turned to Draven casual-like. "He was naked in my shower when I first met him," I said conversationally. "And I couldn't even stay mad because my shower is literally the most awesome shower on the planet."

Draven laughed. "Way to make a splash into someone's life, Rhys."

"That was punny," I deadpanned.

Draven laughed, and those champagne bubbles *exploded* in my chest again. I surreptitiously massaged them away, but I think Draven noticed. He went quiet for a bit. "Want some?" I offered him a piece that was marbled with all the gooey goodness.

"No, thank you. Have you tamed my chef yet?"

I thought of Henri's red face when I'd poked my head in earlier to request our dinner. "He seems to be a little high-strung."

"High-strung might be an understatement."

"Thanks for arranging my play date, and thanks for hanging out with us."

He held out his hand, and I set my plate down and laced my fingers through his.

"I can feel your heartbeat in the webs between your fingers," he said casually.

"Is that a healthy thing for you to be focusing on?" I mean, vampires *could* be hazardous to your health.

"For you or for me?"

I shrugged. "Let's go with both."

He laughed and looked down at our hands clasped together. "It's a comfort to me," he whispered.

I sobered. Yeah, heartbeat equaled life. But Draven didn't want to talk about what I'd seen when he'd snacked on me a few days ago, so I just squeezed his hand a bit, and laid my head on his shoulder as we watched the rest of the movie.

I CAME AWAKE ABRUPTLY and sat up. My eyes tried to see in total darkness, and struggled for a minute until I made out Rhys and Dice on the beanbag chair, curled up with each other. I wanted to *awww* out loud but restrained myself. Barely. Instead, I grabbed another blanket and put it over poor Rhys. Dice had wrapped hers around her like a burrito, or like a girl who didn't like to share. I laughed silently. Rhys had his work cut out for him with her. She was everything awesome, but she was very hard to reach emotionally. I thought it might be a defense mechanism because she saw *so* much about people.

I slipped on my unicorn fuzzy slippers, snapped my fingers to get Zian's attention, and left my room with Zian trailing after me. Another guard was on duty outside of my room. I waited while he spoke to Mesmer in his earpiece, and then they both escorted me to the office.

It hadn't surprised me that Draven had been gone when I woke up. I wasn't sure if vampires as a whole didn't sleep much, or if Draven in particular had insomnia. I *did* know that Draven had said something about vampires not sleeping in the same room as other people, including their spouses. I, myself, didn't mind it a bit. It was comforting to hear the sound of someone else while you slept. At the very least, it meant that whatever came along to eat us had to go through at least one other person first.

I laughed, and Mesmer eyed me. I shrugged my shoulders. "I crack myself up." I tried to explain the joke, but he pulled a Mesmer on me and refused to laugh.

"Spoilsport."

They made me wait as one of them went in and searched the room. Then they made me wait even longer so they could get backup outside the office window and move more of the guards to our side of the villa.

"Leave some guarding Rhys and Dice, though," I said, worried that someone might come for me and find them instead.

Mesmer nodded and said something into his earpiece.

"I have come to the conclusion that it is no fun being kept under lock and key. But I'm really grateful, Mesmer. Thanks for working to keep us safe."

If I wasn't ninety-nine percent sure that gargoyles didn't blush, I might mistake the pinkening of his cheeks for one. Mesmer nodded at me, and then let me enter. Henri came in almost immediately with graham crackers and hot chocolate.

"Hey, Henri. Not sleeping either?"

Henri's golden-blond hair looked disheveled, as though he'd been funneling his hands through it all night, and his eyes looked slightly bloodshot. "Oh no, Henri! What's wrong?" I patted the sofa seat next to me. "Sit down. Tell me all about it." I didn't give him much of an option, but he looked *awful!*

Henri sat delicately, and elegantly served himself some hot chocolate. "It is our daughter, Reece." His shaking hands sloshed hot chocolate on the sofa, and I mopped it up with a bit of water from the pitcher and a rag.

"No worries, continue. What about your daughter?"

I wanted to hold his hand but thought he might die of shock. So instead, I tried to let him know with the rest of my body language that I was completely dialed in to whatever he had on his mind.

"The mansion on the island has hired her to be their chef."

I hummed in thought. "But isn't that good news, Henri? Your family's special brand of wizardry lends itself to being head chef. Isn't that what she wanted?"

I'd found out my first week that while Henri was an amazing chef that could cook nearly anything, it turned out that it was a special brand of wizardry, and that his whole *family* were amazing chefs. He called it chef magic, and never in my most realistic daydreams would I have dreamed that such a thing existed. A magic that lent itself to making tasty dishes? Sign me up! They had passed their special brand of magic down generation after generation through the patriarchal line. Sadly, because Henri had only one child, a girl, the likelihood of their magic dying with her was just about a sure thing. It had been a miracle that Reece had gotten it when no other females in the line had.

Henri sighed. "Yes, but she cannot tell me anything about her employer! He made her sign an NDA that prohibits her from even stating if it is a family that lives in the big house or a single occupant!"

"Oh, Henri. I had to sign one here. I'm sure you did too. These bigwig paranormals are just protecting themselves."

"But I am her father!"

I did pat his hand then, trying to calm him. "Yes, that *is* true. And if it were my own daughter, I know I would be wary of the situation." I sat and thought for a few minutes. "What if I asked Draven to come with us to meet the family that lives there?"

"Or single, *male* occupant!" His voice went pitchy on that statement, and I winced.

"Is that what has you so worried?"

"No! Yes!" He ran his hands through his hair, the resulting mess sticking up every which way. "I don't know." He huffed. "I want Reece to find someone special, like I did many years ago with her mother, but she's our only child." His eyes went a bit watery, and I patted his hand some more.

"I don't have any children yet, Henri, but I imagine letting them go must be very difficult." I thought for a moment. "Wait, Henri, isn't she around my age?"

"Yes."

I laughed. "Oh, my friend. You have to let her leave the nest some time!"

Henri sighed again. "Yes, I must. But only if she finds someone really special." He had become steady enough to sip his cocoa without splashing it everywhere. "Will you ask Master Leto? I don't want to be a bother, but I'm just not comfortable with her taking the job without knowing what sort of situation she'd be living in."

I smiled in reassurance. "I'll ask him. And if he can't make it, for whatever reason, we'll just go ourselves, and drag my army with me."

Mesmer snickered in the corner, and Henri grimaced.

"You know what I'm craving, Henri?"

Henri sat up straight. "What, miss? I will make it! For your kindness to me and my family."

"Lasagna, a salad, and really garlicky breadsticks."

Henri popped up like someone had stabbed him in the butt and hurried out the door without even saying goodbye.

"That was kind of you."

I shrieked and jumped a foot. Which was really impressive, considering I had been sitting down. Hot chocolate rained down everywhere around me, including on Zian, who growled a little, then sighed and started cleaning his fur.

Mesmer was chortling in the corner, and I could hear the other guards stationed outside the window laughing too.

"Mesmer! I thought I asked you to *warn* me when the vampire was in the room!"

Mesmer looked very stoic, but his gray eyes were creased around the corners in mirth.

Draven stepped out of the shadows, and I glared at him. "I'm getting you a bell that you can wear around your neck."

He laughed. "Oh, cara mia. You're good for the soul." He tried to dab some of the chocolate off, but I growled and grabbed the rag. I wet it and scrubbed it off my skin and then got down on my hands and knees and attempted to mop it up.

"What do you mean, it was kind?" I glared at my ruined pajamas. No amount of stain remover would get this out.

Draven handed me a clean, damp rag. "Henri cooks and bakes when he's stressed. You provided an outlet for him."

"Well, no point wasting a fidgety chef."

Draven laughed again.

I sighed as I dumped all the rags on the table. "Have you been here the whole time?"

185

Draven was drinking something in a bone china teacup that smelled heavenly. "Yes. I had some work I wanted to finish up."

I tutted at him. "Your brain never sleeps." That would be difficult. I wondered if vampires used more brainpower than humans did? Or if their thought processes were just faster? Hmm, food for thought. "I don't have that problem."

He canted his head to the side. "You have others. We all have something."

"Truth." I smiled and tried to snuggle back into the damp sofa, but laid against Zian instead. He was comfy, and not as damp. Zian grumbled but adjusted his enormous body so that I had space, and I laughed as he smacked his lips and chuffed at me.

"You're a big baby."

Zian sneezed on me and chuffed when I poked him. "Laugh it up furball."

I felt toasty by the fire. The nights were getting colder, and the big villa sometimes got drafty in the colder weather. "Will you go with us?" I eyed Draven, who I found looking at me with what some might consider fondness. My heart sped up at the emotions in his eyes, but I battled the gooey feelings back ruthlessly. Draven had friend-zoned me, and I was stuck there for the foreseeable future.

"I'll have to. If we're starting a battle, the general needs to be with his troops."

"Harty har har." I rolled my eyes at him. "Hilarious."

"I thought so," Mesmer said from the corner.

"No comments from the peanut gallery! And you're on my list, mister! You have two jobs with me, keep me alive, and let me know when the vampire is near!"

"He pays me better than you do."

"I pay in food! Delicious, yummy, food! You can't tell me Henri makes you better food than what he makes me!"

Draven started laughing, even as Mesmer said, "I get paid very well by Master Leto. I even get health and dental benefits."

"What do you need dental benefits for? Your teeth are stone!"

The guards outside laughed at that one, and Mesmer shot me an "I'll get back at you later look," then stepped outside the door briefly to confer with the other guards.

Which left me alone with Draven again. Did anyone else but me know how hard it was to slow your heart rate down when there's a vampire that can hear your heartbeat around you? *Especially* as I didn't want to give said vampire any ammunition to use on me, if, say, he realized how very much my crush was turning into actual, acute feelings? Yeah, *so* not easy. *Steady. Breaths.* I'd found another trick was to get my mind on something else quickly. I searched for a topic.

"Any luck finding someone that's interested in developing a matter-to matter-transport?"

Zian's head was resting on Draven's lap for scratches, and I tried not to be jealous of my familiar.

"No, unfortunately. That would really make things convenient, wouldn't it? If someone could invent that?"

I got too warm, so I plopped down onto the sofa again. "For sure. But it would also change the economy forever after."

He nodded. "It would, but it would help save the planet. We would need fewer fossil fuels because people would just transport to work."

"Car companies would fold, though. So many people would lose jobs."

He smiled at me. "These are big thoughts for two a.m."

I sighed. "Yeah. Couldn't sleep. I kept jolting awake."

Draven was quiet for a few minutes. The sound of the fire crackling filled the silence. "I've meant to ask you. Have you heard from your adopted cousin recently?"

I frowned. "Glade?"

He nodded.

"No. I have no desire to hear from him. Why?"

He ran his fingers through Zian's thick fur. "I did some digging into your background."

I was three seconds from protesting before I realized, duh! Of *course* the master vampire would dig into his employee's backgrounds prior to hiring them. My mouth snapped shut.

"I came across some very skeevy information regarding what should have been your inheritance. He's run through most of the money, but I know how he can repay you, and the house is, of course, yours."

The first thing that occurred to me? A master vampire used the word skeevy. The second? *I knew that rat fink stole my inheritance!*

I growled, and by default Zian growled too in support. "That rat fink wicket monger!"

Draven blinked at my colorful vocabulary and smiled. "It's in process."

"What does that mean?"

Zian flopped his ten-ton head onto my lap to comfort me, and my breath gushed out in a wheeze. "Easy boy. I need all of those parts."

"It means I have some people working on it. I have a lawyer extricating him from your inheritance, and several people working on liquidating his assets so that he can pay back the money he stole from you."

"Legally?"

He smiled angelically. On him, with his beauty and curls, you could almost believe it, if you didn't notice the glacial look in his eyes. "Mostly."

I winced and tried not to imagine what 'mostly' entailed.

"Normally, I like to fight my own battles, but thank you, Draven. I really appreciate it. And not on that note at all," I said, completely changing the subject, "I would like to hire a bodyguard or two for Dice. I think she's in some kind of trouble, and I don't want to just trust that whoever is after her isn't paranormal."

"Already done."

I blinked in shock. "Wait...really?"

"She's important to you, and she needs help. I've already handled it."

"Wow, you're like a one person stop-shop for getting things done! You can confess, you have a huge to-do list, don't you?" I smiled blindingly. "Do you want to borrow my ta-da-done pile?"

He laughed. "I like to keep busy. It helps quiet my thoughts."

"Yeah, I really like my downtime too much to work that hard. I'm not lazy, per se. I just need more down-time than the average person."

His gaze turned serious. "It's because you're an empath. It's to protect and rejuvenate yourself. Plus, can you imagine what would happen to your rainmaking abilities if you didn't sequester yourself away from people from time to time and relax?" He smirked. "It would be constant hailstorms, tornados, and tsunamis. So, on behalf of Moonhaven Cove, we thank you for watching movies and relaxing in the jacuzzi."

"If only I could do those things together! Then I could really get my rest and relax on!" I laughed, not really serious. Well, maybe a little serious.

"We have a flat screen that comes out of the wall in front of the jacuzzi. The controls are on the side of the tub." He smirked at me, and I laughed and rolled my eyes.

"Of course you do. We should call this the Leto Playboy Villa instead of just the Leto Villa."

His eyebrow went up a tiny bit. "Ah, but I'm not a playboy. That requires one, that I be a boy, and two, that I play around. Neither applies."

I sighed internally at that. Yep. I could confirm that he was a mature vampire who didn't play games with people. I appreciated it, but I couldn't help but hope he'd consider dating again. Preferably with me.

"I appreciate that." We sat in silence for a bit, before I said, "So, we take the troops to the mansion on the island tomorrow?"

He laughed and nodded.

CHAPTER II
MIA

I wanted to hold Henri's hand as we stood on the grand porch outside of the island mansion the next day. To soothe him, because it definitely wasn't *me* that needed soothing. Everywhere I looked, there was evidence of wealth: expensive cars, an army of gardeners and other staff, marble statues of exotic animals. It made my head spin, and it also made me appreciate the Leto Villa more. Draven had made it more homey, and less mausoleum-like.

Except, there was someone inside that was in a lot of pain, and they didn't feel at all stone-like to me.

"Draven, someone's in pain," I whispered. He was standing behind me, looking around the property with interest. He nodded his understanding, but Henri must have had elephant hearing because he whipped around and looked at me in horror.

"Is it Reece?"

I squinted in thought. "No. It's a male."

Henri sighed in relief, and I patted his shoulder. Finally, the wide double doors swung open, and a butler in proper butler attire, and who looked about a thousand years old, stood before us. He had a shock of white hair that fuzzed out in all directions around his head, and his eyes were a pure gold.

I tried not to gape. "We're expected by the master of the house," Draven said from behind me.

I closed my mouth before anyone could catch my stunned surprise as we all followed the clearly arthritic butler into a large foyer. I looked ahead to the main room as they took my sweater and tried not to wheeze. Gargling gargoyles, the ceilings were at least fifty feet high!

All around the top of the main room was a mezzanine that was filled with statues, paintings, and musical instruments. The ceiling was shaped like a dome and, what I assumed was glass and *not* diamonds, was cut into a million different shaped prisms that threw sparkling lights along the hardwood floors beneath our feet.

A big dog came gamboling down the massive staircase, and I backed up a little, trying to get out of his way. He was huge!

"He's a Bernese Mountain dog," a husky voice said.

I followed the sound of the voice to an open door on the ground level. A man stood there, leaning heavily on a cane with some kind of large bird on the top. It reminded me of a phoenix from books. It would be so cool if phoenixes were actually real. I would have to ask Rhys about that later.

The man had hair the color of soot, and he was very large, both in height and breadth. His chest, arms, and legs were massive, yet, to me, he looked frail.

Because I now knew where the feeling of pain was coming from.

He dipped his head to Draven and then to me and Henri.

We'd left the rest of the bodyguards outside, and Henri's wife couldn't come, so it was just us and our army of bodyguards. "It's an honor, Master Leto." He slowly, and painfully, made his way to a roomy leather sofa along the wall, and sank in with a slight sigh. "But if you don't mind my asking, why are you here?"

The dog settled at his master's feet, nose sniffing the room energetically, trying to determine who we were. Or, probably more like he smelled Zian on me. Since Henri seemed frozen, and Draven was eying me, waiting for me to say something, I huffed at them, and moved to seat myself on the adjoining sofa.

I stuck my hand out. "Hi, I'm Mia, friend of the gray-haired gentlemen over there, and Master Leto's executive assistant. You just hired a new chef named Reece?"

The man shook my hand. His hand was malformed, but still strong, and he stared into my eyes for a few moments before he pulled his hand away. "An empath?" he said, almost to himself. "And...a rainmaker. Hmm, both powerful abilities."

And then he grimaced. "I'm sorry you have to feel my pain, love." He spoke low, probably so Henri wouldn't hear, but he couldn't speak so low that the vampire in the room couldn't hear him.

"I'm sorry you're *in* so much pain," I said.

He nodded, and I could tell that would be all he'd say on the subject. "Now, yes, I hired Reece a few weeks ago. She's an excellent chef." He looked at Henri. "Is there something wrong with my having hired her?"

Henri spluttered, and I wanted to smile. This was Henri's worst imaginings. A handsome, though scarred, single male had employed his daughter.

Draven sat beside me, and the man shook his head in frustration with himself. "I'm sorry. I forgot to introduce myself. My name is Tylen Evermore. I hope you'll forgive me. My mind is not what it once was."

Draven and I nodded, but Henri was still spluttering, standing twenty feet away from us.

I laughed, covering it with a hand, before I said, "Henri is worried you'll mistreat Reece, his daughter. She signed the NDA, you see, and he was worried about the household she'd gotten hired by."

Tylen nodded, as though this was a completely normal response, and I had to admit that it seemed to be. Parents worried about their children always. It didn't matter if they were four or eighty-four; they never stopped worrying. Tylen pushed a gray button that nearly blended in with the wall behind the sofa, and a bright, chiming bell sounded somewhere in the mansion.

A beautiful woman came through a swinging door, dusting the flour off of her bright blue skirt and thick teal sweater. Her bright blonde hair was up in a messy bun, but a good chunk of it had fallen out. It was long, probably waist length. She shoved it behind her ear, revealing a sweet face with slightly pink cheeks, alabaster skin, and bright blue eyes.

In short, Reece was adorable. She was like a Care Bear, except for grown-ups. I wanted to put her in my pocket and take her home with me.

There were so many emotions pinging around the room, my mind was spinning a little. Relief from Henri that his daughter looked to be okay, something deep from Tylen behind me, and a bright spot of embarrassment from Reece. "Yes, My Lord?"

Tylen scowled. "Tylen, Reece. I am not a lord."

Reece fidgeted, looking like she disagreed with that statement, and I jumped up and crossed over to her.

Men! Poor Reece was seriously uncomfortable.

I held my hand out to her. "Hi, I'm Mia. I live in the Leto Villa. I'm Draven's dubious executive assistant and resident pain in the butt." Draven chuckled as I smiled at her, hoping to ease her tension.

She smiled shyly and took my hand. "Hi. It's nice to meet you. I'm Reece." She spotted her dad behind me and blinked at him in confusion.

I winced. Yep. Dear old Dad came to check up on you. But Reece didn't yell or get more embarrassed. She sidestepped me neatly and just about tackle-hugged Henri. I could sense it wasn't because she felt she needed saving, she just really missed and loved her dad.

Aww.

Henri was spluttering and patting her back as she squeezed him tight.

I laughed at the two of them, feeling a twinge of jealousy at the cute daddy-daughter moment.

"I told you I was fine. Mr. Evermore is a good employer," she told him in exasperation.

Tylen hissed in pain as his dog bumped his leg, and the dog whined in sympathy. Then the dog sighed and laid his head on his master's foot, looking up at his master with love in his big doggy eyes.

I plopped myself onto the floor next to the great behemoth and offered my hand. "His name's Huggles," Tylen murmured, his eyes following Reece's movements like a hawk.

I spluttered out a laugh and then clapped my hand over

my mouth. Tylen focused his molten, silver eyes on me. "My five-year-old niece named him," he said in self-defense.

I nodded. Yep. That would do it.

Huggles finally licked my hand in hello, then he sniffled all along my skinny jeans and my ankle boots. "Hugs, leave her be," Tylen growled.

Hugs sneezed, spraying everyone around him in a ten-foot radius, and Tylen and Draven scowled while I laughed, and mopped it up with my sweater.

Tylen eyed him with disfavor. "Thank you for that," he rasped. "Always so appreciated."

"He smells my tiger on me."

"Your familiar?"

I blinked. "Yes." Then I lowered my voice to a whisper, "How'd you know what I am?"

I could hear father and daughter chatting behind me as Tylen pursed his lips, pulling the scars on his face, making them whiten and flatten in a snarl against his cheek. "I have three powerful gifts in wizardry. Everything else I'm very weak in. My three are air manipulation, I can talk to and understand animals—and they can understand me on a basic level—and divining. It's an almost extinct branch of wizardry that allows me, through touch, to sense the gifts of another being. Your gifts are very strong, so you're easier to read than many."

Draven murmured, "It also allows him to see small snippets of the future."

Tylen nodded, though most of his attention was still focused on his chef and her father.

I felt so awful for him. It was easy to see with my eyes how much pain he was in, but empathically, it was so much worse. It didn't feel like his pain, but my own. At least emotionally. There was always an emotional fallout for me from the chronic, physical pain of others.

"It's okay," Draven murmured, when dark storm-clouds started gathering outside. He rubbed my back and continued to murmur assurances to me as I leaned against him, letting his presence soothe and comfort me. I felt so powerless sometimes. Feeling what others felt, but not being able to help, was painful.

The front door knocker clacked loudly, and the butler let Mesmer in. "Master Leto, there's a storm kicking up outside. We might want to head back to the villa."

Bless his sweet gray heart. He must be worried about lightning striking the human.

It couldn't have been Draven he was worried about, because a brief storm could do nothing but bring cool, sun-free relief to a vampire. And I don't think it was Henri. I got the feeling Henri didn't like Mesmer all that much, and the feeling seemed mutual.

I sighed as Draven chuckled behind me. "It's okay, Mesmer. I just need to chill out. Give me a minute." I closed my eyes to Mesmer's confused expression and breathed in and out slowly. With each exhale, I tried to let go of my frustrations regarding those I couldn't help, and with each inhale I resolved that even if I couldn't do much for some people, I would keep trying to do what I could in my sphere of influence. Which, I cheered myself, was a lot bigger because I was part of the Leto household. The Leto household was a big name in the paranormal community.

As I continued to do my breathing, I could see the room gradually lighten behind my closed eyelids. The room went silent as the others realized what was happening. My eyes popped open.

"There. No storm."

"My island appreciates it," Tylen said wryly.

Suddenly, there was a loud cacophony from outside: barks, roars, men shouting, yowls and hisses. It basically sounded like a zoo was seconds away from attacking us.

I stood quickly; Mesmer stood in front of me. His gun was already out and aimed at the door; his gray arm quickly bulked up to his alternate stone form and was very steady. Henri held Reece close, and Draven and Tylen were both standing as well, though Tylen had his eyes closed in concentration.

A large cat burst through one of the front windows, shattering it into a zillion pieces. Hugs barked and growled like crazy, and I pounced on Mesmer's arm as he moved to shoot the large feline.

"It's Zian, Mesmer! Don't shoot!"

Zian ran to me and herded me to the back of the room. I allowed him to, not knowing what was going on. As soon as he got me there, the front doors slammed open, and paranormals poured in through the opening.

Pandemonium broke out. Zian had backed me into the corner, and he hadn't let me move yet. Tylen's bodyguards and Draven's guards arrived at the same time. Mesmer moved to stand beside Zian, and they both took down anything that came toward me. I grabbed a heavy candlestick off a side table and bashed a few heads that got too close to our little group in the corner. No way was I just standing there, letting everyone else risk their lives without doing something.

"Vampires," Mesmer cursed after shooting one, and it did nothing. Then he dumped the bullets in his gun onto the floor, loaded gold-plated ones, and started firing again.

Draven had rounded up Reece and Henri and shoved them my way at the beginning of the attack. I could see him now. He blurred from one mercenary to the next, taking them down with precision and speed.

I trembled and the skies outside grew black with clouds again. Thunder rolled across the island, concussing the mansion with a loud *boom*. Lightning streaked the windows.

Tylen stood to my right, protecting Reece and her father. His walking stick was now a sword, and he ran anyone through that got too close. Then, the melee grew even more confused when animals thundered in. An elephant picked up a man with his trunk through the open door and smashed him into a marble statue. Monkeys covered people from head to toe and dragged them down to the floor. All kinds of tropical birds flew in through the broken window and harassed and pecked, their beaks drawing blood.

The men started taking out the animals, which infuriated Tylen. He roared and drew a gun, shooting the mercenaries who'd hurt them, then made a loud screeching sound, circled his hand twice in the air, and pointed outside. The animals scattered and disappeared through the door and broken window.

Silence.

Absolute silence.

A blast of thunder shook the house, almost knocking me onto my butt in surprise. I kneeled and rubbed Zian's fur in gratefulness before I felt the prickling sense of eyes on me. I quickly glanced at the window. Someone stood there. Fury radiated off of him, and he had cold, gray eyes.

"Draven!" I shouted, pointing.

But he was gone. There was no sign of him. "The

vampire from The Laughing Elf. He was there, at the window!"

I blinked and Draven was gone, whooshing air was the only sign of his passing. I could see him out the window, in the exact place the other vampire had been, sniffing the area, but then I blinked again and he was gone.

Vampires were *fast!*

Zian nudged me, and I came to my feet.

Henri and Tylen were both checking on Reece. She looked embarrassed at all the attention.

Tylen crossed to me. "I'm sorry this happened while you were on my island. Let me get this cleaned up and we can talk."

I nodded, still dumbstruck from the fight.

My cell rang. "Hello?"

"You okay?"

I spluttered. "I think you have the wrong number."

"Hilarious, Mia. I was swimming with Zian in the Leto pool and he suddenly ditched me and took off. And he was moving *fast*. I was worried."

I could hear it in his voice. It made warmth blossom in my chest. I felt loved. "Call me back with video chat."

He signed off and called me back, and I showed him the room of bodies.

When I flipped the phone back around to my face, Rhys' face was pale. "That vampire isn't giving up, is he?"

"It doesn't look like it. He must have tracked us here. Thankfully, Tylen has a ton of guards as well, and everyone helped fight them off."

Rhys nodded, his swirly purple eyes looking thoughtful. "Did Zian get there in time?"

"Just barely. He shattered the window and came in like a

spy in a spy movie, except way cooler!" I was a little enthused about this. Zian was a rockstar in my eyes.

Rhys laughed. "Only you, Starshine. Only you. Well, I'll let you get to it. Come by the club tonight?"

"Do I get in free?"

"Nope. Not tonight. Penance for terrifying me."

"Aww, come on! I'm the best friend! You're supposed to let me in for free! I have to put up with your overly affectionate butt all the time!"

Rhys roared with laughter and signed off.

I growled and shoved my phone back into my back pocket. Reece was looking over at me with interest. "Elves!" I hissed to her. "Honestly, they think they're the world's gift to humanity."

She smiled. "That's because they're treated that way by most. Elves are revered in our world."

I patted her arm. "You're sweet, Reece, but you have so much to learn about elves. There's absolutely *nothing* to revere about them. They're royal pains! They steal your hot water, kiss you when you'd rather kiss a skunk, and generally bug and annoy you until you want to run away to the circus."

Reece moved closer. "Do you *like* Rhys?" she whispered.

"No!" I protested. "Eww, he's like my brother!"

She laughed. "Well, that makes sense then. And yes, elves are very affectionate. It's fortunate they are, because they can also be a little proud."

"Yeah, that's not Rhys. He's got no pride at all."

Reece laughed, then sobered as Tylen came back. Still no sign of my employer.

Tylen grabbed one of Reece's hands, and Henri glowered at him. They were too busy staring at each other to notice. I pulled Henri to the side by his suit-coat sleeve, and whispered, "I think she's all good here, Henri. We should leave them be."

Henri looked like he wanted to protest, but sighed instead. "You're right. She has to grow up sometime."

I wanted to laugh. I mean, Reece was *my* age, late twenties, and he was only just now realizing she needed to grow up. It dawned on me then that *this* was the reason Reece had taken the job. For one, she seemed to have a very compassionate heart, and two, at the Leto Villa, she was always under the thumb of her dad, who was also our head chef. Here, she could spread her wings, have the kitchen all to herself, and have a very handsome employer to ogle. Win-win.

I said my goodbyes and walked outside with Henri, Mesmer, and Zian. Two of whom crowded around me tighter than a tick on a hound. I showed them my space bubble, and they both looked at me like I was crazy. "Come on, guys! Space bubble! Breathing room!" I pantomimed the space around me currently taken by hulking forms and tried to shove them away from me. "A girl needs room to breathe!" I protested when they refused to budge.

Zian snapped lazily at me, and Mesmer just flat-out ignored me. Overprotective, hulking brutes. "Just wait, I believe in paybacks." I sulked.

"Forgive them for trying to keep you alive," Draven said, suddenly at my side.

"Oh sure, you move for *him*," I growled at Zian, who sneezed at me in answer.

I sighed.

"I'm feeling a little overwhelmed right now. And I'm scared. They attacked us again, and I feel like simultaneously hiding my head in the sand in the hopes that all of this will go away and going on a Rambo streak with guns strapped to my chest and grenades attached to my belt. My emotions are all jumbled."

Draven smiled. "As amusing as that would be to see, try to let us help protect you. It helps us feel manly and like we are the smallest bit necessary."

I appreciated that they tried to protect me very much. In fact, it was what was keeping me alive during all of this craziness. I shuddered. I was not a fan of murderous vampires. I could barely handle the one in my life that *wasn't* in a constant murderous rage.

I glanced up at Draven. "Sure. I can let the big, powerful protectors feel needed. My gift to you guys," I teased. "But it's only to help your self-esteem! Not because I might need it."

Mesmer looked like he was trying really hard not to crack a smile. "Don't chip a tooth fighting back a smile there, Mes."

He cuffed the back of my head lightly, exactly like a big brother would, and I smiled.

Ahh, family.

CHAPTER 12
DRAVEN & MIA

"I don't understand why you have to be there tonight." Mia said.

I cocked an eyebrow at her. "We were just attacked not seven hours ago."

"I *know* that! I was there! But I already have Mesmer, and Rhys will stay with me at the club."

I wanted to smile but knew that would be the wrong move. Mia was very adamant that she could do things for herself. I knew it stemmed from her raising herself through her late teens and working her fingers to the bone to provide for herself, but in this, she was wrong. I admired her tenacity and determined spirit, but I wouldn't be letting her out of my sight anytime soon. Every time we had a close call, I had the horrible thought that *this* would be the time that I would lose her. *This* would be the moment my enemy took her from me, too. It drove a spike of fear into my belly, driving me to seek more and more desperate measures to keep her safe.

Currently, she had four guards tailing her, as well as

Mesmer and myself, and two trackers that Mesmer had cleverly hidden in her personal things. One in her phone, the other in the lining of her purse.

She also had Rhys, to whom I had recently expressed my appreciation for saving Mia's life by gifting him with a townhome. It had surprised me when he'd accepted it. I think Mia had something to do with it. Something about it being in a pretty part of town, and within walking distance to her favorite doughnut shop, Diggity Dog Doughnuts. The doughnut shop was owned by wolf shifters, who thought the name was hilarious. I found it less so. It didn't make the doughnuts sound appetizing. Also, because I knew Mia would be with Rhys a lot, I made sure there was security on the premises of the townhome I gifted him. I think that was one of the key reasons Rhys had accepted it. He loved Mia. He didn't want to see her get hurt.

I downshifted as I hugged a corner on the turn and gazed at Mia, appreciating her beauty.

I found it mystifying when others talked about the dreadfulness of getting older; that you started feeling it as you hit the triple digits. I'd found it to be untrue, and I'd been in quadruple digits for a while now. Our minds were so fascinating to me. My mind still felt young, like I was in my thirties. I wondered sometimes if we eternally felt young. That it was just our experiences that aged us. What if you'd been given a body that didn't age, and a mind that felt perpetually youthful, like with vampires? What age did that actually make me?

These thoughts and more crowded my mind as I looked over at Mia. I knew my mind was picking this apart because of my attraction to her. The discrepancy in our ages had troubled me for a time, but only until I realized that vampirism was akin to drinking from the fountain of youth. I would never look old. And my brain still felt youthful. The only thing that had perhaps aged was my soul. But that was, to my mind, a good thing. Experience was an excellent teacher.

Since my wife had been slain, I'd been attracted to different women. But I'd never acted on it because the more I'd gotten to know them, the more I'd become certain that Charisse would be the only love of my life, and that all others would forever pale in comparison.

But when I was around Mia, she became even *more* beautiful to me. There was a sparkle in her eyes that hinted at the mischievousness that lurked beneath. She was warm and caring and she made me laugh. She brought me out of my thoughts and out of my secluded shell. All she had to do was ask, and I practically jumped at the chance to take her places, just to be around her. She brought warmth to my life. To me. All the parts of me that had shut down after Charisse died were coming to life again.

It left me reeling, but reeling in a good way.

And it left me justifiably terrified.

Which brought me back to tonight.

"I'll pay your cover charge to make up for my odious presence." I teased her.

She scowled at me. "No, you will not! I can pick up my own tab."

Her sharp movements tilted her headpiece, and she hastily threw a hand up to catch it and set it right.

"Your feather is askew," I said, nodding my head at her bedraggled feather. It looked like Zian had gnawed on it.

Mia tried to straighten the feather, muttering under her

breath. I was right. It sounded like Zian had thought it was a toy.

I smiled as I took the country roads at a speed not advisable for most species. I was the safest driver I knew. Just because I drove at the speed of light didn't mean I wasn't fully in control.

"You look beautiful," I said softly.

Mia blushed and smoothed her dress. "Thank you."

Tonight was Roaring Twenties night at the club, and Mia had dressed to the nines. She had on a gold and black beaded flapper dress that cinched at her waist and ended in beaded tassels. Her hair ornament was a dazzling and glittering headpiece with golden feathers. On her neck was a long pearl necklace that was knotted three times down the center of her body and draped to her belly button. Her stockings were fishnet black, and she had on glittery chandelier earrings to complete the outfit.

In short, she was irresistible, and I intended to dance the night away with her and not let anyone else near her. I was feeling a little possessive tonight, which surprised me. I couldn't ever remember feeling possessive with Charisse.

"Will you dance with me tonight?"

She blushed again, and a splash of warmth infused my chest. "Rhys will want to dance with me as well."

"I can share, I suppose." But only with Rhys, I silently told myself.

She gawped at me, and I laughed. If my fangs were down, I'd be flashing them. She always made me laugh with her facial expressions.

"Who are you and what have you done with Draven Leto?" she demanded. "You do realize you're flirting with me right now?"

I smirked. "Is that what it's called, cara mia?"

She spluttered and started laughing. "Yes, Draven, welcome to the twenty-first century." She patted my leg like I was a doddering old man and laughed when I playfully growled at her.

This. This was why I was falling for her. She made me feel alive again. And she was so natural around me! It didn't seem to matter to her that I was more deadly than her cat; she treated me as if I were just a man, and she was just a girl. And I loved her for that. To be just a man to her. Just a friend. Just a lover. Not a killer. It warmed my heart that she'd seen me at my most deadly today, and she didn't shy away from me. She hadn't even missed a beat, she just kept right on treating me like the most ordinary, wonderful thing in the world.

I needed to know if she was still entertaining the idea of us. Which was why I intended to make a move tonight. Her reaction would tell me either way, and I felt an excited thrum deep in my chest at the thought of holding Mia all night long.

Let the night begin!

It was official. Draven's long life had finally driven him crazy. He helped me from the car—some expensive sports car that looked like it could get us to space without any problems whatsoever—and paid my cover at the club even though I tried, and failed, to pay my own way. He was way faster with the money hand off.

Vampires!

The club was gorgeous! The chandeliers sparkled a soft

white, candles dotted every table, the band was playing an upbeat jazz number, and the big screen had a picture of a moonlit night in New Orleans. Clear balloons were strung and twisted across the club above the crowd, and feathers were everywhere in the decorations. People were lined up in front of the gigantic screen of New Orleans, using it for a photo background. Dancers were swinging and jiving on the dance floor, and Rhys and Dice were manning the bar.

The bar was incredibly busy, but I wanted a sweet tea, and Rhys had just learned how to make it properly for me. I was one of the few customers that ordered it, but he kept it stocked and brewed just for me.

I grabbed Draven's hand and led him through the throng until we reached the bar. Dice was wearing a miniskirt, spike heels, a tee shirt with a skull on it, and leather finger-less gloves. She had a chain belt around her waist that had feathers dangling down in honor of the theme of the evening. Her hair was an electric silver today.

Rhys was rocking a blue suede suit. I swear, was it impossible for immortals to have bad hair days? To look homely? Even when Rhys wore sweats, he was more good-looking than he had any right to be. And even though I'd never seen Draven in sweats, I had a feeling it would be the same for him.

Rhys kissed me full on the lips when I leaned across the bar for a hug. "Will you stop doing that!?" I hissed as I grabbed a swig of someone's drink and apologized after I washed the taste of Rhys off my lips. "Seriously, elves are waaaayyyy too affectionate!"

Dice hugged me and flicked Rhys on the ear as she went to fill an order. "Dice, does he do that with you?"

She slid the patron their drink and came back to us. "Nah, he tries to act cool around me."

She smirked when Rhys spluttered. Draven laughed and put his arm around my waist. I looked at him, blinking at him in confusion. Seriously, I thought it was entirely possible that aliens had swapped bodies with Draven. He was acting so peculiar! Draven just laughed at my expression and closed my mouth, which was gawping at him in astonishment.

Rhys raised an eyebrow at the arm placement and then followed Dice around as she served drinks and proceeded to remind her, loudly, of all the ways that he was a cool and clever elf.

Dice wasn't having it. She had his number. The paranormal world at large revered elves, more so star elves, but Rhys was a serious goofball. Yes, he was gorgeous, but seriously, he was a goofball.

"You're really doing this?" I asked Draven, with my eye on his hand at my waist.

"Doing what?"

I turned in his arms and looked up at him. I was so close I could smell the lime and forest on his skin. "Don't be coy and don't play dumb. You're the smartest person I know."

His chocolate-brown eyes looked down at me. I wanted to reach up and run my fingers through his curls, just to see how they felt against my fingers. And then I just shrugged and did it. He was being all lovey-dovey at the moment. I thought I might be able to get away with it. His hair was really soft and didn't have any product in it to make it all gunky. A girl appreciated those types of things.

"A little while ago, you were telling me you wanted to be just friends." I tried to keep the hurt that had caused out of my voice. It didn't matter if his reasons had been completely valid. It still hadn't felt good to get rejected.

He sighed. "Is this where you warn me not to mess with your head or your feelings?"

I nodded. "And also to remind you that my best friend is a star elf and will bury you six-feet under if you hurt me."

We both looked to where Rhys was serving a drink to a svelte man with a handlebar mustache. Rhys wasn't looking at the man, though, he was looking at Draven, and his swirly nebula eyes were cold with promised violence.

I shivered.

Yep, it was official. My best friend could be crazy scary. I was just grateful he was on *my* side. It was worth all of his wayward affection when I could see how clearly Rhys loved me. Who knew? And my biggest worry had been a fear that Dice would see more into Rhys' affection than there was. But nope, she seemed to read him perfectly.

I kept forgetting she could do that.

"You are interested, right? I'm not projecting my feelings onto you?"

Aww, the sweetie. His eyes were aglow with concern that he had overstepped.

I reached up and touched his cheek. His skin was warm, and there was a bit of stubble on his jawline. I pulled him down to me, and then *oohmphed* in surprise when he lifted me up so my legs were locked around his waist, and his hands were on my lower back, holding me up, and then he kissed me.

I'd only been kissed one other time in my life, but it was clear from the moment his soft lips touched mine that there would forever be a before and after. Before Draven and after Draven. Our mouths moved in sync, as though we had done this a million times before. A buzz started in my head, like I'd been drinking steadily for a while, even though I hadn't. Up felt like down, and down felt like up. My stomach *swooped* and danced, my heart *thudded,* and there was a feeling in my chest like champagne bubbles popping. The jazz filtered around us; the voices of the crowd creating a wall of background noise.

And then his arms went under me, lifting me, cradling me, and I felt cocooned and warm and safe. The noise filtered to a soft glow, and I melted into him. My insides went from champagne bubbles to melted chocolate, just that fast.

It lasted maybe a minute, but it felt like a lifetime before I pulled back and looked at him with a face that probably resembled a cartoon owl. I was panting slightly, and I... What had just happened? Draven had kissed me, right? I didn't just have a seizure or something and imagine that?

I wanted to pull him back to me and kiss him again. I wanted to go take a walk in the brisk night air and cool off. I wanted to ask the people surrounding us on the dance floor if they'd just seen him kiss me so I could have irrefutable proof I wasn't losing my mind.

"Mia?"

Draven was asking me something, but I was having a hard time focusing.

"Mia, you with me?"

"Umm, hmm, yeah. I'm with you."

His smile was gentle. "I was just asking if you wanted to dance."

"We *are* dancing."

Draven looked down at our feet, which weren't moving. I don't know why this fact surprised me. I looked down at my wayward feet encased in shimmering heels and scowled. I'd really thought we'd been dancing the whole time.

Draven laughed and gently pulled me closer as he released my feet to the ground. He tugged me toward the middle of the dance floor.

"But my sweet tea!" I waved my hand, trying to get Rhys' attention, but nope, he was flirting unsuccessfully with Dice.

Seriously, when was that elf going to learn? Dice knew all of his moves before he made them. He needed to be genuine with her, and not put on the act he was putting on. But I remembered what he'd told me the first night we met. How he was still hurting. How he didn't think he was ready for love again yet. He was probably acting this way because he didn't want to get serious with anyone. And Dice knew it, so she put up with his Romeo act.

I sighed and let them be, bemoaning my lack of sweet tea.

Draven curled his arms around me, and while everyone else was jiving and shimmying and laughing and sweating up a storm, I was slow-dancing with a vampire, with my head resting against the curve of his neck, and his chin resting on the top of my head.

I don't think I opened my eyes the entire rest of the time we were in the club.

On the drive home, he held my hand.

I tried to remember if I'd held hands with someone before. Someone who mattered. I'd maybe held hands with my adopted parents a few times? I couldn't remember. My memories of that time were fuzzy.

The country roads were winding, and for once in his life, Draven was driving leisurely. He had one hand on the wheel, barely steering with his fingertips, and the other was holding mine. I glanced at our hands clasped together and then glanced up at the stars.

The top was down on the car because I no longer cared if my hair turned into a bird's nest. The wind was whipping my curls everywhere. And even though I'd wrapped a hair tie around my hair in a bun, strands kept escaping and tickling my face.

"You've lived this whole other life," I blurted out suddenly. My brain had been constantly churning facts like this at me since we'd left the club. I kept remembering the images I'd seen in his mind. The woman that had been killed, and him sobbing over her body. The wars that he'd fought in. The immense measure of time that he'd been alive.

I don't know why this was hitting me this way. I had known these things before; I'd just never put them together with the possibility of us being together. In my mind, it was like Draven and his life as a vampire differed from the Draven that I worked with day in and out. I'd separated them somehow. But they weren't separate. My Draven, my boss Draven, was a vampire who'd lived almost a millennium.

A millennium.

I tried to wrap my brain around that.

The longer I sat there thinking, the more I tallied up all the pluses on his side, and all the minuses on my own. It was impossible for me to match him in wisdom, raw power, wealth, or cleverness. I considered myself to have *some* wisdom, and to be *mildly* clever, but after spending all this time with Draven recently, I'd come to see that he was

WANTED: VAMPIRE'S ASSISTANT

fiendishly clever. Like, clever to the tenth degree. He was nothing short of brilliant.

If that wasn't intimidating enough, he was also humble, kind, and sweet. I mean, yes, he could be overbearing and way too protective, but I knew that was in part because of his experiences.

"You've gotten quiet. Are you thinking yourself into a corner?"

I glanced at him, then away. "Maybe."

He squeezed my hand. "This is hard for me, too."

I fidgeted.

"Really, it is," he said. I was certain I wasn't ready or willing to attempt being with someone yet."

My heart squeezed. "How long has it been?"

"A few hundred years."

"That's a *really* long time to be alone."

He smiled. "My kind are less changeable than mortals. Change takes more time for us, and the effects of change last longer. We don't flit from thing to thing, from flower to flower, as mortals do. When genuine change, lasting change, takes place within us, it becomes a part of us in a way that's difficult to excise. My wife has been gone nearly three hundred years, but in some ways, it feels like it happened yesterday."

"Change is hard," I agreed. In a softer voice, I said, "I'm sorry about the loss of your wife."

He squeezed my hand again, and we drove the rest of the way in silence.

That night, he left me at my door with a kiss to my forehead, and I spent the rest of the night snuggled with Zian, trying to picture the days ahead. I had no idea what was going to happen. No idea if we could work and date, no idea if we were a good fit romantically at all. I really had no idea about any of it. And that was terrifying to me.

I dialed Rhys. "Will you let me stay with you if I get kicked out of here?" I asked without waiting for a greeting.

"Well, hello to you too, Starshine." Rhys' voice was warm and sultry. He was teasing me like he didn't have a care in the world.

It was annoying when I was freaking out so badly. I wanted someone to freak out with me! That's what best friends were *for*!

"I'm serious!" I hissed. "If things go badly between me and Draven, I might need a place to stay until I can find work."

"You'll work for me, of course."

I looked at the phone in frustration, then hung up without warning. I called back using video chat.

He answered. He was lying in bed shirtless, one hand propped behind his head. His purple nebula eyes looked sleepy, and his silver hair was all askew. "You hung up on me, darling."

"I'm coming over. I need best friend advice."

He shot up, and the sheet slipped down to his waist. "*Seriously*, don't answer video chat if you aren't wearing clothing! New rule!" I complain-hissed as I covered my eyes like his nakedness had seared me with a laser, or like the sun had burned holes in my retinas. "What is wrong with you? Are you entirely lacking in modesty?"

"Yes."

I growled at him and attempted looking through the smallest space between my fingers. "I'm coming over."

"You can't. There's a crazed killer trying to kill you! I'll come over there." He got up, presumably to put on clothes, and I shrieked and shoved a pillow over my face. I wasn't a prude, but come on!

"Seriously," I complained. "Clo-thing. It's a thing, Rhys!"

He laughed at me, and I growled and hung up.

Zian growl-chuffed, and I laughed, feeling vindicated. "Right? He has no sense of decency."

Zian did that funny thing where he attempted to answer me back using whines and chuffs and growls, and I laughed and kissed his nose. "You're the best familiar ever."

Thirty minutes later, Rhys arrived, let in by one of the guards, and I opened my bedroom door and yanked him in. I tackled him down to the floor in a hug, and he laughed as he squeezed me.

"What? What's happening?"

Zian tried to lie over the top of our legs, and I pushed him off, then dragged Rhys to the beanbag, where I proceeded to push him down onto it and then curled up next to him.

"Draven kissed me!" I said without preamble.

"I know, Starshine. I was there."

Oh. Yeah.

Rhys' eyebrow went up. "It looked...consensual?"

"Yes?"

"That's not supposed to be a question. It either was or wasn't."

I sighed and sank back into the beanbag, letting it support my head and neck. "Yes, it was, but...Geezer, he's like almost a millennium old!"

"Yep, he's a dirty old man for going after someone so young," Rhys said with a smirk.

I smacked his arm. "Seriously, he's so much *more* than I am."

"More what?"

I threw my arms wide. "More of everything! Wiser, smarter, stronger, and there's certainly a difference in our economic situations."

Rhys grabbed my hand and threaded his fingers through mine, probably trying to pin it down so I didn't flail and smack him in the face again.

"I can promise he's not noticing the differences you are. He seems happy."

I turned my head to look at my best friend with skepticism. "Won't this stuff come up later, though? The disparity between us?"

Rhys looked thoughtful. "Maybe in some form. But you'll work through it. It's not like he's thinking about how much less intelligent you are, or how he can buy several small countries and you can maybe buy a pack of underwear."

He laughed when I smacked his arm.

"I'm serious. It's a non-issue with him. You're the one making it into one."

"You think?"

"Fairly certain. I'm not him, but I *am* a guy."

"Yeah, but you're an elf; he's a vampire."

"Eh," he shrugged. "Now, my shower is broken. Can I use yours?"

"Lies! You just like me for my shower!"

He laughed as he grabbed a towel from the closet. "What can I say? Your shower is sweet nirvana."

I waved a queenly hand toward my bathroom, giving him permission while I digested our conversation.

A tap on the door interrupted my thoughts.

"Come in!"

Draven poked his head in. He listened to Rhys singing in the shower for a moment. "Rhys is here?"

"Yep. He's stealing my shower again. There's got to be a better shower somewhere else in this villa. Every time he uses mine, he makes it smell like his bath products," I complained. "Even when he doesn't bring any!"

And I didn't know how he managed it. I'd scoured my bathroom for a hidden stash of his beauty products, but could find nothing.

Draven blinked at me and then smiled. "I'm sure he has a secret stash somewhere."

I invited him in and sat down on the bed. "So, what's up? You just checking on me?"

"More like making sure that Rhys isn't getting into trouble."

"Umm hmm." I eyed him. I didn't think that was it. "Jealous?" His eyes flashed red and then back to his lovely brown. Guessed it in one. "You really shouldn't be," I assured him. "I'm like a sister to him. You know elves are just super affectionate."

"So I've heard." He fussed with his blue, silk bathrobe before coming to the point of his late-night visit. "I'd like to take you to dinner tomorrow, if you're amenable?"

"Take me to dinner, right? Not, *have* me for dinner?"

His eyes flashed red again, but stayed red this time, and I swallowed. Right. Don't tease the vampire.

"Take you to dinner," he said blandly.

I laughed and hugged him, trying to quell his obvious awkwardness. When was the last time Draven had asked someone out on a date? "I'd love to. Are there any amazing Mexican restaurants nearby?" Mmm, he smelled good. I tried to sniff him unobtrusively, but obviously failed because his shoulders shook in laughter. *Argh, caught.*

"Yes, there's Tres Hermanas. A Mexican restaurant owned by three witch sisters. I've eaten there a few times. The food is authentic cuisine and has gotten rave reviews."

"Can't wait." I looked up at him. "Meet in the entrance hall at six?"

He nodded. "I'll make a reservation. It's always busy for dinner." He cuddled me close for a minute, then kissed me and left.

As I listened to Rhys whistle in the shower, I realized I was overthinking everything again. Draven had flirted with *me* tonight and kissed *me*. I'd been staying in the friend-zone where he'd put me since the night I'd been attacked at Rhys' club. And I'd been doing an admirable job of keeping my feelings under wraps, if I did say so myself.

So Draven must have already thought of and dismissed all the things I was worried about. He processed things much quicker than I did, and I was sure he didn't share my worries. I resolved to set them all aside. At least for now.

If I kept fidgeting and worrying about everything, I'd just make myself and the people around me miserable. I didn't want that.

Le sigh. I sometimes longed for the days when it was just me in my dingy apartment. All I'd had to worry about then was myself, and of course, the next rent check. Oh, and that little thing called food. And break-ins were common in the area, so I was always worrying about getting robbed, or, more accurately, being home while my apartment was getting robbed.

I laughed. Okay, so I'd still had a lot of worries. They'd just been different worries.

I palmed my phone and hit a few buttons.

"Yes."

I snickered to myself. Mesmer was always the epitome of brevity, especially on the phone.

"I can't sleep, and Rhys is here. Do you have time for a few rounds of poker?"

"I'll be there in a few minutes."

CHAPTER 13
MIA

Around four or so, a note had been delivered to my desk indicating that I should dress casually for the evening. I'd laughed as Draven had attempted to look indifferent about the delivery of the note by burying himself in paperwork, and signing the million documents I'd left on his desk for him.

I remembered his half smile with a curl of warmth that settled in my tummy as I got ready.

Draven was the complete package. This both thrilled me and made me slightly nauseous because *I didn't have anything to wear!* Seriously, I needed to go shopping, stat!

I rummaged in the back of my walk-in closet for a pair of black skinny jeans and then shrieked in delight when I found a cream cable-knit sweater that I knew was warm and looked cute on me. I paired it with brown ankle boots that had faux fur lining and were insanely warm and then made my way to my bathroom to apply my makeup and do my hair.

After curling my hair and pinning back my bangs in a

swoopy style, I finished off my makeup with gold eyeliner. Finally, I opened my jewelry case and found the pair I'd been thinking would go with the outfit, a cream dangle set that was both delicate and pretty.

Zian sniffed me and sneezed as I added another spritz of perfume. It smelled like vanilla and chocolate. One of my favorite scents to wear when the weather was cold.

I laughed as he tried to cover his nose and grumbled at me in disgust. "Yes, but people like it. I'm assuming vampires like it, too."

Zian eyed me in disbelief, and I shrugged. "It's true. I guess I'll see tonight, though. I know their sense of smell is really strong. Maybe perfume is too much."

Well, it was too late now. I couldn't wash it off and still make it to the foyer in time.

I said a hurried goodbye to Zian and rushed down to the foyer, not wanting to be late, and made it just as the clock chimed six.

It didn't matter, because Draven was already there waiting for me.

Holy Hannah, the man wore jeans *well*.

I resisted the urge to fan myself.

Draven had on a dark-gray cable-knit sweater, similar to mine but more fitted, and dark-wash blue jeans.

I looked down at his feet.

Blue Converse.

If I could have gotten away with sighing in appreciation right then, I would have. Seriously, he was wearing Converse? Le sigh.

"Wow, you look so nice," I stammered, making him laugh.

"I think I need to dress down more often. You're looking

at me like you usually ogle the chocolate-chocolate-chip muffins that Henri makes for you by the dozen."

Yes. Yes, I was.

Down girl.

And it was even more ridiculous because my heart flipped at his laugh, and those champagne bubbles popped in my chest.

What the heck *was* that?

I massaged my chest absently, completely missing the solemnity return to Draven's eyes.

He offered his arm, and we went out into the cool autumn evening.

The restaurant was eclectic, no doubt encompassing the three sisters' tastes. A fun, vibrant energy surrounded it. The parking lot was full, yet Draven still managed to find a spot close to the entrance. There was a huge park with a lake on the side of the restaurant that Draven told me they used as an entertainment venue for all kinds of things: weddings, concerts, Easter egg hunts for the kids. It was beautiful and very green. Trees lined the lake and river, and even though autumn had come to Moonhaven Cove, some flowers still lined the walks.

We were seated by a beautiful woman who introduced herself as Rose. Her sienna hair was pulled up in a bun, and her emerald eyes looked timeless. "What can I get started for you?" she asked, as she pulled a pad and pen out of her apron.

I glanced down at the menu and saw that they did virgin drinks. "Virgin piña colada, please."

Rose stepped aside as a server brought out two large bowls of homemade chips and salsa. The server left quickly, and Rose finished taking our drinks. Draven surprised me and ordered a mocha.

"I didn't know you drank coffee! Does it do anything for you?"

Draven scooped salsa onto a chip and munched on it before answering. "Sadly, it doesn't. I just like the taste. Coffee is too bitter, and hot chocolate is too sweet. Mocha hits both notes perfectly for me."

I smiled. Yep, that sounded about right. It amazed me how similar Draven and I were. He and I enjoyed a lot of the same things, and even though he was ancient, we shared similar thoughts on diverse subjects.

And what differences we had so far had only made things more interesting between us. I could definitely say that of the two of us, Draven was more intense. I was much more chill and relaxed than he was; than he would ever be, most likely. Draven didn't relax well. Like, at all, really.

"Watch a movie with me tonight?" He smiled and nodded. I tapped my boot against his Converse and felt like all was right in the world as he snuggled my foot between his larger feet beneath the table.

I ordered the chicken fajitas, and he chose a beef enchilada plate, and we talked long into the night. He asked me about the different jobs I'd had, and I told him several funny stories about my bosses, some of whom had seemed literally crazy.

"Where were you born?"

Draven put his fork down and took a sip of his mocha. His beautiful brown curls glinted in the candlelight, and I wanted so badly to run my fingers through them again. Maybe tonight during the movie.

"I was born in the province of Ferrara in Italy to an

Italian farming family. We made our living selling vegetables and wool at the nearby markets."

Draven fiddled with his drink, lost in long-ago memories. "One winter, a sickness swept through our small community. It killed by the hundreds. By the end of that winter, I'd lost my whole family."

I gasped softly and reached for his hand. Our eyes met across the table, and I could read the pain in them. "I made my way to the *Abbazia di Pomposa,* or Abby of Pomposa, and asked for shelter. A few kind monks took me under their wings and broadened my education greatly. As a poor farmer, I hadn't even learned how to read or write. The monks changed that. When I came of age, I kept many of the records from the library, and assisted with a great many tasks around the abbazia."

I scooted my chair closer to Draven, and leaned my head on his shoulder, wanting to be closer to him. His story was breaking my heart.

"One night, a man came, seeking shelter and a place to sleep for the night. The monks let him in. During the night, he let others in, and by morning, they had slaughtered everyone. I later found out that I had been turned because of my supposed beauty."

He sounded bitter about that fact.

"You are beautiful—for a man, at least—but I'm sorry it's caused you pain."

He kissed the side of my head.

Our trip home was quiet as I thought about his childhood and his turning. Both had been such traumatic events. I was sure he'd long since dealt with them. When he'd been speaking of the experiences, I'd felt only distant pain from him. More like a memory of pain than anything else. Still, it made me sad that he'd been through so much. It made me want to fill his days with laughter and fun to make up for all the harshness of his former days.

We cuddled on the beanbag with Zian at our feet as we watched Big Hero 6. I ran my fingers through his curls and watched in amusement as they sprang back into place almost immediately. Right around the time Hiro was bot-fighting, Draven fell asleep, curled up around me as though he could and *would* protect me from anything that might try to hurt me.

Our bodyguards were outside, and I felt confident they would at least give us some warning if someone who wanted to kill us barged in.

Maybe.

Hopefully.

At least Mesmer would.

I tried not to take too many liberties with Draven's person as he slept, and instead got a little misty eyed that he was comfortable enough to sleep around me. I knew what that meant for a vampire: complete and utter trust. Some vampire couples who'd been together for *years* had never slept in the same room as each other. Or so I'd been told.

I felt deeply honored by his gift of trust.

I tried not to make too much noise as I slurped down the chocolate shake Henri had made for me, then set it aside and snuggled fully into Draven's side, stealing his warmth.

It amazed me yet again that Draven was warm. The books and movies about vampires *lied*. Perhaps in his youth, Draven had been mad with bloodlust, but he sure wasn't now. He had more control around blood than I had around chocolate! And he ate. As a matter of fact, he ate with gusto, making little noises of satisfaction, and little hums that always made me secretly smile. And he was crazy smart. The list went on and on. Draven was nothing like a fictional vampire.

And I was so happy about that. Fictional vampires did not sound like my cup of sweet tea.

Zian was snoring at our side, so I gave him a gentle nudge with my foot to get him to stop. He rolled over onto his back, smacking his lips, probably dreaming of a juicy steak.

My attention was caught by the movie again as I thought about our dilemma with the vampire that kept coming after us. I had hesitated to mention it to Draven, but after I'd seen the vampire through the window, after they had attacked us the last time, I'd recognized him from somewhere other than Rhys's club.

He'd been in the flash of images I'd seen from Draven's memories. The vampire with the cold gray eyes that had made me think of icebergs hidden in the ocean. You barely saw the tip, but some of them were so very deep. I got the same shivery feeling around our attacker.

I didn't know what it meant, but I think it meant that we were in trouble.

Now that I thought about it, I'd seen the vampire three times now, and Rhys and Mesmer once, but Draven had yet to see his face.

He obviously knew him from his past, though.

I shivered.

It made me wonder if he was the same person who'd killed Draven's wife. I cuddled into Draven more deeply and tried to push any and all bad thoughts from my mind.

I was watching a good movie, and I was getting snuggled by the best vampire on the planet, whom I happened to think was amazing. I didn't want my night ruined by scary thoughts.

Instead, I thought of Draven's face as the candlelight had flickered on it over dinner. And I thought of his smirk as he sat next to me beside the pool. And I thought of a million other little snippets of interactions and memories between us...and drifted to sleep peacefully.

CHAPTER 14
MIA

As I neared the doughnut shop near Rhys' townhouse, I pondered to myself how much difference eight months could make.

I'd come in April, and it was now December. I had bundled against the cold in my favorite teal coat with a hood, and Christmas decorations were everywhere around town. Garland hung from light posts, store fronts had been decorated with lights and frosty background scenes, wreaths were literally everywhere I looked...

The weather wizards had made it snow so the people of Moonhaven could have a white Christmas. We'd gotten a few inches so far, and I was absolutely giddy. It made the whole town look like a postcard, especially at night.

My boots had extra traction, so I wasn't slipping and sliding everywhere as I ate my doughnut and looked at storefronts. I hadn't gotten a gift yet for Draven, and it was only three days until Christmas.

Honestly, what did you give the vampire who had everything?

My thoughts had been running in circles on this. Initially, I'd tried around November to ask oh-so-casual questions about his tastes. Until he'd looked at me as if he knew exactly what I was doing with a small smile on his lips, and I'd had to back off.

Dang vampire. He was too smart for his own good.

And did he give me a single idea? Nope. Nada. Zilch.

So here I was, looking into each storefront, desperately hoping that something jumped out at me and shouted *Draven*.

I was thinking maybe several small gifts. Like, a new shaving set, and a bowling ball, and a... Wait.

I stopped dead, and Mesmer nearly smacked into the back of me. I turned with a gasp. "I know what to get him!" I nearly shouted into Mesmer's face.

Poor Mesmer backed up a step and merely raised a black eyebrow at me. "His lordship?"

"Yes!" I fist bumped him, and then hissed and shook out my hand while he smirked at me.

Never fist bump a Gargoyle. Seriously, they're rock.

"We have several stops to make." I swung my arm through his, and we started down the sidewalk again.

Coming out of a shop ahead of us was the blond from the tea shop those months ago. She still looked perfect, while I looked like a bedraggled kitty chew-toy, but eh, semantics. She had multiple bags on her arms and was chatting noisily on the phone with someone.

She stopped when she noticed Mesmer and me. Her eyes were a chilly, pale blue. They were so cold I involuntarily shivered. Until just a moment ago I'd been perfectly cozy and warm in my coat, gloves and beanie, but I felt ice-cold now.

She scoffed as she looked me up and down. "But you're so grungy and plain! What on earth does he see in you?"

Grungy?

Plain?

Seriously?

I kept my face impassive. "I'm assuming that's a rhetorical question?"

She made a sound of disgust and barreled past us, slamming into me hard as she did so, which, If I hadn't been arm in arm with Mesmer, would have knocked me flat.

Mesmer reached one long arm out to stop her, but I patted his side and he let her go. It wasn't worth my time. I hated drama.

I watched the paragon walk away and then eyed Mes in gratitude.

"Thanks for letting me handle that myself."

He nodded. "She hurt you. I can call Sheriff Finn and file a report against her?"

"If she continues, we will, but I'm content to let it be for now."

He nodded. "If that is what you want."

"Yes." I sighed, then shook it off and resumed our walk to our first destination. "So, Mes, do you have someone special in your life?"

Mesmer looked at me incredulously.

"What?" I laughed. "It's okay for friends to ask that of each other, right?"

"Have you been reading that *How to be a Friend for Dummies* book again?"

I could feel my cheeks turn pink. "Noooo!" I fanned my face with my free hand desperately. "I don't have a book like that!"

"Hah!"

"So, is that a yes?" I asked, ignoring his snooping into books he shouldn't know I had.

Mesmer sighed. "No. No one special in my life."

"Do you want someone special?"

He thought about that for a bit. "I'm in my eighty-third year. I would like to find a partner I can share my life with. But I worry about her safety with me. My job is dangerous. My world is dangerous. How can I bring someone into my life, and ask her to share it with me, when I know there is a good possibility that my job will spill over into my life and put her in jeopardy?"

I blinked. "First, wow, that's the most words I've heard you put together, like, ever. And second?" I thought for a bit. "Mes, life is full of dangers. I know it's cliché, but I can literally get hit by a bus and be gone tomorrow. So can this mystery woman of yours." I looked up at him. "Look at Draven and me. I'm in danger, and I know he regrets that, but I also think when weighed up against us being in each other's lives, or not being in each other's lives, we choose to be grateful we're together, despite the circumstances. Because I've done the whole alone thing. And I can tell you it stinks. Having someone special in your life makes all the difference."

And wow, had I just sounded like a *Hallmark* card. I scrunched my nose at him. "Sorry for the sap."

Mesmer laughed.

I skidded to a stop on the walkway and gaped at him. "You laughed."

Mes shrugged, a happy glitter in his dark eyes. "It happens from time to time."

"I've known you for eight months and this is the first time

I've heard you laugh like that. Like a full belly laugh. Usually, you kind of quietly chuckle like you're afraid to really let go."

Mesmer's cheeks were turning pink. I pointed at them and whisper-shouted, "Oh my gosh! You're blushing!"

Mesmer scowled at me and glanced around us, shushing me with his hands. Shoppers had stopped to stare at us, and I made a sorry face and scooted closer to Mes so I could whisper more quietly. "I thought I was imagining things that day on the island. You blushed then too!" I accused. I didn't know gargoyles could blush!

His blush deepened, and, prancing pixies, all I could think was that it was possibly the most adorable thing ever. I wisely kept that to myself because Mes was brawny enough to snap me in half and use me as a toothpick.

"Mes, you know you're handsome, right? And you have that whole military-type thing going for you? Women eat that up."

If anything, his blush burned brighter, and I gaped at him in a stupor. "Has no one told you this before? But, I, but, how?" I stuttered. It just seemed so wrong! Seriously! Mesmer was hot with two t's! He was a little on the quiet side, but some girls loved that! And, he had an amazing job —that I knew, because I kept the books—paid *very* well.

Mes shook his head. "I haven't...dated anyone. I haven't gone on a single date."

I nearly gasped again in surprise. I moved so close to him that I was practically Scotchgard on his coat. "Have you kissed anyone?" I whispered.

Still blushing, but looking as if he would rather be anywhere but answering my very nosy questions, he shook his head.

"Mesmer, we have *got* to get you kissed!"

He shook his head. "No."

"No? No? But kissing is so fun! Jump on the kissing bandwagon! The smooching train! The pucker pony!"

He couldn't help but laugh again at my ridiculousness, and I shimmied in place in celebration for making him laugh deeply again. I was on a roll!

"Who's joining the smooching train?"

I squealed, but Mesmer merely blinked at me with an eyebrow raised. "You could have warned me he was coming up behind me."

His smile was a secret smile, and I knew it was because letting the paranormals in my life scare the crud out of me amused him.

"You're getting coal in your stocking."

He winked.

I turned to Rhys. "You're intruding on my Christmas shopping."

He pretended that my words wounded him by lurching around, clutching his chest, and I smacked his arm. "People are staring, weirdo."

He laughed and kissed me before I could blink.

I spluttered and used Mes' jacket to get the Rhys cooties off. "Stop doing that!" I squealed. "I have Rhysphobia now because you keep kissing me." Rhys pouted, and I shook my finger. "Nopity nope! You don't get to pout. My lips are off limits."

He shrugged, and I had pity on him. Dumb star elf couldn't help it. Honestly, I'd never known a more cuddly race. It was hilarious because they were cuddly, but strangely antisocial at the same time. They were some of the most powerful supernaturals in the world, and others both feared and revered them for it.

It had obviously gone to their heads, but...I felt a little bad for them. And then I'd told Rhys it was his job to go out and make lots of babies to repopulate his species. He'd laughed at me the whole week. He would stop for a half-day or so, then look at me again remembering my words and bust up laughing again.

Literally.

The whole week.

To get back at him, like any good little sister/best friend would do, I'd unfriended him on Paramate, the social online hang-out for supernaturals. And then felt terrible a week later when he kept texting me crying emojis and sad GIFs and friended him again.

Ugh. Star elves.

I threaded my other arm through Rhys' elbow, and we started walking again. "So," I said, looking at him, "I have several stops to make before we can head to the villa. Care to make a wager?"

Interest sparked his nebula eyes. "What kind of wager?"

"Mes will be our judge. You and I will go into each establishment and get what I need, but we will each have a character that the other person gives us, and we need to stay in that character the whole time we're in each place. For example, we're heading into the bowling alley. I want you to be an eighteenth-century British chap who's slightly deaf and very forgetful." I grinned up at him, unable to contain my excitement.

Rhys nodded. "And I want you to be an elderly lady that periodically yells out, 'Has anyone seen my teeth?'"

I giggled.

Game. On.

CHAPTER 15
MIA

When I got home, I was tired and sore and feeling icky. Also, I was ready for some alone time.

It wasn't Mesmer or Rhys; it was the crowds.

For as long as I could remember, crowds got to me. They made me feel penned in and crabby, and like I was slowly suffocating. Now, knowing that I was an empath, that feeling made so much sense.

I stripped in my room, and put on a new tankini set that was black with cute ruffled shorts and black mesh across the upper part of my chest, slipped my sandals on, grabbed my towel, and Zian and I were off.

I slunk through the halls, so tired of people that I didn't want to see *anyone*. Including my newly-minted boyfriend. Not that I didn't like his company, but I was all peopled out.

The pool area was quiet, and the nighttime lights were on, so there was enough light for me to see by without stubbing my toe.

I slipped into the inky, dark water, hissed at the temperature, and then let out an enormous sigh of relief.

Zian didn't like the hot tub, and I wasn't entirely sure it was healthy for him, so he laid down beside where I rested my head against the smooth concrete of the spa.

I didn't even want to talk to *Zian*, I was that peopled out, and Zian seemed to sense my mood, because he left me alone. He just closed his eyes and kept me company.

Of course, Mesmer and the other guards were outside of my visual range, keeping an eye on me, but I pretended they weren't there, and that I was all alone as I breathed in and out several times deeply. Each breath released a little more tension in my shoulders.

Finally, feeling peaceful, I laid my head back again and closed my eyes.

The sound of the waterfall over the pool was the only sound for a few minutes.

Draven gave me a half hour and then came out in board shorts. I didn't understand how the vampire could make board shorts look classy, but he managed.

I smiled at him in welcome.

"Better?" he asked as he slid in next to me.

"Much. Thanks for giving me some space to detox from the crowds."

He shrugged. "I've known an empath or two in my lifetime. I know you guys need it."

I cuddled into his side and laid my head down on his shoulder, but couldn't find a comfortable position. I shifted and squirmed until Draven had mercy on me and cuddled me to his chest. I sighed in relief as the water lapped over us.

"I got your Christmas and birthday gifts today," I told

him. His birthday fell on the twenty-sixth, but my gift was all one piece, so he was getting it all together.

"Really?" His eyebrow arched. "I told you not to get me anything."

"Yeah, no. That's not happening, and you knew it. Who *does* that? Not get their new-ish...person a Christmas or birthday gift?"

He chuckled. "Their new person? And we've been dating for a few months now."

I squirmed, embarrassed. "Well, I don't know exactly what to call you."

He laughed darkly and *swoop* went my stomach. "Your lover?"

"Not yet, you're not!"

"Your friend?"

"Yeeesssssss?"

"That's a question?"

I flicked my eyes to his face, able to see his slight frown in the darkness. "Not that we aren't friends!" I assured him. "Just, we're sort of dating?"

"If you only think we're 'sort of' dating, then I must be doing something very wrong."

I darted my eyes to his again, ready to make all kinds of assurances, when I caught the slight quirk of his lips. I splashed him, growling. "Are you laughing at me?"

He laughed and wrapped his arms around me. "You're adorable."

"Adorable like yipping puppies?"

"Adorable like Mia."

I smiled and closed my eyes.

There were only a few minutes of quiet before he asked, "So, what did you get me?"

I cracked up. "Dentures, hernia cream, and over-the-hill balloons in black."

He tickled my side. "Very funny."

I cackled. "It's true! I also got black gauze streamers so we can celebrate your agedness in style. I also found someone to spell a band so they look like skeletons as they play for the Christmas party."

He chuckled and leaned his head back, looking up at the stars. "I'll never be bored with you, will I?"

"Nope!"

"And all these decorations, are they going in the room being set up for the Christmas party?"

I gasped, scandalized. "No! They're going in the office!"

He laughed and cuddled me closer. "Mia, Mia, you're so good for me. I hope I'm equally good for you."

I wanted to say something funny and blow off his statement/question, but I knew I shouldn't. It felt like he was really searching for an honest answer, and I paused to think about it, and really give it the attention a serious question like that needed.

Was Draven good for me?

"Yes, Draven," I assured him. "You're *very* good for me. But I'm not going to get sappy!" I warned him, shaking my finger at him.

He shrugged, and there was a twinkle in his brown eyes. "Mesmer tells me you got pretty sappy tonight. And what's this about the 'pucker pony'?"

"Messsmmmmerrrr!! That was a secret!"

A gargoyle chuckled from the shadows.

241

THE NIGHT of our Christmas party dawned cold and clear. The temperature was hovering in the forties and enchanted snow continued falling on our beautiful seaside town.

I was standing at the door with Draven as we welcomed guests, but Rhys, like the little kid he was, kept flicking little paper wads at me. It looked like there was snow at my feet because he'd flicked so many.

I growled and swung around to slug him as the doorbell rang again. I gave him the dirtiest look I could manage and turned back around just in time for Aiwin to pull the door open with all of his stately aplomb and announce, "Mr. Tylen Evermore and Miss Reece Allais." Aiwin moved his ear closer to Reece's whispering mouth and then announced, "And Mr. Hugs."

Aiwin looked at the enormous dog in distaste, and I laughed, hugging Reece and shaking Tyler's hand. "I'm so glad everyone made it! The roads are a nightmare right now!"

Tylen frowned. His intense eyes literally looked like molten silver and they were so cool! "We didn't have any difficulties. We took the sleigh."

"You took the what?!"

He shrugged and pointed out the door to a full-on Santa sleigh pulled by five snowy-white reindeer.

"Oh. My. Gosh." I squeezed Draven's arm so tightly that he had to pull my death-grip off of him finger by finger.

"I'm sure he'd be willing to take you for a spin," Draven said wryly.

"But...the guests!"

"I'll be here to greet them. Go say hello to the reindeer."

I literally squealed and jumped up and down like I was five before I yanked my coat, scarf, and gloves off the coatrack, and dragged Reece behind me. And because I dragged Reece with me, Tylen came with as well. Rhys and Dice hurried out after us, not wanting to be left out either, pulling on their outerwear quickly. It was a whole sleigh-viewing party.

The sleigh was off white with gold trim along all the edges, had more swoops and curves than a mandala, and looked fast!

"*Ohmygosh* it's beautiful."

The reindeer stood stately and calm as I petted them. I looked at Reece. "Is this not all your five-year-old dreams coming true?"

She grinned. "You should have seen me when I first saw them pull up outside the mansion."

I laughed.

We all piled in, Rhys and I fighting over the best seat in the middle of the forward-facing bench. I won, of course. There may have been some light shoving involved.

Rhys glowered at me from the middle of the rear-facing seat, and I smiled beatifically while Dice laughed at our shenanigans.

There were heated blankets that were still somehow warm, probably through magic, and were so cozy that I sighed in delight as I laid one over Reece, Dice and me.

Tylen clicked his tongue, and the reindeer were off, hooves clopping on the wet, slushy snow in near-synchronous movement.

"*Oh*," I said, breathing in the night's stillness. It was *beautiful*. There was a light dusting of snow over everything. Lights down by the shore gleamed from the boats moored in the harbor, and the small lighthouse out on a tiny island about a quarter mile offshore was lit up like a beacon.

"It's beautiful, isn't it?" Dice said.

"It really is." I turned to her. "I used to hate this time of year."

She raised an eyebrow and I shrugged, feeling silly for my confession. "Just—bad memories, I suppose."

She nodded, and I knew Dice understood. She, after all, was still running from her own bad memories.

I just hoped they didn't catch up with her.

Rhys looked disturbed by our conversation, his nebula eyes darting from Dice to me and then back again.

I shrugged and smiled softly at him. What could you do? Not everyone had good Christmas and holiday memories. For some, including me before this Christmas, the holidays were a painful reminder of everything that was missing in people's lives.

I sat back in contentment. The feelings in the sleigh were warm, peaceful, and happy. It was a nice break from the worry over the vampire-that-shall-not-be-named attacking them.

The only downer was Tylen's pain. It made me want to go home and research all the ways, both magical and non-magical, that we might be able to help him.

Rhys, who always seemed to know what I was thinking, smiled sadly at me and said, "You have a hero complex."

"I don't!" Wanting to help people did not a hero complex make. It just meant that I cared about them. There was nothing wrong with compassion. He quirked a grin and shook his head, his eyes still looking sad. I knew he worried about me. He'd told me more than once that I was too tenderhearted, and my inability to separate other's pain from myself would keep hurting me until I learned to keep them separate.

Dice looked behind us, able to hear something, and we all followed suit. "Hugs! Here, boy!"

Tylen groaned while the sleigh driver made a pit stop to pick up Hugs, who'd caught up to us.

He jumped into the sleigh and gave kisses and licks to everyone before settling near his master's legs. Then he sighed a gigantic sigh, as if all was right in his world.

Speaking of his master... "Thank you for allowing us into your home a few weeks ago."

Tylen shrugged. "I knew you came with Reece's father. I couldn't turn him away." *Not even if I wanted to,* his expression seemed to say.

"You don't like visitors?"

He gave me a look. "No."

"But you're so kind!"

He glowered at me. "Take that back!"

Reece busted up laughing and huddled closer to me for warmth.

"I will *not.* You're just misunderstood." I should know. I could feel what he felt. Even though to the world he acted like a big grump, inside he was very kind.

Tylen looked at me in something akin to horror and I rolled my eyes. "Empath, yeah?"

He muttered something under his breath about empaths before he held his hand out to Reece, who ditched us girls to go snuggle next to him.

"I see how it is. What about girl power?"

Reece shrugged. "I'm warmer with him."

"I'll have you know that I'm a very warm person!" I protested.

Dice laughed and slung an arm around my shoulder. "Yep, you're warm all right."

THE CHRISTMAS PARTY was a smashing success. To keep things fun, we'd recreated several bridal and baby shower games for the holiday season. At the door, everyone got a pin that they clipped to their sweaters. On it, they were directed not to say Christmas or Holidays, and if someone did, you got their pin. Those with the most at the end won a prize that Draven and I had picked out together. It was hilarious to go around the different groups as they chatted and visited and hear how they tried to explain their plans for the holidays, or what they did for Christmas, without using those particular words.

Henri, who not only catered the party but got to attend along with the rest of the staff, was a serial pin swiper. He seemed to have ears like a bat and could hear someone from across the room mention one of the forbidden words.

We also had a game where the participants had to name a Christmas song after only a few bars. And since some of those titles had the word Christmas in them, it became this hilarious thing where they tried to shout out the answer but had to pantomime Holiday or Christmas, which Draven refused to accept as a legal guess.

One of the werewolves who owned Diggity Dog Doughnuts looked like he was going to rip Draven's throat out when Draven kicked him out of the game for refusing to say the full title of the song because the werewolf didn't want to lose his pin.

Personally, I thought it was a little cruel to expect them to lose one game to win another, but Draven had loved the idea, and I laughed and let him have his fun. He had a very valid reason for it, even though I think he got a little too much enjoyment out of riling people. *All* the prizes were amazing getaways to various places, and he didn't want a single person to win *every* prize. He wanted to spread them out amongst everyone. It was a good idea. But, whooee, it made some people mad. Especially werewolves.

Not every werewolf had a short temper. There were a few that did the dance off that were amazingly cool and levelheaded. It made me cheer them on because they were so tenacious...and talented dancers.

"Enjoying yourself?"

"Eh."

Draven laughed as he danced with me on our sparkling dance floor. He'd had a spell put on the ballroom to make it look like a winter wonderland. There were three arches into the room that had strings of white lights and real frost-tipped greenery grown over the arch. The light strings hung down on each side and created three magical doorways.

Real snow fell, but never touched the floor where it would melt and make the floor wet and slick, so we got the beauty of snow, but not the mess. Green garlands and red poinsettias decorated tables laden with food and drinks. We had a white and milk chocolate fountain, which was my favorite, with every available dipping goodie known to man, paranormal, or child. White lights were strung above us to create a magical canopy, and the dance floor was dark with little pinpricks of light gleaming off of it like stars.

The room took my breath away.

So, it was safe to say I was having an *amazing* time, which Draven well knew.

I smiled at him. "You?"

"I'm here with you," he said. "How could it not be wonderful?"

I squirmed. "Falafel flutes, you are a mushy, mushy vampire."

He tipped his head back and laughed uproariously, and then he drew me into his chest and arms and snuggled with me. "Only with you," he whispered.

More mush, but I allowed it because he was both warm and happy. It was a big change from when I'd first come for the interview eight months ago.

I looked up at him. At his wild, brown curls, and his warm chocolate eyes, at the five-o'clock shadow that never seemed to go away no matter how much he shaved, and I realized...I loved him.

I loved Draven. I loved a vampire.

It hadn't come all at once, like most people believed it came, but instead it had come little by little. Each moment we spent together building onto the next, and the next, until my heart had all of these happy moments within it that were all filled with Draven. With his goodness, his smile, his intelligence and humor. His laugh that made bubbles burst in my chest. The way he treated me like I was precious to him.

And I knew I *was* precious to him.

I cuddled in closer and closed my eyes. It wasn't the right time to tell him, but I vowed I would tell him soon. Even if he wasn't at the same place as I was in his feelings for me, it was still something he'd want to know.

I extricated myself from Draven's arms when the song was over and went to hunt for my best friend. I needed to talk with someone about this. How did you tell someone you loved them?

He was dancing with Dice, and it looked like they were arguing with each other. Uh oh. I winced when she stopped hissing at him as I drew closer.

"Can I cut in?" I asked, trying to look angelic as Dice shifted her frown to me.

"He's all yours," she growled.

Ouch. And Rhys looked crushed. Maybe right then wasn't the best time to ask Rhys about love. So I pulled up my big-girl panties and was there for my bestie.

"What's wrong?" I asked in a gentle voice.

Rhys' nebula eyes looked bruised and exhausted. He sighed and shrugged while leading me around the room masterfully. My bestie could dance! Like *Dancing with the Stars,* dance! "I wanted to talk to her about why she's on the run."

Oh. Yeah, I couldn't imagine that went well.

"I'm sorry, Rhys. Maybe it's too soon? It might take a while for her to trust us more. It feels like she's been through the wringer, ya know?" I tried not to fumble or step on his toes as he spun me out of his arms and then spun me back in. "I know we want her to trust us *right now* so we can help, but it has to come in her own time."

Rhys pursed his lips. "I just want her to be safe."

"I know. I really do. I want to help as well. But we have to let her reach out to us on this one." I stopped dancing and gave him a hug before I pulled his gift out of my pocket, unable to wait another minute to give it to him. It was four tickets to see an Angel's game. "Happy festivities!"

He laughed at my work-around for the word Christmas and dragged me off the dance floor to open it. When he saw what it was, he looked at me in adorable confusion. "Thank you? What is this?"

I laughed. "It's to a baseball game! I have a contact who gave us these for next season. They're for a field level hospitality suite so we can be comfy and well-fed as we watch your first-ever baseball game!" I made jazz hands in a *tada* celebration, but Rhys continued to look at me like I was speaking a foreign language.

"I only recognized maybe five words out of what you just said."

I laughed and snuck into his back pocket for his phone. I pulled up an Angel's game on *YouTube* and hit play. "Study, my friend. You need to be completely fluent in baseball by the time we go. And the great thing is, you can bring Dice, and I can bring Draven!" I wanted to jump up and down in excitement. Seriously, suites were insanely expensive, but my contact was a kindly old man who'd owed me a favor. His only son was a professional baseball pitcher and was able to score us the tickets.

Rhys hugged me in thanks, glued to the game on his phone, and we went our separate ways.

By around two the next morning, the party was winding down. People were finding their coats and bags and saying their goodbyes. I was feeling like I might need a mocha to give me the *umph* I needed before I could seek my bed, so I sought out the coffee bar and had them give me a double shot of espresso. Yum. I sipped and sighed. Seriously. Loved. Chocolate.

After that I felt like I could go run a marathon in six inches of snow. I was bouncing around from departing group to departing group, giving hugs and saying my goodbyes, while Draven was keeping me in his line of sight like I was a slightly spazzy ping-pong ball.

After the last guest had departed, I turned around,

leaning against the door, feeling hyper, but also weighed down with exhaustion. I was really regretting that mocha right then. "Lancing leeks, that was a busy night!"

Draven laughed as he pulled me away from the door. "Lancing leeks? That's a new one."

I pursed my lips in disapproval. "There is to be no laughing at my fantastic curse words."

Still dragging me, he looked back at me somberly. "I wasn't laughing, my lady. I was expressing my astonishment at your wide and varied uses of the English language."

My laugh echoed around the empty ballroom. "So, basically in Draven speak, you just said the same thing I did, but outsmarted me by saying it in such a complimentary way that I can't possibly be mad at you?"

His eyes glittered with laughter.

Yep. Outsmarted by my vampire.

I didn't even feel bad about it. I was outsmarted by him often. That was what came from dating a thousand-year-old vampire who, it sometimes seemed like, knew *everything*. It was a good thing I had a healthy self-esteem. And it was also a good thing he was adorable, because being a know-it-all could get very annoying after a while. But Draven made it fun. And he was so clever that I couldn't ever be mad at him for it.

Half the time, I let him win a disagreement because I knew the other half of the time, he was letting me win. It worked out in the end. And the things we really couldn't seem to see eye-to-eye on, we talked about until we were both in consensus.

I had no idea what other relationships were like, but I had to say, others were welcome to their young guys with their limited experience and Peter Pan syndrome. But for me, I was very happy with my vampire.

We sat in his sitting room, which was decorated in cream and brown leather, and exchanged gifts.

I bit my lip as Draven opened mine. I'd had a leather journal worked up, with pockets for envelopes glued onto the heavy cardstock pages. In every envelope was a fun date that I wanted to go on with him. There was bowling and arcades, movie tickets, restaurants, a themed night at The Laughing Elf, and a ton more. But I was really nervous. Seriously, what *did* you get the vampire who had everything?

Draven was quiet as he paged through the journal. He opened each envelope carefully and slowly until he had a whole lap-full of tickets and vouchers; then he looked at me, and I could see it in his eyes.

I gulped.

"I love you, Mia."

I blinked my stinging eyes and said tremulously, "I love you too." I swallowed again, feeling like I was choking on too much emotion. "I just realized it tonight."

He smiled. "I've known for a while."

"Well, you *are* quicker than I am," I sassed, and leaned into his chest.

He laughed and snuggled me closer, my gift to him falling to the couch. After a few minutes, I couldn't stand the suspense anymore.

"What'd you get me?" I wanted my gift. I'd waited and waited for it and he'd been more secretive than 007 about it. Forbidding staff from giving me hints, threatening Mesmer within an inch of his life if he let anything slip. I was bouncing in the seat, vibrating with excitement. It wasn't my first Christmas gift, but it was my first with Draven, and that made all the difference.

He smiled his secret smile and grabbed my hand. We wound through several rooms and hallways before he opened a door with a key. "You locked it!" I accused, half offended, and half admiring that he seemed to know me so well after so little time together. I was totally the type to find, unwrap, and then re-wrap my Christmas gifts so it didn't look like I'd seen them.

He chuckled as the door opened and I swear my jaw probably hit my chest, I was in such awe. There was a huge bay window on one side of the room, a snack bar loaded with lots of goodies on the other side, and along one wall of windows, looking out at the winter wonderland outside, was a white, baby grand piano with a silver padded bench seat.

My breath caught, and I blinked rapidly again. My stupid eyes were stinging from all the dust in the unused room, obviously. It had nothing to do with the incredibly thoughtful gift in front of me.

Draven pulled me toward him so my back was resting against his chest as he cuddled me closer. "You said you wanted to learn," he murmured in my ear. "It comes with piano lessons."

I was still too choked up to say anything, but Draven seemed to understand. I dragged him with me to run my hands over the smooth, satiny finish. I sat on the bench seat and marveled at its comfiness. I opened the fallboard and revealed the long line of white and black keys, trying out a few in the lower range. And then I simply sat there.

I thought back to all the times when I was young. Losing my parents, and then losing my foster parents. Working my fingers to the bone and not getting anywhere except a crummy apartment in a rough neighborhood. Never having enough food, and if I did, it was only because I'd elected to skip the electric bill that month and freeze.

I remembered all the times I'd worked back-to-back shifts to try to stay afloat, and all the times I'd fallen asleep in my waitressing uniform because I'd been too tired to change into my pajamas for bed. I remembered the loneliness, and the sorrow, and how they'd eaten through me until I'd felt raw and broken, and so very, very ancient.

All of those things flitted quickly through my mind as I looked down at those keys. "I think you're my gift for all those difficult years," I said quietly. I couldn't look at him as I said it, and I totally won the cheese of the year award, but —he really was.

Draven's breath caught, and then his warm body covered mine from the back as he hugged me from behind again. Then he sat on the seat with me. We sat in stillness in my new music room with my head resting on his shoulder and his chin resting on my head as the sun slowly rose on December twenty-sixth.

CHAPTER 16
MIA

Winter was beautiful in Moonhaven Cove. The enchanted snow still fell, but the town managed through magic to keep the streets, driveways, and sidewalks clear of it.

It was cold.

I enjoyed the cold, I always had, but I could tell there were those around me that did *not* enjoy it.

Who would have thought a star elf could be so persnickety? "Are you sure you're wearing enough clothing?" I said, trying to stifle my laughter as we walked through the forest nearest the villa, following the gushing river. I'd needed a breath of fresh air and some exercise, and Draven had requested politely that I take Rhys. I also had Mesmer and assorted guards back a little behind us, so Rhys and I felt pretty isolated, even though we weren't.

Rhys, who was bundled up in two super-soft sweaters, snow boots that hit just below his knees, a pair of pants that had fleece material inside of them for insulation, a beanie, ear warmers, and a face mask that wrapped around his face, only letting his eyes peep through, glared at me.

"Not all of us have the money for a high fae charm!"

I reached into my jacket and wrapped my hand around my new heating charm that Draven had insisted I take with me. "Yeah, these things are awesome!" I gushed. I mean, I didn't even think I needed the jacket, I was *that* warm!

Rhys looked like he wanted to toss me in a snowdrift. I cleared my throat and tried to assume a very stoic expression. "Yeah, they're really no big deal."

Crunch, crunch, crunch, went our footsteps as silence lulled for a minute. Followed by the distant crunching of the guards' footsteps. "Then you won't mind if I borrow it, will you?"

Well, his lips *did* look a little blue. He gave me nebula puppy-dog eyes, and I caved. "Ugh, alright! But don't tell Draven! He'll kill me." I looked behind to Mesmer and the others. "You all are sworn to secrecy!"

Mesmer nodded, and my heart actually warmed as I handed Rhys my charm. It was a silver panda key-chain that glowed faintly with magic. "Huh, I think Mesmer likes me better than Draven."

"*Aaaahhhhhh,*" Rhys sighed. "That's better." Then he flicked the ends of my hair. "Of course he likes you better. You're fun, and Draven is a fuddy duddy."

I pinched him and he howled like I'd thrown him in boiling lava. "Why do I get pinched when I compliment you!?"

"Because you said something mean about Draven."

He scowled at me, then forgave me in an instant, and swung an arm around my shoulders. "How sure are we that

Mesmer likes you? He could just be setting up a long con, and go in for the kill later."

I twisted to see Mesmer again. Only Mesmer could look adorable in a dark-blue puff coat and black tactical pants. "Mes, you going to kill me later?"

Mesmer, who always registered in my empath senses as a slow moving, powerful storm, shrugged and said, "I'm more likely to kill Rhys. He sometimes annoys me."

I was curious about this. Rhys had annoyed Mesmer? I mean, I knew he'd annoyed me a time or two, but Mesmer wasn't quick to anger. "How?"

Mesmer glared at Rhys. "He keeps sneaking into your showers."

I laughed and swung back around. Yep, that would do it. After the first few times, Draven had asked Rhys to shower in a different bathroom of the villa, or, hey, here was a thought, at his own home! But Rhys loved to tweak Draven and Mesmer's noses, and he found new and creative ways to sneak past the villa's barrier spells, and past the mass of guards, to steal some time in my shower. His excuse was that none of the other showers available to him relaxed him as much as mine did. Personally, I thought it was because he loved me and liked being around me. And with him and Dice being on the outs right now, he was becoming downright needy!

A loud popping sound ripped through the still forest, and, I don't know if I hit the floor because of instinct, or something knocked me down, but I found myself eating snow before I could blink.

My ears were ringing, and I shook my head a little to get them to stop. I tried flipping over onto my back to see what was happening, but before I could make the attempt, Rhys was there, flipping me over gently and cursing up a blue streak. One of his hands was above us, giving power to one of his hardened starlight domes of magic.

There were rapid pings against the dome that hit with enough force that they created cracks, but after a second, the cracks smoothed again. It befuddled me for a moment, my sluggish brain trying desperately to catch up. I could hear Mesmer roar and burst into his full gargoyle form, and the other guards, werewolves and other shifters, shift immediately and take off running.

They rushed away, chasing after someone.

Rhys was saying something, over and over, and I tried to focus my attention on him, but his words kept slipping and sliding around like a badly tuned TV.

I gave up on hearing him and tried to read his lips because of the ringing in my ears, and that's when the pain hit. Had I been shot? I didn't know why I wasn't freaking out about it, but I wasn't. My thought processes were sluggish and hazy. I recognized, distantly, that I was probably in shock. "Oh," I said, as I looked down and saw my white coat stained with red. "I really liked this coat," I said inanely, shivering.

My hearing tuned back in and I could hear Rhys growl at me, "It's just a stupid coat, Mia." He said as he stripped out of his own coat and one of his sweaters. He balled them both up and pushed them into my shoulder, holding it tightly there. He wasn't even shivering from the cold which confused me until my sluggish brain reminded me that I'd given him my heating charm.

He took the charm off and shoved it into the hand opposite my wounded shoulder. "But you'll be cold!" I slurred. There were some weird things happening with the trees.

They moved and swirled around us. I closed my eyes; the swirling was making me nauseous.

"Mia," Rhys growled. "Just accept the stupid charm!"

I thought this was unfair. I was only trying to be a good friend! Chapter twenty-one in my book talked about the importance of thinking of others, and how important it was to be selfless sometimes in friendships.

I think I blacked out a little for a time. I came to again with Rhys vibrating with cold above me as he huddled close to me, keeping us both under the cover of his shield. I looked at him, and my heart ached to see his red-rimmed, glossy eyes.

With more effort than I thought it should take, I moved my good hand and wrapped it around Rhys' ankle. It was the only part of him I could reach as he crouched over me, but I was satisfied, because the charm was working for both of us now. Rhys' shivering stopped, and he looked down at my face.

I licked my dry-as-the-Sahara lips. "I didn't want you to be cold," I whispered weakly.

He chuckled darkly. "Stars, I love you, you little brat. Stop getting hurt! You won't have to worry about me finding a mate because I'll be dead of a heart attack!"

I smiled and closed my eyes. He was such a drama queen.

I could hear howling as the wolves closed in on someone, then growling and fighting. Then what sounded like angry howling. Was that a thing? Suddenly, Draven was outside the bubble.

"Draven," I whispered. Rhys' head whipped around, verifying it was Draven, then he let him in by dropping the barrier, and reformed it quickly once Draven was inside.

"How did you know to come?" Rhys murmured.

"I felt her."

My blinks seemed to be getting longer. It was hard for me to keep my eyes open, but I really, really tried because I wanted to see Draven's face. He took over, putting pressure on the wound so Rhys could focus on making his barrier as impenetrable as possible.

Rhys shifted so that his back was to us, still in a crouch, and held up both hands to push more power into his starlight barrier. It glowed with deep silver-white magic and pulsed like a quasar.

Draven pulled me into his lap, still keeping pressure on my shoulder, and I scoffed at myself for being a diva when I'd just mentally accused Rhys of the same thing. Weren't people shot at all the time in movies, and most of them seemed to still be able to run down the bad guys and drive themselves to the hospital afterwards. What was wrong with me?

And then I looked down at my white coat again, and my eyes widened.

Oh.

Yeah, I was bleeding to death.

Draven was swearing and growling as he put more pressure on the wound, but I was still losing it too fast. Maybe the bullet had nicked an artery? Didn't that happen sometimes? Wasn't *anyone* around here a doctor?

It wasn't until Draven said, "Shh, just rest," that I realized I'd been whispering all my thoughts aloud in one long continuous stream. He turned to Rhys. "Why is she losing blood so quickly?" he demanded, his voice taut with fear.

Rhys shook his head in frustration. "I *don't know!*"

I licked my lips again. Seriously, my mouth was so

lacking in moisture, I was contemplating licking the snow. It would feel cool and soothing on my tongue and down my burning throat. "The heat charm," I said, my brain fighting to think clearly.

Rhys spun, realizing I was still keeping both of us warm with the heat charm that was between his ankle and my hand. Draven took it from me and put it in Rhys' pocket.

"She needs the cold. A lower body temperature will reduce her blood flow."

Rhys nodded, focusing on the shield again. We could still hear shouts from the direction of the forest, but they were growing fainter as the guards and whoever had shot at us went deeper in.

Draven started packing snow around me while speaking to someone in a low growl on his cell phone. "She needs a life-flight. I'm *losing* her. Get someone out here *now!*" He let the phone fall from his ear as he tried to offer comfort.

"Just a little longer," he promised. I was shivering so hard it was making my teeth rattle. I whimpered, having a sudden sympathy for people that worked every day in arctic temperatures.

Mesmer finally came to stand next to the shield and nodded at Rhys, who dropped it. "We chased him, Lord Draven. But he threw himself off a cliff rather than be captured. We verified that he's dead. He's a known associate of the vampire Alessandro."

Draven swore in every language he knew. There were quite a few languages in there that I blinked at. One of them had sounded like Klingon.

Draven handed me to Mesmer, who cuddled me in his arms like I was a baby foal. "Fly her to the hospital," he choked out. "Get her there fast. She's fading."

I protested weakly. I wanted Draven and Rhys with me!

"I'll come as quickly as I can," he promised, leaning over me so that I could see the promise in his eyes. "And Rhys will come as well."

I nodded as Mesmer's wings shot out and lifted us off the ground, heading with all speed toward the midtown hospital. As we passed over a sleepy hamlet of nice houses, I lost all sense, and blacked out again.

I remembered flashes after that.

The bright lights of the hospital, the controlled chaos of the medical team as they ran beside Mesmer while directing him somewhere with me, a brighter light shoved in my face, Draven growling at a doctor, Rhys, with his arm wrapped around Draven's front, trying to get him to leave the medical staff alone to do their jobs.

I smelled antiseptic and the scent that was distinctly hospital before I scrunched my nose and fought the light that speared through my retinas.

"Lights," I whispered.

Then I sighed as the lights dimmed and fell back into the abyss.

I woke up with Draven in my hospital bed with me. He had situated me between his legs and let me recline on his chest so I would be more comfortable. I had gauze covering my shoulder and chest, and I came to with the very real certainty that I'd just escaped certain death.

My thoughts were still fuzzy, but I looked at my guys with complete adoration. Dice was probably holding down The Laughing Elf, but Rhys was passed out in the only chair in the room with his mouth hanging open, yet still managing to look like a model for *Abercrombie*, and Draven had his arms wrapped around me like he was afraid I was going to sprout wings and fly away from him. Flowers, teddy bears, and mylar balloons covered every available surface of my room, even lined up along the window ledge. I gawped at them in amazement before I attempted to sit up a little.

I made it about halfway up when I had to stop and hissed in pain. Crying crawdaddies that *hurt.* Moving was a terrible idea. Like, the worst idea ever. I carefully laid back down, trying not to damage anything too much or wake Draven or Rhys up.

But of course, Draven, like the vampire he was, came awake as soon as my body registered that I was in pain. "What?" he asked in a panicked voice. "What's wrong?" His hands hovered over me as if he sought to diagnose whatever ailed me by just his hands alone.

"I'm okay," I assured him. "Just sore." I tried to smile and was sure it ended up more a rictus grimace when Draven's eyes went even wilder with concern.

He slammed a finger down on the button to pump drugs into my system, and I hissed as he moved, the movement pulling on the tubes and needles in my arm. But then I sighed in sweet relief, and my shoulders slumped in relaxation.

Ahhh. Painkillers were the best!

Draven cuddled me, very carefully, closer to him, and I breathed him in. "I vaguely remember you threatening to cut off the doctor's fingers," I whispered.

He smile-grimaced at me, and then shrugged. "He wasn't moving quickly enough. I wanted him to appreciate that his life would be very short if he didn't save you."

I patted his knee. "Yeah, big guy. Let's try not to go

around threatening nice people who save lives for a living, yeah? It's really rude. Not to mention counterproductive."

He flashed his canines at me, but there was no humor in the grin. "He needed inducement to move faster."

I laughed and then groaned in pain. "No making me laugh," I protested.

Draven wrapped his arms around me and kissed my forehead, then my closed eyelids, one by one. I was suddenly exhausted again. "Stop getting shot at," he said hoarsely, his voice choked with emotion.

I sighed against his chest. I would certainly *try!*

CHAPTER 17
DRAVEN

I was pacing, there was a roiling sensation in my stomach, my heart felt like lead, and I was truly tired of playing hide and seek with the vampire that kept threatening me and mine.

I didn't need to understand the reasons behind his attacks. He and I had never had bad blood between us, and I had done nothing to bring this level of focus and abuse upon us. Alessandro was a vampire almost as old as I was, and had had years to learn the art of war. Just as I had.

The thought was not at all comforting.

In my efforts to protect us, I kept throwing more and more men into our protection, but it was akin to using duct tape on a sinking ship. The men held off the inevitable for now, but they wouldn't be able to prevent our destruction indefinitely.

Only I and one other could. And I would need his help.

I'd been in contact, a long time ago, with a high elf. The elves were an ancient race, nearly the most ancient race on the planet next to the dragons and the vampires. There weren't many left upon the mainlands (Rhys was an anomaly and had broken off from the elves for reasons of his own). They'd gone into seclusion to their own hidden lands a long time ago. But there were a few who enjoyed interacting with the infant races, and who offered their help from time to time, if properly induced to do so.

And I'd found him.

The prince of the elves.

It was him that I was waiting on, this cold, blustery day. Virion Trysvaris. A high elf with a special tracking ability. This particular high elf was also known for his healing ability, and I wanted him near for Mia.

Mia.

I sighed and ran my hands through my curly hair.

There was a myth in the ancient tongue of vampire scholars that spoke of a bond that happened between souls that were each other's mirror. Only the most ancient of vampires and the most devoted of scholars knew of it, and that was because it was considered to be mythical.

It was known as *Arisma*.

I didn't remember all the particulars, but I *did* remember that a couple who had Arisma could feel what the other felt.

I had been in my study the other night, when I'd suddenly felt a burst of terror, shock and pain. And I'd known instinctively that the feelings were coming from Mia. I'd tracked her through the pull in my chest, and found her on the ground bleeding out.

To say that I was terrified would be an understatement.

It was such a vivid reminder of what had happened with my wife that I'd staggered in shock for a moment before I'd grimly gotten hold of myself and rushed to her.

It was only now, after the emergency, that I realized what it meant. We were Arisma. Mirror souls.

The knowledge brought both joy and fear. Joy, that I'd found something that most vampires, most beings, would never know, would never understand. But terror because she was so fragile and could easily be taken from me.

I wanted to protect her for whatever length of time she was given to me to protect.

To that end, I needed to utilize Virion's tracking skills to track down the vampire who kept sending henchmen after us.

I left my study and sought out Mia, somehow unsurprised to find her in our office. I wanted to laugh at the elaborate set up she had going, but I also wanted to pick her up and put her back in bed. The wound had proved to be too much for Rhys' brand of magic. She was still in so much pain that it made me grind my teeth at the impotence I felt. I needed the elf prince, and I needed him *soon*.

Mia sat in a reclining chair she'd had brought into the office. The table was laden with her favorite foods and drinks, and soft music played in the background. She had her feet up, and someone had moved her desk so that it sat right next to her chair in the middle of the room. A fire burned brightly in the fireplace, and Zian, of course, was lying in front of it with a happy sigh.

Mia had stacks of papers on her little lap desk that she was using. She was making notes in the margins of some of the most recent blueprints that we'd been sent, giving me her opinion on whether the designs would work in the human world, and what the most cost-effective marketing strategy might be. She couldn't tell whether the blueprints would actually net a workable project yet; I was currently teaching her, but it was a lot to learn. She did know enough now to give me details on how the proposed project would work, and whether it would be successful in the human world.

Mia's guards were by the windows. One was keeping an eye outside, looking for any trace of movement, while the other was looking at Mia in frustration and helplessness.

I laughed silently. I knew that feeling so very well.

Zian blinked a bleary eye at me before closing it again, and rolled a bit more to the right so the fire could warm his other side.

I shook my head at the scene that the four made.

I dismissed the guards with a pointed look to stand outside the door. They left so silently that Mia, whose brow was scrunched as she puzzled over a new schematic, didn't hear or notice them.

"I see you're giving your guards minor panic attacks."

Her head shot up, and her copper eyes found me. "Draven? I didn't even hear you come in!"

I came around and sat on the couch across from her as I studied the piles and piles of paperwork surrounding her. She flushed and looked slightly guilty. I wanted to laugh, but didn't. She wasn't a child, my Mia. She could do what she wanted. It was just that she wasn't supposed to be doing *anything* at the moment. Doctor's orders.

I didn't mention this to her. She knew what her limits were, and I wasn't going to remind her that humans were fragile again either. Whenever I did, she got a particularly mulish look in her eyes that told me she was going to prove everyone wrong about that.

Now that we were Arisma, I thought she might be able to siphon a bit of my healing ability, but that didn't look to be the case yet. I wanted to groan. Nothing was working as I thought it might; as I wanted it to. I knew enough of life to know that things rarely did, but I'd hoped that just *once* things would line up in orderly little boxes, behaving as they should.

Perhaps it was the architect and tinkerer in me that wished it so.

Then again, Mia had been unexpected. And she didn't particularly fit in orderly little boxes either. I smiled at the thought, and she blinked at me.

"What are you grinning about?"

I shrugged and changed the subject. "I have someone coming today who I hope will be able to heal you." I hesitated and then sighed. "He'll also hopefully help me track down Alessandro."

She sat up so suddenly that all the papers on her lap scattered and slid to the gleaming hardwood floor. Mia winced and gasped at the pain the sudden movement had caused, and I kneeled at her feet before I even registered that I'd intended to move. I set the papers to the side in an orderly stack and held her icy hands.

"I must find him, Mia. He's gotten through our guard too many times, and I can't keep you in seclusion here under house arrest. It's cruel to do so, even though I want to keep you safe."

"What if he's...?"

"Too much for us?" I gave her a feral grin. "He won't be. He's clever, I'll give you that, and persistent, but my team and I will take care of him. Permanently."

I could feel the blood boil in my veins at the thought.

"You've gone all assassin-y on me again," she said with a sigh.

I shrugged. I had no problems killing someone that came after my family or friends. It was a matter of survival, not preference.

She pursed her lips but dropped the subject. I leaned in to kiss her, missing the taste of her lips, when the door suddenly slammed open with such force that the handle smashed through the wood paneling on the wall and got stuck.

Mesmer stomped into the room in full gargoyle form with someone trapped inside of his large stone wings. The giant gargoyle stopped, but didn't release his prisoner. His face was impassive, like he had all the time in the world. I cleared my throat, but before I could speak, a sardonic tenor voice said, "You can release me now. We're obviously where you wanted me to be."

Mesmer grunted but didn't release his passenger. The person sighed. "I won't hurt them. Just let me out."

Mesmer's head tilted down, and he searched the face of whomever he held. When he was certain that the being would keep his word, he released them.

Virion, the high elf prince. He looked a little worse for the wear. His long copper hair was snarled, he had dark smudges under his green and gold eyes, and his fine clothes were shredded. Like the elves of old, he wore what looked like a long, split tunic and close-fitting pants. Over his tunic was a lightweight vest of mythril. He had golden gauntlets on his wrists and forearms with elven scrolling on them, a pair of golden greaves that went from just above his knees down to just above his ankles, and twin curved blades that were strapped to his back. The blades were singing softly.

In short, Virion looked like someone you didn't want to mess with. I wasn't without claws myself, but I knew if it came to a death match between he and I, that I would not win. It was only my desperation to protect Mia that drove me to such lengths as stealing Virion, the last surviving high elven prince of a line that had been slaughtered.

One copper eyebrow winged upward as Virion took me in.

Mesmer, trying to give us privacy to talk, yanked the door out of the wood paneling, pulling a whole chunk of paneling off, and shut it, standing out in the hall.

"Prince Virion."

"Master vampire." His gaze went to Mia. His eyes softened for a moment before they swung back to me and hardened. "Please tell me you didn't kidnap me to heal one who is already on the mend."

I, in fact, *did* do that. "That among other things." With a smile on my lips, I said, "Thank you for coming so quickly."

Mia gasped. "*You kidnapped a prince!*" She tried to stand, and then swayed. Before I could help her, Virion was there, holding her steady. A twinge of jealousy burned through me when Mia looked at the elf in awe. I shut the feeling down immediately. I had no time for pettiness. Besides, I wasn't a petty vampire. It did twinge a bit when the person you loved and were bonded to was in awe of another male, though.

"I could have prevented it, but I was bored," Virion said.

Mia laughed. Her eyes were crossed in dizziness, and she looked a little green, but she laughed in genuine delight, and then moaned, putting a hand to her forehead. "I'm so sorry. I was shot, and Draven's been a little worried about me. He's been fussing over me like a hen with her chicks. But he shouldn't have resorted to *kidnapping!*"

I winced at the look she gave me. Yeah, she was upset with me. She had every right to be, really, but I didn't like the feel of us being out of sync. And I wouldn't have changed my decision, so it was a moot point. The only thing I felt bad about was the necessity of the action, not the action itself.

Zian sniffed Virion's greaves, wrinkling his big nose as he did so at the magic they were slathered in, and snuffling his boots. He started licking them, and the high elf merely gave him a look and shook his head. The tiger pouted and went back to the fire, sighing greatly. It was tough being an animal around a high elf. They emitted so much magical energy that was in tune with nature that animals basically adopted them on the spot. Even Zian, who adored Mia, wanted Virion's attention and love. And when he didn't get it, he pouted.

It was amusing seeing a cat who weighed two hundred-fifty pounds pout.

Virion seated Mia again and pulled a chair closer to her. "I'm a farmer, you see. Harvest has been long over for the season and my coffers are filled with money from my sales." He patted her hand, releasing it. I snorted at this. Yes, like he needed the money. "Winter can be long and boring," Virion continued, ignoring me. "So, when an insistent gargoyle kidnapped me, I went with it. I figured, if nothing else, I would get some diversion when we got to our destination."

I sat at the other end of the couch, watching Mia charm Virion. I almost laughed. I don't even think the elf realized she was doing it, and I knew for certain Mia didn't. It was in her nature to soothe others, being the empath that she was. It came naturally to her. As naturally as breathing did.

"Are your," Mia cocked her head, listening, "singing blades okay? They feel—is that confusion?" Her brow puckered. "And there is a second aura coming from you. One is calm, the other feels...disgruntled."

I covered my smile with my hands when Virion looked startled, and took that as my cue to give her time to charm him to our side without me underfoot.

I stood and dipped my head in a slight bow to Virion, then kissed Mia's forehead. "Call me if you need me." She nodded, and I turned back to the captive prince. "I'll let you and Mia get acquainted. I am needed elsewhere." Virion nodded regally at me, regarding me with eyes that told me I was not what he had expected. I smiled. He was *exactly* as I had expected. I had no worries that he would hurt Mia, and I had every hope that he would help me hunt down the scum that had almost killed her.

CHAPTER 18
MIA

Okay, Draven really needed to not kidnap people, and I hope he knew we *would* talk about that later. You know, when I could stand without passing out. *That* later.

I puzzled over Virion. The ears tipped me off—I snorted at my unintended pun—that he was in the elf or fae family. My bet was high elf. I couldn't really say why. He just felt a bit like Rhys to me.

His hair was literally bronze, like my eyes, which was all kinds of weird to me, and his eyes were a vibrant emerald green with a handful of gold dust thrown in. The gold dust glowed when he used his magic. I had no idea what magic he currently had active, because I could only see it in his eyes, but it was something. Rhys' eyes did the same thing when his magic was active.

I slumped back in the chair and tried not to whimper. It turned out that I was allergic to heavy-duty painkillers. I'd had an interesting night parked in my bathroom from just taking a half dose. After that night, I'd not been interested in trying a different type or brand. Throwing up all night does that to a girl. Just no.

So, I was getting by with over-the-counter stuff, and it didn't even *touch* the pain. Seriously, at this point I felt like the stuff in the bottle might as well be candy for all the good it was doing me. But still, I faithfully took eight hundred mg every four hours like it said on the bottle.

I grumbled silently to myself.

All this to say, that I was seriously in a lot of pain, and absolutely any position that I tried made me hiss. I couldn't get comfortable, and I was beyond cranky. To distract myself, I'd come down here, had the guards move some things around for me, and distracted myself with work. It had been working well until Virion had shown up via gargoyle delivery.

Virion had curved twin swords that were literally singing. I didn't know if pain was making me loopy, but I could still hear them singing and sighing softly to themselves. I couldn't make out the words, and for some reason that comforted me. When I could start making out the words, I was definitely going back to bed and staying there until I got at least five hours of sleep.

And Virion's aura was...off. For one, he had two of them. I think one was actually Virion the person, and the other...? I wasn't sure, but it felt like a part of Virion.

"You're sensing my magic."

"What now?"

Virion smiled. "Elven magic is sentient."

Ooooohhhh, well, that explained so much. If Rhys was a high elf, why didn't he have two auras? I would ask him later. "Soooo, your magic is a bit cranky at the moment?"

He nodded. "I restrained it from defending us, of course.

I sensed no malice in the gargoyle. I was curious enough to entertain him; my magic was not."

"Oh, so it was mad it didn't get to attack and defend you both?"

"Exactly."

I thought about this. "You know, I can't say that I blame it." I mean, really, people that were kidnapped had every right to do all that they could to get away.

I sighed. "I'm so sorry they kidnapped you. We've been having...a crazy time lately. We've got a master vampire trying to kill us, well he's really just been coming after *me* lately. Which, don't get me wrong, I don't want him to go after Draven again as well; it's just irritating. This is like the third time I've been injured by this loony." I leaned my head back against the cushion and closed my eyes. "He shot me this time. Last time he poisoned me. The time before that he shot out the glass at The Tea Hobbit, and before that he tried to blow up my car. It was this huge disaster that could have gotten a lot of people hurt or killed, but Mesmer drove the car into the lake, which limited the explosion."

I peered blearily at him. I couldn't pinpoint his expression exactly, but I thought I saw sympathy in there. I wanted him to understand why Draven had felt the situation desperate enough. "To be honest, I'm not sure what all your type of elf can do. I'm assuming from what you said that you can heal?"

He nodded. "My line can also track just about anything: magic, beings, blood, etc. We have a few other abilities as well."

I groaned. "So that's why they stole you. I'm so sorry, Virion. I think Draven's going a little crazy. He's had people on this for months, literally months, but this vampire is like a ghost, and he almost always uses someone else to do his dirty work for him." Well, except for the one time. And boy, had that poisoning felt personal.

Virion sat back, his hands comfortably resting on his knees. "To what end, though?"

"What do you mean?"

"I mean, what is the purpose of his psychological warfare? Is he truly trying to kill you, or just harry you?"

I rubbed my temples, trying to soothe my migraine. "Well, I think the poison definitely was trying to kill me. This time with the shooting, too. Draven's been shot at as well. I think we've just been really blessed to have amazing people watching our backs who are good at their jobs and have a lot of magic. I have a friend, Rhys, who's a star elf."

"One of my brethren is here?" Virion sat up in his chair, more alert.

I smiled. "Yeah, he's my best friend. In fact, I'm expecting him any minute now. He's usually by to check on me several times a day, so you'll meet him if you decide to hang out for a bit."

I winced. I really needed to word that better. But how did you say, please-oh-please-oh-please heal me so I can sleep for three hours together? And, while you're at it, can you please track the bad guy down for us so we can kill him? Thank you ever so much.

Virion slid to his knees in front of me, and I blinked at him, startled. He moved with such grace and speed that I hadn't even seen him twitch before he was right in front of me.

Whoa. Elves were cool. Then again, I was a little biased. "I will heal you now," he said.

"Wait, really?" I swear I almost got teary. I might get to

sleep? Like, for a few hours in a row? "That would be really lovely," I whispered hoarsely. My emotions, stupid empathic emotions, were all over the place. I wanted to cry, to cheer, and to sleep, all simultaneously.

The gold dust burned brighter in his eyes as he put his hand over the bandage and focused his magic into the wound. It felt like hot fireflies were flitting about inside my wound, about a million of them, and then there was this searing heat that made me cry out in shock, and then numbness. Blessed numbness.

"If I weren't with Draven I would seriously kiss you right now," I said, completely blissed out by the no-pain.

Virion smirked. "Not even a little one?"

What was it with these guys? I reached for his hand and kissed it, not lingering in the slightest, but trying to get across to him how grateful I was. "Thank you," I said sincerely.

He winked at me, and then finally went to pet my pouting tiger. I had never seen Zian behave that way before. He was acting more like a puppy who wanted cuddles than a two-hundred-fifty-pound giant cat.

This elf was like Dr. Doolittle, and I was sort of awed by that.

Suddenly, Zian and Virion both stood up, their ears cocked toward something they heard outside. If it wasn't so alarming, I would have thought it was adorable.

And then I heard glass shattering, like everywhere, all at once. Even the room we were in. Before I could blink, Virion had pulled out his twin swords, which were singing what sounded like a battle dirge now, and started crossing swords with the soldiers who had gotten through the wards of the villa somehow.

I half stood on my chair, ready to leap or run or fight or *something,* when Zian parked his butt in front of me, watching the surrounding fight with eyes that were as sharp as a sword.

I couldn't just sit here!

I bolted to Draven's desk, desperate for anything to defend myself with, and came across his letter opener. It would have to work.

A man yanked me back by my hair, and I stabbed the letter opener behind me blindly. I must have hit something because he shouted and released me. Especially once Zian took a bite out of his leg.

Draven!

I dashed from the room and skid out into the hallway.

It was a madhouse!

In the hallway alone, there were several fights happening. Our guards and staff were holding their own, and I was fervently grateful for that. I left the hallway at a run, carefully dashing around everyone so I didn't die perforated and of unnatural causes. My most desperate wish was to die of ancient age, in my sleep, right next to Draven. Definitely not with a three-foot sword sticking out of my chest.

I hit the foyer in my stockinged feet and slid along the tiles. My eyes widened as I took in the surrounding melee. Henri was using frying pans, one in each hand, to defend himself with. Mesmer was fighting two other gargoyles with his bare hands. The sound of them slamming into each other was as loud as a rockslide.

In every corner, staff and guards tried to hold off the attackers. Rhys and Draven were not in this room. I wasn't even sure if Rhys was here. Virion was following me. He and Zian were both protecting me as I ran through the villa in search of Draven. I dodged around fights and came up with a frying pan like Henri, and I exchanged my letter opener for a butcher knife. I had a vague idea that I could use the pan like a shield, but also a weapon.

I paused for a moment, trying to see if I could feel Draven. I felt a slight drag toward the front lawn, so I ran for it.

I stumbled to a halt at the scene in front of me. Draven was fighting with a vampire, their movements faster than anything I could follow clearly. I knew it was Draven because just as I was watching, the other vampire scored a hit, and Draven got slammed into the side of the building, pausing the fight for a few brief seconds. I blinked when Draven snarled and jumped back into a fight that was so fast it made my head spin.

Alessandro had finally come in person again.

Rhys was in the courtyard. He had a long sword, curved like Virion's, and was taking on those around the main vampire fight. Mesmer threw the two gargoyles through the front door and joined us on the lawn. Everywhere I looked, there were people battling for survival.

I needed...

With a gasp, I ran for the toy garage. I skidded to a stop at the blue, tricked-out dune buggy, strapped on a helmet, and turned the key to start it up. It was built for deep sand with the wide, craggy tires, and light build, but it would have to do. I shoved it in reverse to back out of the garage, and then shoved it into first and gunned it.

I wanted to head straight to Draven, but I didn't. I needed to trust that he could handle himself right now. But I *could* help the rest of the staff. I sailed along at a fast clip, and jerked the wheel, gunning for a werewolf trying to come up on Rhys' blind side. As a star elf, I didn't think he *had* a blind side, but whatever.

I braced for the impact and rammed into the werewolf at thirty-five miles an hour. The werewolf went sailing over Rhys' head and landed in the fountain. Ugh, it was going to take forever to get the ick out of the fountain now.

Seeing that he was down, I looked for another. I used every driving trick Mesmer and Draven had taught me, and a few I made up as I systematically took people out. Just then, the radio that had been belting out a show tune changed songs. "Eye of the Tiger" came on.

I smiled.

And I could tell from the shifter in front of me that it was not a nice smile.

I wanted to high five myself. Evil smile? Check.

I ran him over.

When there were no more bad guys to run over, I sat idling in the buggy, and watched with the rest of the staff as Draven took hit after hit from his opponent. Although, he got in some hits on Alessandro as well. They seemed to be equal in fighting abilities, and that was not a good thing to my way of thinking.

Rhys hopped into the seat next to me, covered in blood and dirt, and I let him know with my eyes how grateful I was that he was okay. Then I turned back to Draven with my heart in my throat.

"Alessandro is a brother of sorts to Draven. They were created by the same sire," Rhys said quietly. His eyes flicked to mine. "It turns out their sire is the king of the vampires."

I whipped toward Rhys in shock. My eyes wide. He nodded. "Alessandro said that their sire is finally fading. He's eliminating all of his competition for the throne."

I puzzled through all of this as quickly as I could. Out of the corner of my eye, I saw Rhys throw a dagger with unerring accuracy, and a panther shifter went down.

"We can't physically help. It's part of their succession laws." His eyes were trying to tell me something, and I blinked at him in confusion for a few seconds, replaying what he'd just said in mind again, trying to find the clue.

Duh.

Physically. Can't help physically.

I turned back to the fight, determined, and clutched for Rhys' hand, threading my fingers through his. I needed to borrow his stability for a bit. His emotions were heightened but curiously very stable, while mine were all over the place. The skin to skin contact would help me stay calm.

Rhys nodded, his eyes continuously scanning around us. Mesmer had taken his gargoyles down and was standing near my driver's side door with his arms folded over his chest. The rest of the guards were surrounding the buggy behind us in a half circle, waiting and watching.

I focused on Draven and tried to figure out how I could help him from a distance, without it being obvious that I was helping. I couldn't use the more obvious weather magic because it would be visible, and I didn't know of any way to use my empathic ability at a distance. I didn't even think I *could* use it offensively. It was more just an insight type of magic.

Grrrrr.

I focused on Draven with my heart in my throat. He was taking more hits as his reflexes got slower and slower. He had to win this fight. I'd just *found* him, and it was for galloping gargoyles sure I wasn't going to lose him now.

I growled, my brain frantically trying to come up with a solution.

Don't you dare give up, Draven.

For an instant, his eyes shot to me in shock, and I blinked in surprise. Had he heard me? No...that wasn't possible. Draven threw himself back into the fight.

Huh, he was moving quicker than he had been.

I would ponder that later.

I needed a solution *now!*

The only thing that was sneaky enough that I could think of was an article I'd once read on barometric pressure. In the article, it had said that when people claimed they could predict bad weather because of their joints, they were likely right because a drop in barometric pressure led to expanding tissues within our bodies. The expanding tissues put pressure on our joints and caused pain.

But I had two problems with this. One, I didn't know how I could drop barometric pressure in an isolated bubble just outside the other vampire. I couldn't let the drop in pressure hit Draven as well, so it would have to be somehow *inside* the other vampire. And two, I didn't know if that was at all possible. And if it was, I didn't know if it was enough to help. At most, I thought it would make the other vampire incredibly uncomfortable, and that didn't seem like it would help all that much. But it was all I had at the moment.

I focused my weather magic on the vampire and tried to imagine in my mind his body slowly filling with the atmospheric pressure surrounding him. I imagined it leaking like a slow sieve into his system through the pores of his skin. Then, I focused on making that pressure inside of him lower in steady increments. I knew our bodies maintained atmospheric pressure normally so that the outside air pressure didn't hurt us, so I had no idea what would happen here. I just knew that it wasn't traceable, and it was the only thing I could think of on the fly.

I was so focused on what I was doing that I didn't at first feel Rhys squeezing my hand in a death grip. When he about took my hand off, I blinked and my awareness was outside of myself again and on the fight. The other vampire was noticeably slower now and looked like he was in a considerable amount of pain.

My heart in my throat again, I watched as the other vampire's attacks grew more vicious, in desperation now to win the fight, and no longer sure that he would. His cocky smirk gone, the vampire flipped Draven over him and stabbed him in the side with the long dagger in his hand. I gasped, but Draven didn't let the dagger in his side stop him as he reached behind him with both hands and—

I scrunched my eyes shut quickly, then opened them when everyone around me started cheering. I jumped over the dune buggy door and ran for Draven, hitting his chest at a dead run. He *oomphed* as I hit him, and I winced and pulled back quickly.

"Sorry, so sorry. You're alive!" And then I grabbed his shirt and shook him a little. "Don't do that again! Seriously, I think I had seven coronaries." And then I stopped shaking him and slid my arms around him, trying to avoid the dagger in his side as I held him close to me and just relished in the fact that my favorite person in the known world was not dead.

Virion, most helpfully, came up beside us and *yanked* the dagger out without any warning, making Draven wince, and then *smacked* his hand down onto the wound, healing it.

I couldn't tell if Draven wanted to smash his fist into

Virion's face after that or give him a bro hug. My money was on the face smashing, but Draven surprised me by pulling Virion into a hug instead. A hug in which Virion did not reciprocate. He stiffened, as if he had no clue what to do with either a vampire hugging him, or the hug in general, I couldn't tell.

For that matter, I leaped toward him and wrapped my arms around him in a hug as well. Both of us kind of squishing him in between us in an embarrassing display of gratitude. Also, I might have laid it on extra thick because I knew how uncomfortable Virion was with our display, and I was evil like that.

I wanted to cackle madly.

Virion patted us awkwardly in a *'There, there, you gushy, helpless people, can you please get off me now?'* move, and I laughed. "Virion, all the hugs for you. All the hugs. As a matter of fact—" I looked around at all the staff and the guards surrounding us. "Doesn't he deserve hugs, guys?"

They agreed that Virion needed hugs, because soon, Virion was in the middle of the biggest hug pile known to man, women, children, and paranormals. At least fifty people surrounded us, smiles and smirks and relief showing on their faces, as we all hugged Virion.

And Mesmer, funny, awesome Mesmer, said, "Still glad you didn't fight me, boy?" in his deep, full gargoyle voice.

Virion sighed and then laughed. "Lesson learned."

EPILOGUE

That evening I sat with Draven in the Great Room. We were cuddling by the fire, Zian was somewhere at our feet, and I was so drowsy that I was struggling to stay awake.

It took a lot out of a girl to be healed, and then have an epic battle on the front lawn.

And then a hazy thought came to mind, and I sat up, suddenly so awake that I could even math right then. And I don't math. Ever.

"Draven..." I hesitated, cleared my throat, and then said, "You killed the other vampire." It wasn't a question.

"Yes?" I could see he knew where I was going with this because his eyes were laughing at me.

"So, you're now King of the Vampires."

He nodded somberly.

I blinked.

I blinked again.

"What does that make me?"

"Right now?"

I nodded.

"Nothing." He slowly drew something out of his pocket, and I blinked at the gorgeous opal and tungsten band. My building freak-out softened into muted joy. It was exactly something I would have picked out myself. I didn't like rocks on my fingers. "But if you agree to marry me, you can be my queen."

His face looked earnest and serious. His eyes were brightened by the fire dancing in front of us, the flames kissing our faces. He held the ring out to me, and I slowly reached for it, slipping it onto my ring finger.

"It fits." I looked at him. "That means I get to keep it, right?"

He shook his head. "I'm afraid you only get to keep it if you marry me." He said this as though he was very sorry to break this news to me, but he just couldn't do anything about the terms of this agreement.

I wanted to bust up laughing, but managed to keep it all in.

"But it fits so well!"

Draven's eyes danced, and he bit his lip, clearing his throat. "I had it sized to fit you perfectly."

"And I have to marry you to keep it?" I asked, as though I were just making sure of the terms of the deal.

He nodded seriously.

I sighed. "Then I guess I'll have to marry you. I really like the ring."

We looked at each other, and then the joy cracked us wide open, and we smiled and laughed, and he *oomphed* as I launched myself onto his lap, kissing his face wherever I could reach.

He laughed at me, and just went with it.

Zian looked at us like we were crazy, but crazy beings he was fond of. I patted his head and gave him a good scratch when he put his huge head on the cushion next to us, watching our antics with a puzzled, furry expression.

"Mesmer, I'm getting married!" I called to the bodyguard in the corner of the room, hiding in the shadows.

"Congratulations, my lady," came his wry voice.

"Aww, Mes, are we making you uncomfortable with our affection?"

"Yes." It went without saying that it was his duty to deal with it.

I cackled. "You could turn around and face the corner?" I suggested in an overly sweet tone.

Draven's eyes were smiling again, but there was an evil look to them now. "Yes, like a time out," he agreed.

I started laughing as Mes looked at both of us with his patented gargoyle look of disgruntlement. "Are you two finished yet?" he drawled sarcastically.

I looked at Draven, Draven looked at me, and we both said, "Nope!"

Mesmer sighed the hugest sigh, and I could tell...he was really looking forward to a lifetime of guarding us.

I sent Mes an air kiss and snuggled my chin into Draven's neck. "Did Virion go home?"

Draven's huff of laughter fluttered through my hair. "He took a room at the Docile Duke."

I blinked, startled. "The hotel on Main Street that prides itself on treating its patrons like they're royalty, and has eighteenth-century English design and staff?"

He nodded. "The very same."

I thought about that. Virion being waited upon by his own butler, sitting in a tea room while the ladies crocheted, and I choked on gleeful laughter. Virion was awesome and awe-inspiring, but he also was not really fond of emotions on any scale and did not seem to like ridiculousness of any kind. Like, at *all*. It was really difficult to imagine him taking tea with little old ladies and stuffy gentlemen.

"Why?"

Draven shrugged. "Said he wasn't ready to go home yet. I have to assume that a high elven warrior-farmer knows what he's doing."

I shook my head. Warrior-farmer. Virion was certainly interesting.

"Rhys took off. He said he had paperwork at The Laughing Elf, but I think he just wanted to check on Dice." I wiggled my eyebrows, and Draven smoothed them with a tender look.

"He loves her," he said.

I sat up. "Really? I thought, well, I thought he cared about her a lot, but I wasn't sure it had progressed to love yet."

"Trust me," Draven said dryly, "I recognize the signs."

I kissed his chin and frowned in thought. "Dice is still struggling. If he loves her, he's going to have to be patient. She's like a wild horse that just wants freedom and safety."

"Saw many wild horses in Manhattan?" Draven asked with a smirk.

I smacked his chest lightly. "Funny. You know what I mean. That pixie will not fall easily. She's too scared, and too determined to stay single."

"You have no faith in Rhys?"

I scrunched my nose. "Of course I do! I just...feel bad for him, you know? Our relationship has been so easy in comparison with theirs."

Mesmer suddenly sounded like he was choking on a chicken wing over in the corner, and Draven was goggling at me and mouthing the word *easy,* but without any sound coming out. Then he threw his head back and laughed. It filled the whole space around us, literally echoing in the vast room. What had I said that was so funny?

He gathered me to him tenderly after chortling so hard that he was nearly out of breath. "Ah, Mia. You are a treasure."

Well, *yes,* I was. I ignored the continued sniggers from Mesmer and cuddled with Draven again. Eventually, the warmth of the fire worked its magic on me, and I drowsed. Before I fell fully asleep, my thoughts went to Rhys and Dice. I wanted to help them but didn't know how. I would think of something.

My last thought was of Virion taking tea with a stuffy and snooty elderly lady who was critiquing his holding of a teacup. *"Pinkies out, young man. Pinkies out."*

I smiled and drifted off.

ABOUT THE AUTHOR

Dusty Rose grew up in a little town in California. She herds constantly migrating teenagers in her daytime hours, and loves music, plays, movies and books. She fervently believes in the strength of the human spirit, that laughter is one of the best possible medicines, and that happily ever after isn't just something we read about in fairytales.

Printed in Great Britain
by Amazon

39784985R00165